OUTCAST BREED

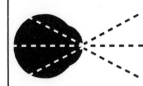

OUTCAST BREED

A WESTERN TRIO

MAX BRAND®

THORNDIKE PRESS

A part of Gale, Cengage Learning

GALE
CENGAGE Learning·

Detroit • New York • San Francisco • New Haven, Conn • Waterville, Maine • London

GALE
CENGAGE Learning®

LIBRARY OF CONGRESS CATALOGING-IN-PUBLICATION DATA

Brand, Max, 1892–1944.
   Outcast breed : a western trio / by Max Brand.
     p. cm. — (Thorndike Press large print western)
   ISBN-13: 978-1-4104-4322-9 (hardcover)
   ISBN-10: 1-4104-4322-1 (hardcover)
   1. Frontier and pioneer life—West (U.S.)—Fiction. 2. Large type books.
   I. Title.
   PS3511.A87O77 2011b
   813'.52—dc22
                                   2011033339

Published in 2011 by arrangement with Golden West Literary Agency.

ADDITIONAL COPYRIGHT INFORMATION

CONTENTS

■ ■ ■ ■

Carcajou's Trail

■ ■ ■ ■

In 1932 Frederick Faust published thirteen serials and twenty-three short novels in the pages of Street & Smith's *Western Story Magazine;* additionally a three-part serial appeared in *Sport Story* and a six-part serial appeared in *Argosy.* "Carcajou's Trail" appeared in the March 26th issue of *Western Story Magazine* under the Max Brand byline. A tale of greed and deceit, its protagonist is a larger-than-life character who, in an effort to escape the clutches of the law, heads to the Yukon where he becomes involved in the search for a gold mine with an unlikely group including a blind man, a woman, and a dog with killer instincts.

I

Two boats were just in from Juneau, and Dyea was filled with excited men and howling dogs. Over in Chilkoot Pass, where misery and folly crowded in together, men were laboring, but no one between the mountains and the sea could realize the importance of the man who stood at Steuermann's Bar in Dyea. This man was John Banner. That name never became famous in the North, but ask any of the old-timers if they ever heard of a fellow nicknamed Carcajou.

Carcajou is French-Canadian for wolverine, and it is worthwhile knowing something about the animal before you try to comprehend the man. The wolverine is the largest weasel, as a matter of fact, but it looks like a little humpbacked caricature of a bear. Some of the Indians call it skunk bear. It has short legs and a long, weasel body. It has claws with which it can chisel through yards of frozen ground to get at a buried cache that the keenest sense of smell in all the world has enabled it to locate. It has the biting power of a wolf and the tenacity of a bulldog. It is stronger, pound for pound, than any animal in the world. A one-hundred-and-twenty-pound timber wolf simply turns aside and gives up the trail when it sees the wolverine come padding toward it, for it knows that the smaller animal will not budge from the path and that it is better to tamper with dynamite than with the compressed ferocity of this beast. The strength of the wolverine is explained by the fact that there is not a straight line in it. Legs, back, neck, body, all are curves that loop into one another and give continual reinforcement. But the strength of spirit is greater than the strength of flesh.

The Indians say that the soul of the carcajou is the soul of Satan. At any rate, it combines the terrible blood lust of the weasel with the patience of a grizzly bear. It is the only one of the weasel family distinguished for intelligence, and it seems as though the wits of the entire species are concentrated in that one small brain, for trappers will tell you that nothing that lives in the wilderness compares with the carcajou for diabolical cleverness. There are stories about old and cunning trappers with many years of experience who had been driven from fine trapping grounds by the ferocious cunning of the wolverine that will follow the trap lines, avoiding all poisoned bait, and ruin the pelts of the trapped creatures it does not devour. It has been known to work for long days, carefully prying and tugging, trying one leverage after another, until it has found a way into a ponderously built log cache. Thus men have died when, at the end of the long winter marches, they have found the cache gone.

This is not a full portrait of the carcajou. It is only a sketch, and, if you wish to get even an inkling of the true nature of the beast, you must go far North and abandon yourself for many a long winter evening to the talk of the French-Canadian trappers who will tell you tales in which the carcajou gradually ceases to be animal and passes into that legendary realm between flesh and fancy, where only the werewolf exists.

Bearing all of these things in mind, look now behind the doors of Steuermann's through the mist of steam and smoke at John Banner, who is to receive his new baptism of blood and to be renamed Carcajou before this day is an hour older. At first sight there is nothing unusual about him. He is simply a fellow of middle height, looking rather plump and, on the whole, lethargic. You will guess his weight at a hundred and sixty, and thereby you will make your first mistake, because there are twenty extra pounds under the loose clothes. Look again to note the depth and roundness of the barrel of the man. Gradually you see that here is a man composed of nothing but curves that loop and subtly reinforce one another. The shoulders slope into arms big at the top and tapering down to a perfectly round wrist. The hand that holds the glass of whiskey on the edge of the bar is daintily and delicately made. Perhaps the length of the thumb is rather unusual. Still, look as closely as you can, there is nothing very unusual about him, except that you begin to feel that perhaps what seems plumpness is not fat at all. At least, the line of the cheek bone and the jaw is clear cut and firm enough. Perhaps under the clothes the body of the man is like India rubber, firm and resilient.

So much for John Banner at this moment. More is to come. In the meantime, there were other people in that barroom worthy of attention. Just inside the door, pushing back the furred hood from his face, was Bill

Roads, a huge, raw-boned, powerful man. He looked over the crowd with the air of one who hopes to find a face. When his glance rested on the form of John Banner, it was plain that he had arrived at the object of his quest, his face contorted, and a light flared in his eyes. He started weaving through the crowd, with his gaze fixed upon the goal, and one hand dropped into the deep pocket of his coat.

Down the bar, not far from Banner, stood a pair of big French-Canadians, smiling men, contented with themselves. They had made one fortune inside, and they were going after another. Wise in the ways of the wilderness, their strength was more than doubled, because they were devoted friends, each ready to guard the back of the other against every danger, and ever on the watch to give needed help. Beyond the French-Canadians, there was an odd group of three, a group whose importance was to appear later. Jimmy Slade was there, and Charley Horn, their ruffian natures clearly appearing in their faces, and between them was that good old man, Tom Painter — Old Tom to most men. He was not so very old, either, not more, say, than fifty-nine or sixty, but men of that age are old for the far North. There was about his face an air of gentle

15

resignation, as of one who has endured much pain and prepares to endure yet more before the end will come. The bartender, after filling a glass, pushed it across the bar and inside the grasp of the waiting hand of Old Tom. Then the veteran looked up with a smile, and the eyes were empty, totally darkened. Even a child could tell that he was blind.

Steuermann stared at him, hard. "Are you going inside, Old Tom?" he asked.

"Going back inside once more, the last time, Steuermann," said Old Tom.

"Along with these here friends of yours?" asked the bartender.

"You ain't met 'em yet, I guess," said Old Tom. "Here's Charley Horn on my right and Jim Slade on my left. Shake hands with Steuermann, boys, will you?"

They extended their hands with muttered words of greeting. Their eyes, keen and suspicious, probed at the mind of Steuermann, as though wondering how far he might suspect them of dark deeds. He, however, had looked at them before and did not feel that it was necessary to look again. Dark deeds were exactly what the pair seemed equipped for. Worse faces than these had been turned toward the Chilkoot. There was nothing strange about that. Only, why

16

were they companions of a blind man? That was a question worth an answer.

"You'll find the trail sort of rough, won't you, Tom?" asked Steuermann.

"I can walk pretty good with a stick to feel the way," answered Old Tom. "Besides, we've got a good outfit, and I guess I'll have to ride a mighty big part of the way."

"A long way, eh?" asked Steuermann.

"All ways are long up this far North, ain't they?" answered Jimmy Slade, cutting in sharply.

"Oh, any way will be a pretty long way for me, Steuermann," said Old Tom.

The bartender just shrugged his shoulders. It had not been his intention to ask prying questions. It was merely that pity and interest bubbled up in him as he saw the helpless veteran and the two roughnecks who were his escort.

This conversation took place while big Bill Roads worked his way in from the door toward his man. He did not come up from the side, but from behind, where Banner stood at the bar with a glass of whiskey poised in his hand. He was close behind his quarry when the men on the right and left of him pressed suddenly back, for they saw that Roads had drawn a gun and at the same instant shouted: "Hands up, Banner, or take

17

it in the back!"

Banner moved to throw up his hands, but as the right hand rose above his shoulder it flung the whiskey out of the glass straight behind him. Perhaps this was partly fortune; perhaps in greater part it was uncanny skill in locating the speaker by the mere sound of his voice. But certainly a few drops of the stinging liquor splashed into the eyes of Roads.

He fired twice, fanning the hammer with the thumb of his right hand, the two bullets smashing through the mirror behind the bar, the pride of Steuermann, and left two small holes surrounded by the white of powdered glass, from which the cracks extended outward in long, wavering lines. The second shot was the last that Roads could fire, for Banner was at him by that time.

He did not strike with his fists, but he caught hold of big Roads with his hands, and, as though the touch were molten lead, Roads yelled with pain and fear for help. Then he went down. There was something grisly about the sudden paralysis that seized on Roads. It was as though the spider had been stung by the poison of the smaller wasp, as if an electric shock had numbed all of the vital nerve centers. He still writhed and struggled, but blindly, helplessly, with rapidly decreasing strength.

Then the bystanders saw, with horror, what was happening, as Roads suddenly stopped struggling and began to scream. There were no words, no appeals for help, but simply terrible shrieking. Banner had his elbows on the shoulders of the fallen man and, with his hands interlocked under the chin of Roads, was forcing back his head farther and farther to break his neck.

II

They lunged for Banner then. They laid on him powerful hands, only to find that their fingers, under his clothes, impinged on quivering masses of corded strength on which they could get no hold. The French-Canadians were among the first to try to pry the killer from his victim. One of them, after a mighty effort, muttered through his teeth to his friend: "Carcajou."

That was how the nickname originated — Carcajou. And the hoarse screams of the victim began to be throttled by the distance to which his head had been forced back. The windpipe was closing. The spinal column itself would snap and shatter presently.

Charley Horn was among those present, bending over the twisting, struggling men, his hands on his knees. He was laughing under his breath, a very horrible sound to those who heard it. But now he reached down and struck with the edge of his hand across the top of the neck of Banner. It was enough. For half a second the killer was paralyzed, and in that moment he was torn from the victim.

He stood back by the bar, looking down at big Roads. His face was utterly immobile, except that there was a slight cut in his upper lip, and the red tip of his tongue was touching the wound thoughtfully, tasting his own blood.

"What were you trying to do . . . murder that man?" shouted Steuermann, shaking his fist under the nose of Banner. "A carcajou is what you are! A regular murdering wolverine!"

Carcajou lifted his glance and stared at Steuermann. It was only a glance, but it made Steuermann snatch out a revolver from beneath the bar. Carcajou laid his left hand on the edge of the bar. "I'd put that gun down if I were you," he said.

It was the first time that he had spoken, and there was such a passionless calm in his voice that those who heard could not believe their ears. Steuermann was a brave man, as he had proved over and over again, but he put down the gun. People remembered that afterward, and not a man who was present blamed him for taking water at that particular moment, and from that particular man.

Carcajou left the saloon, stepping lightly, unconcernedly through the crowd, asking the pardon of those he shouldered against, and always speaking in that same impassive voice that might have seemed perfectly gentle had not the others seen what he had done.

But now he was gone, and poor Bill Roads was stretched on a table near the stove, gasping for breath. They forgot that they had seen him try to shoot a man from behind. In fact, it did not seem to be a man, but a monster superhumanly evil. Besides, as they opened his coat to give him air, they saw the badge of a federal officer of the law. They poured a stiff drink of whiskey down his throat. His head was pillowed on a rolled-up coat.

"How is it?" asked Steuermann, who had taken charge.

"I don't know. My neck may be broken. I heard the bones snapping, I thought." He closed his eyes and gasped again. Then, his eyes still closed, he muttered: "I thought I had him at last. Ten thousand miles, and I thought that I had him at last."

One who had been a doctor in quieter days of his life took charge of the injured man, fingered the back of Roads's neck, moved his head up and down. "That neck isn't broken," he said. "You'll be all right, but you need to be put to bed. You've had a shock, man, and that's why your temperature came up so fast. Get him into a bed quick, some of you boys."

"Get Banner, first," pleaded Bill Roads. "Get Banner, and let me go hang. I don't care what happens to me. I only care that he's caught."

"We'll attend to him later on," said Steuermann. "We ain't got time to gather him in just now. Take it easy, man. Take it easy. Don't go and burn yourself up. What kind of a crook is this here Banner, this here Carcajou?"

"Crook? He's more than a crook. He's a fiend. He's a jungle cat. He came out of the New York slums. There's nothing but Satan in him. Get him dead or alive. There's a reward. I don't want any share. There's ten thousand dollars."

Ten thousand dollars! It was a fortune. With it a man could go back to civilization without ever enduring the strain and daring the dangers of the terrible venture into the inside. He would have his stake ready-made. Yet not a man left the saloon on the blood trail.

To be sure, Horn looked at Jimmy Slade, but Slade muttered: "Ten thousand dollars ain't enough to buy the amount of prussic acid that you'd need to bump off that bird. Bullets, they wouldn't be no good. They'd just bounce off the surface, is all."

The blind man had asked no questions, but he waited with a troubled face, looking down always.

"Just a bird that hopped in here and done a gun play and got flopped on his back for his trouble," said Charley Horn. "That's all, Old Tom. There wa'n't no real trouble at all. Not the killing kind, but the gent that done the shooting pretty near got his neck broke." He chuckled a little. A hard man was Charley Horn, just a trifle harder than Jimmy Slade, although there was not much to choose between.

"Too bad, too bad," said Old Tom. "When folks get this far North, they seem to think that they've left kindness and decency behind 'em . . . sometimes. And that's too bad, too."

His two evil-faced companions glanced askance at one another. Somebody was try-

23

ing to say to Bill Roads: "What's this gent done? This Carcajou?"

"Banner? Carcajou? What does carcajou mean?"

"A weasel with the meanness of a weasel, the brain of a grizzly, and the most of a bear's strength, too."

"You've found the right name for him, then," said Roads. "But talking about him is no good. I'd have to spend days telling you what he's done. I'd have to tell you how I've done nothing but follow him for two years, and follow him I still will, working for the government or working for myself. I'll crawl on my hands around the whole world, but finally I'll split his skull with a bullet, or run a knife through his heart. He's got to die."

He was panting as he spoke these last words. Then a spasm of pain got him once more, and he groaned.

The others listened to him with a singular respect. A two-year-old blood trail is very interesting, indeed. Yet the thought of the $10,000 reward did not induce a single man there to leave the saloon and track down the enemy of society. The trouble was that they had seen too much and too intimately the dealings of John Banner in that same room. They did not want to find themselves flattened on the ground with the hands of the monster on their throats.

"It's a funny thing," said Steuermann, shaking his head, although *funny* was not really the word that he wanted. "It's a funny thing that he didn't take a shorter way of murdering you, man, when he had you spread out like that."

"What's killing more or less to him?" asked the officer of the law. "What does that matter to a demon like Banner? Not a thing! Killing, bit by bit, with his hands, that's what would please him. Three mortal times he could have killed me on this trail, and three times he's refused to shoot . . . he's tried to get at me with his hands every time."

They listened with horror. There was hardly a man in that room with delicate sensibilities, but what they heard was sufficient to make them sick. After that, if $50,000 had been offered, instead of $10,000, it would not have been enough to get any man, or any four men, out of that room on the trail of Carcajou.

Steuermann found, at this point, a chance to draw Jimmy Slade to one side. Ordinarily he would not have dreamed of talking as he was about to talk now. But enough had happened to excite him highly, and his tongue broke loose from the usually severely imposed restraints.

"Slade," he said, "I've got to ask you a question. Where do you intend to go with Old Tom?"

Slade looked boldly and contemptuously into the eyes of the bartender. "Ask me again another way," he said. "I don't understand that kind of language."

Steuermann darkened and drew back a little. "All right," he said. "Only, brother, I wanna tell you one thing."

"Tell it soft and low, then," said Slade, growing uglier every moment.

"I'll tell you this. Old Tom ain't a stranger up here."

"No?"

"No, he's not a stranger. And if he goes in blind with you and your side-kicker, there's gonna be a whole lot of us anxious to see him come out again."

Slade stepped closer to the other. "Now, whatcha mean by that?" he demanded savagely.

"You know what I mean," said Steuermann without flinching. "I've told you what I mean, and I guess you understand the language all right."

"Say it over once more, brother," said Slade through his teeth.

"I'll say it over," answered the bartender. "We'll be looking to see you and Horn come out with Old Tom still alongside of you."

"And where else would he be?" demanded Slade.

"Dead of frostbite, somewhere inside," said Steuermann, and turned back behind his bar.

III

When the newly named Carcajou stepped outside the saloon, he stood for a moment and breathed in the air, pure, free from smoke — free, it also seemed to him, even from the language of man. Within the doors he could hear the murmur of voices that had been loosed the moment he left the room, but he regarded this not at all, except as a sign of his freedom. Mankind meant nothing to Carcajou, except insofar as the race furnished for him interesting enemies. Now and then the race was close, now and again the fight was hard, but the victory was always his. There might be, somewhere on the planet, men swifter, stronger, fiercer, more cunning than he, but he had never met such a one. Having gone unconquered all of his days, he expected to remain so to the end. As for friends, he never had known one, male or female, who valued him as much as they valued the price on his head. That price was of long standing, from the time he was fifteen, in fact. Doubtless the price would not have been placed had his age been known. At fifteen he had looked twenty, at least. At twenty-five he looked still hardly more than twenty. Ten years of breaking and evading the law had not aged him.

The reason that he paused now was not because he did not know where to go. It was simply that he was hesitating, wondering whether he really wished that famous man of the law, Bill Roads, dead or alive. He could have killed Roads easily enough. But if Roads were off the trail, what would remain to make things really interesting for him? Who would be able to make him sleep like a wolf, with one eye open? Who would be able to make him keep constantly on the alert, waiting and peering about for danger?

Bill Roads was, on the whole, the most formidable enemy that he had ever known. Four times Roads had come in close contact with him. Four times he had defeated the enemy. This day he had wished to kill the man, but on the whole he was rather glad that he had not. One does not wish to subtract from life all of its spice. When he had reached this conclusion, he nodded slightly and set off down the street.

It was snowing, a fall of large, crisp flakes that came down in wavering strokes of dimness before his eyes. Where they touched his face, they did not seem very cold. There was a pleasant sound of them underfoot. The air was not yet iced. It was rather moist and still. Straight down the street he could see still the leaden waters of the sea.

On the whole he was content. Actual happiness he never knew, except when he was cracking a safe, say, or at grips with a foeman. But now he was fairly well pleased with himself. He had discovered that life in the States was growing a little too warm for him. He might, it was true, avoid the law for another few months, but he knew that there were too many posters about him here and there. $10,000 is a large enough sum of money to put brains in the most stupid and courage in the cowardly. It was not exactly that he was afraid to remain in the wide mileage of the States. It was simply that he considered it unwise to put his head in the lion's mouth. He had evaded destruction a hundred times, to be sure, but in the end the luck would turn against him and he would go down. It would be small comfort to him if he lay one day gasping on his back, grasping at the mud with his mighty hands, if he knew that the bullet that laid him low had been fired by a tyro who chance had favored. So he had determined to leave the country, and he had made his way toward the great white North.

He intended to go inland, and there he would be lost among the shifting crowds of miners for perhaps a year. When he came out again, no doubt the memory of him would be slightly dimmer in the minds of the police. After that, he could take a trip around the world and let his repute become still less familiar. When he returned to New York — well, then the old world would not know him, and he would begin the nefarious practices that he loved once more.

This was his general plan of campaign. This was his strategy. As for tactics, he was prepared to deal with each situation as it arose. He was not one to worry about the future. As he had dealt with Bill Roads in the saloon, so he had dealt with other enemies from time to time, and so he would deal with them again in the future. It must not be thought that he had a blind confidence in himself. He seriously had waited, all the days of his life, to find another man superior to himself in power, in speed, and cruelly quick decision. He did not pray to encounter such a dreadful foe, but he yearned for the meeting as a child may yearn to have a younger brother born.

Striding down the street, he passed a gap between the buildings on his left and heard the shouting of a small crowd, the snarling of a dog, the curses of a man. It was not a pretty scene. A big crate had been opened in the space between the buildings, and a dog on a long chain had been let out of the crate. Just outside the length of chain stood a man with a club, and, as the dog rushed at him, he beat the beast to the ground again and again.

You'll never break that dog that way, said Carcajou to himself. He canted his head to the side as he stood and watched. Perhaps there was enough of the animal in him to make him sympathize with beasts very intimately. Now, at least, he thought that he understood in a flash the entire workings of the brain of the dog.

It was a monster Husky, its blood enriched with many crossings of the timber wolf, but of a size that the wolf never attains. What could the other strain or strains be? It was a frightful mongrel. That much was clear. It had the mousy, immense head of an Irish wolfhound. It had also the stature of that terrific beast. But there was the coat of a

31

wolf, and the weight in the shoulders and in the quarters was more than an Irish wolf-hound would ever be likely to show. He would not venture to guess lightly at the total burden of this frightful thing — two hundred pounds, perhaps, or even more.

As it lay flat on the ground, it seemed less. When it rose into the air at the dog breaker, it seemed as huge as a bear. Now the monster arose from the mud and snow, shook himself, and crouched without charging. His head was bleeding. No matter whether he charged high or low, the club always met him, swinging in that expert hand. Always the exactly timed blow crashed down upon his head. So he waited, now, panting with fury rather than with effort, and, lolling out his long red tongue, he looked at the dog breaker with eyes redder still.

The latter shouted with angry triumph and shook his left fist, cursing. "Come on, you!" he yelled. "I've got plenty more of the same kind left!"

It was plain from the triumph in his tone that he had dreaded this encounter.

Carcajou stepped up and said: "You'll never break him that way."

The dog breaker moved back out of range of the monster and turned furiously on this mere human antagonist. The brute in him mantled in his face, and there was little but brute in his composition.

"You'll tell me how to break dogs, will you?"

"I could tell you a point or two," said Carcajou in that same tone of misleading gentleness. In fact, his voice was never raised. He never had shouted out loud in all his life, since a certain dreadful moment in his childhood.

"You could tell me a point or two, could you, you slab-faced piece of fish, you flounder-faced piece of putty, you!" shouted the dog breaker.

Carcajou stepped closer and with a swift, inescapable movement of his left hand caught the club arm of the other man above the wrist.

The dog breaker looked down. The club fell from his paralyzed hand. The fury left his face. White wonder took its place. "Well," he muttered. "What would you do with him?"

"That's a dog for a dog team, isn't it?" asked Carcajou.

"That ain't a dog. That is a dog team," said the breaker. "That's a man-killer, too."

"Oh, is he?" said Carcajou.

"He worse than killed Larry Patrick last

week. Larry ain't gonna be no more than the sewed-up chunks of a man the rest of his days." Then he added: "What would you do with him, mister?"

"You've got to come to grips with him sooner or later. There's a brain behind those red eyes. You might teach him to be afraid of a club, but one day he'll catch you when you have no club in your hand."

"And then cut your throat, you mean?"

"Yes, unless he's been taught that your empty hands are better than his teeth."

"Empty hands?" repeated the dog breaker, and laughed.

Other people in the crowd joined in his derisive laughter.

"Back up, stranger," said one man, "and let this here show go on. Back up, will you?"

Carcajou looked on the unknown and smiled faintly. There was a certain richness of harvest, he found, in this land of the great white North. Wherever one turned, there were reckless men and a harvest of great danger. Gun or knife or hand, or all three, were ever ready to break out into action. However, he merely said: "For a bet, I'd try my hand with that dog . . . my bare hands, I mean."

The stranger who had invited him to back up cried instantly: "I've got five pounds of gold dust in this poke! Is that enough to make a bet for you?"

"That's about fifteen or sixteen hundred dollars, isn't it?" said Carcajou. "All right. That will do."

Taking out a wallet, he began to count the sum requisite for the wager. The others fell silent.

IV

"Unchain that dog," said Carcajou to the dog breaker.

"I'll have to knock him cold before I can unchain him," said the breaker. "Besides, I wouldn't unchain him. I wouldn't turn loose that big streak of murder inside the town. If you wanna give him room, just walk inside the circle he can run in, brother. That'll be about all."

"All right," said Carcajou. He walked straight up to the dog. It was an amazing thing to those who watched it. There had been excitement enough every time the great brute charged the man with the club; it brought each heart up into the throat to see one with empty hands go straight up to the monster and lay a hand on that bleeding head.

The dog crouched, snarling, but the green

and red gleaming was out of its eyes, or very
dim, at least. Carcajou talked straight down
at him, his voice calm and gentle, as always,
and as always just a suggestion of iron
clanking on iron somewhere in the sound.
They heard what he said, and remembered
it.

"You're not such a bad one. You only think
you're bad," said Carcajou. "You've had a
fool slamming you over the head. But you'd
rather wag your tail and be friends, if you
could find the right man. I'm going to be
the right man for you, boy. You can trust
me."

The dog snarled, but there was a whine
mingling with the snarl. The breaker yelled
suddenly in rage and surprise: "He's a hyp-
notizer! That's what he is!"

At that shout, coming so suddenly, the
great beast shot out his long neck and
dragon's head to seize Carcajou by the arm.
The fangs slashed through the sleeve, cut
the skin, but that was all. Carcajou caught
him by the throat and flung him to the
ground. He looked a little, puny thing,
struggling with the huge brute, and he was
flung here and there by the mighty struggles
of the dog. The claws of the beast tore the
heavy furs of Carcajou to fragments and
gouged his body. Blood dribbled on the

36

snow, the blood of Carcajou. Then the dog made one great, last, convulsive motion and lay still, throttled to the verge of death, with his tongue hanging out of his mouth sidewise like a stream of purple-red blood.

The men who stood around had stopped shouting and jumping about in their excitement. They merely drew together and stared. With every fling from side to side of those dragon-like, gaping jaws, they expected to see the arms or the body of the man gnashed to the bone. But although the strength of the brute was like that of a horse, it was securely held.

Carcajou rose to his knees, patted the head of his victim, took a handful of snow and rubbed off the tongue, still hanging from the jaws, and patted the neck and back of the animal.

"What do you call the name of this little pet?" asked Carcajou of the dog breaker.

The latter answered in newly humble tones: "He ain't got any name. Slaughter would be about the right name for him, I reckon."

"Sure it would," said Carcajou.

He rose to his feet. Slaughter sprang up suddenly and stood on wavering legs, eyes still thrusting from his head, lungs heaving desperately. Carcajou laid his hand a second time on the head of the great brute.

"Now we've been introduced, we can be good friends," said Carcajou.

"You better try sooner to be friendly with a pack of wild wolves," said the dog breaker. "That's what he is. A wild wolf is what he is, and he was runnin' wild when he was trapped."

"You mean," said Carcajou, "that he was running with a wolf pack?"

"Yes, and the leader of it," said the breaker.

"Then he's worth having," said Carcajou. He reached out and took the canvas sack of gold dust from the hand of the silent, gloomy man who had made and lost the bet.

"What's the price you put on this dog?" asked Carcajou.

"On him? No price at all," said the other. "I've worked ten days on him, beatin' him to a pulp every day, but I couldn't tame the beast. If you want him, you can have him for nothin'. Look out. He'll have your throat tore out."

Slaughter had crouched to spring, but Carcajou merely snapped his fingers. "That's all right, brother," he said. "We're not going to have any trouble with one another. Steady, boy."

Slaughter stood straight up and stared at

this strange creature that spoke with the voice of a man but that had in his hands the iron grip of a bear's jaws. The dog stood quietly, waiting for the next move in the game, still murderous, still ready to battle to the death, but acknowledging the force of a mystery that could not be easily solved.

Carcajou stepped to the heavy crate in which the monster have been housed, broke out the iron bolt from the wood, and gathered the chain into his hand.

"We'll go downtown to get some new clothes, Slaughter," he said, and started off down the street.

Slaughter held back, planted his great feet against the snow, but Carcajou walked on, talking slow, taking slow, short steps, and the monster was dragged behind him.

"How long'll that go on before the dog jumps on his back and breaks his neck for him?" one of the men in the group of watchers said to the puzzled dog breaker.

"I dunno," said the dog breaker. "I talk about things that I know. I dunno nothing about gents like that one yonder. I never seen nothing like him before, and so I don't know." He shook his head. "Look at the strength of him," he pointed out. "That dog weighs two hundred pounds, and he's bracing every foot and leg of him to put on the brakes, but still Slaughter had to go along. I dunno. He held the neck of that brute like his hands were vises. I never seen nothing like it, and that's why I say that I don't know."

"Well, could that dog be made into something worthwhile in a dog team?" asked another man.

"You seen for yourself," said the dog breaker. "Slaughter is a dog team. He's sled dog and swing and leader all in one. But if you tried to make him part of a whole team, wouldn't he go and eat the other part?"

Only one man laughed. The others were too intently staring at the strange picture of the great dog as he gradually passed out of sight down the street through the white flurry of the snow.

V

The law might be slightly benumbed in Dyea, but it was not altogether dead, and, therefore, Carcajou could not afford to linger in the town. Bill Roads would be out organizing a posse before long, for one thing. It was very strange that news, and Bill Roads with it, could move so fast. When he thought of this, Carcajou felt a thrusting up of admiration in his heart for Bill Roads.

That man was a man, and no mistake about it.

There were some quick preparations to be made. He bought a new outfit of furs. Already he had acquired a sled, and the pack to go on it, with four excellent dogs. He needed merely to hitch up the dogs, put a thoroughly strong muzzle on his newly acquired monster, harness him in as sled dog, and strike out on the trail. He carried with him on this trip a burden of excess weight that few adventurers took with them. This consisted of an excellent Winchester rifle on the one hand, and under his coat a .45-caliber Colt revolver with the trigger filed off and the sights removed, also. He would rather have traveled without one leg than without that revolver.

He went up Dyea Creek on the run. There was no need of urging his dogs along. He had a good leader that knew its business in picking out the trail, and the three animals behind the leader were constantly trying to hump their way through their harness, because behind them pressed the gaunt giant, Slaughter, red-eyed, silent, but slavering with hatred and rage and pure physical hunger. He wanted, in fact, to get at those other beasts and destroy them. Very small, frightened, and frantic looked the four big

Huskies as they tugged at their traces ahead of the dark beast. He looked to Carcajou more than ever like a vast, long-legged rat. He was the ugliest creature that the man had ever seen. There was something more than animal ugliness — there was a spiritual hideousness about the brute that appalled the mind. But the master was fairly pleased. He was more than ever pleased when it came to the terrible toil up the Chilkoot, where men labored inch by inch forward, groaning under their packs.

He put packs on each of the four dogs, another pack on his own shoulders, and what seemed to him a killing burden on the back of Slaughter. But Slaughter bore it lightly up the way. He had before him the currying tails and quarters of the other animals, and his greed to get at them whipped him forward. He chased the dogs and carried his own mighty load. He also dragged with him Carcajou himself, dangling at the end of a long chain.

Banner laughed a little, going up this famous slope at such a pace. In two trips he brought up the sled's load, and the sled itself. A man stopped him on the second trip.

"Is that a mad dog that you got there?" he asked.

"No, that's not a mad dog. He's only hungry," said Carcajou. "Like him?"

"He looks like the ghost or a dog's nightmare of everything that no dog, or wolf, either, would ever want to be. Tell me truthfully, is he any good?"

"He's as strong as any two others. You can see for yourself."

"Lemme tell you this, cheechako," said the stranger. "You're a fool to take that big bundle of trouble into Alaska. There's enough trouble already inside. You don't have to take fire from the outside and bring it in. You'll burn before you been there very long."

It was rather strange advice, but it was the only word of counsel that Banner received all the way. Other men regarded him not at all, except as an obstacle before them to be cursed or a trail breaker to be accepted with a grunt of satisfaction. But all that mattered essentially to Carcajou Banner was that he was working his way inside.

When he got to Sheep Camp, he rested, as most other people were doing. It had been a strenuous time even for the limitless strength and the tireless nerve of Carcajou, for he was learning a great deal that he never had known before. He was working at the fine art of snowshoeing. He already knew how to handle skis very well from a certain strange and arduous winter of his youth, but he learned more and more about a similar craft now. He learned the knack of tree felling and how to build camp in the most expeditious and comfortable way. He learned that a carefully made camp and a good sleep were necessary even to him in this country.

The rigors of weather and the trail wiped out the large margin that he could usually allow. In a more southern climate he could disregard such trifles as temperature. But in the white North it was a different matter. He could do more than other men, but he had to be careful. A bullet will kill the loftiest giant, and the North will kill the mightiest man almost as quickly as it topples over the weakling, unless brains and forethought are used. But Carcajou had this advantage: that he learned not only as a thinking, reasoning creature, but also in an animal sense. When an old-timer pointed out the signs of coming storm in the horizon mist, Carcajou looked and listened and felt the lesson sink down into his innermost instinct. It was the same with signs on the trail. It was the same also with the handling of the dogs. By the look in their wind-reddened eyes he learned to guess what was in their minds — that is in all except Slaughter's.

That ugly monster was still a sled dog, pulling half the load, tireless as his new master, and hateful as a legion of demons. Every night came feeding time. Every night the muzzle had to be taken from the long head of the brute, and every time the muzzle was off, there was likely to be a fight between Slaughter and Carcajou. The man always won. He learned a wonderful adroitness in handling the spear-like thrust of those fangs, and yet he carried a dozen deep cuts even before he reached Sheep Camp. However, this constant battle pleased him.

Another thing pleased him when he arrived at the camp. This was to find that his reputation had preceded him. Reputation was the one thing he could not do without. Since he was fifteen, it had always been with him. Since the day of his first battle, admiration, dread, and an invincible loathing always had surrounded him. Just as the great timber wolves slink from the path of the wolverine, so men had shrunk from the way of John Banner. And now they were shrinking again, even these fearless adventurers in the Northland.

He had traveled fast from Dyea, but rumor had gone before him on invisible wings. What he had done in Steuermann's was known, and how he had mastered Slaughter with his bare hands was known, also, although both of these tales had been immensely embroidered and built upon. Any tale worth telling by an Arctic campfire is worth telling well. As for those who doubted, one glimpse of the dreadful figure of Slaughter convinced that northern world. They saw the hero carrying with him down the trail the proofs of his heroism.

Thus in Sheep Camp Carcajou found that his fame was established even more firmly than it had been in the slums of New York and the underworld of half a dozen cities. There was the same admiration, dread, and loathing. He devoured this universal tribute with a savage and silent joy. He could not be loved, he knew. Therefore, he reveled in winning enormous hate.

Even the nickname had gone everywhere with him. That was best of all. Nobody knew him as John Banner. Therefore the law would not follow him so easily. It was always Carcajou now. Men who did not know the meaning of the word — and most of the men on the trail did not — nevertheless used it. It came to have a special meaning in their minds, more loathsome, more hated and feared than the animal to which it rightfully belonged.

At Sheep Camp Carcajou found the strange trio: the blind old man together with Charley Horn and Jimmy Slade. They had come in just before him, and he saw them unhitching a magnificent team of twelve dogs with two fine sleds behind the lot. It gave Carcajou a deep thrill of pleasure and suspicion to see the outfit. The whole atmosphere of it reeked with a suggestion of crime not very deeply hidden. There was some purpose in the minds of Slade and Horn that was not present in the mind of the blind man. What could that purpose be?

Well, whatever it was, it did not trouble Carcajou. All weakness he despised. There was no mercy in him. The world gave him hatred; he repaid the world with contempt. Still, it was interesting to observe the trio and ponder on the probabilities of the future. A calm, deep voice spoke within him and told him that Old Tom had not very long to live at the hands of this precious pair.

The arrival of Old Tom was a considerable sensation in Sheep Camp, but not more so than that created by another outfit of a dozen dogs and three people that came in still later. The dogs were as hand-picked as those of Slade and Horn. The drivers were Rush Taylor, a wiry half-breed, Bud Garret, a famous dog puncher in the North, and Anne Kendal, a twenty-year-old girl.

Carcajou went over and looked at the outfit, standing close and staring at it. Slaughter, leashed on a chain and unmuzzled, stood behind him. They had just had their daily battle, and Slaughter, well beaten, could be trusted for a time. It was pleasant to Carcajou to parade the big beast without a muzzle; it was pleasant to turn his back on the monster while the men held their breath. No doubt they hoped against hope to see the beast attack the man with murderous power. What they hoped mattered nothing to John Banner, so long as he had their respect and their attention.

So he stood close while other observers gave plenty of room to him and the four-legged thunderbolt chained to him. He looked with his calm, cold stare at the two men. It was a habit of Banner's to let his eyes rest for a long period directly on the face of anyone he chose to observe. Then, if they chose to resent his scrutiny, they could do so at their peril. That was all the better. In places where he was not known, he had worked up many a pleasant fight by no greater maneuver than this.

So now he stared, according to his old custom, at the men. They made a formidable pair. They were as brown as wind and sun could tan their leathery hides. The white man was almost as dark as the half-breed. They were both big. They moved alertly and quickly even at the end of a long day's march.

It was clear that they were well known. Other men in Sheep Camp hailed them by name, asked their destination, and, when no answer came, began admiring the string of dogs. But no one looked at the girl or spoke to her, and this was a great surprise to Carcajou. Certain ways of men in the North were still very new to him. But he knew little or nothing about women, north or south. They had not appeared in his life. They were unnecessary adjuncts. Now he looked over the girl with the same steady, grim eye he had used on the men.

She was almost as brown as her traveling companions, not beautiful, but handsome enough to give the illusion of beauty in this wilderness. It seemed that she was as much at home on the trail as either of her traveling mates. While they handled the camp apparatus, she went out and worked with the dogs, moving swiftly and fearlessly among the big Huskies. She had a certain touch and way with them that interested Banner.

Presently, standing with her hands on her

hips, as though about to decide what she would do next, she encountered the eye of Carcajou, looked away, crossed her glance on his again, and suddenly let her eyes rest upon him.

That was very odd. Men had looked him straight in the eye from time to time in his life. Generally they had received enough attention later on to wish that they never had let an eye fall upon him. But never had anyone considered him with the same perfectly cold detachment that she showed.

Charley Horn came up to Rush Taylor, the half-breed, and said quietly, but with iron in his voice: "You're following my outfit, Taylor. What d'you mean by it?"

"I go where I please in this part of the world, Horn," said Rush Taylor steadily.

"Maybe you'll please yourself too much one of these days," answered Charley Horn threateningly.

Bud Garret stopped his work and stood straight and still, listening.

"I mean you, too, Garret," said Horn. "We ain't gonna stand being shadowed the way that you've started out to do."

Garret merely shrugged his shoulders, but it was plain that he was ready for action of any sort. For a moment Horn's glance swung from one of them to the other, vengeance in his eye. Then he shrugged his shoulders and walked away.

The girl came straight to Carcajou. "D'you think you know me, stranger?" she asked. "If you don't, my name's Anne Kendal. What's yours?"

He was both affronted and amazed. "I don't carry excess luggage in the way of names," he said. "Any old name will do for me."

"You were staring at me as though I wore stripes," said the girl. "What do you mean by that?"

"People that wear faces will have them looked at," said Carcajou, and sneered at her.

Her eyes pinched a little with scorn and dislike.

"I'll take care of this bird," said Bud Garret, approaching hastily with a dangerous look.

Carcajou took a quick breath of relief. Any man was welcome as an opposite in the place of this girl.

"Back up, Bud," she said. "I don't want trouble started on my account."

"He's been staring at all of us," said Garret. "I'll teach some manners to the half-wit."

"Look out, Bud!" called some one sharply.

"That's Carcajou!"

Bud Garret halted and suddenly grew pale. Then he stiffened his shoulders. "All right," he said. "It ain't the first murdering carrion-eater that I've handled in my time. I'll take him on."

Carcajou did not answer threat with threat. Nothing about him moved except his lips. He wore a contented smile. He picked the place where he would strike home. That was all. But the girl stepped between them.

"This is my trouble," she said, "and I'll finish it." She faced Carcajou. "What have you got to say to me?" she asked.

Carcajou paused. There was nothing he wanted to say. There was only an emptiness in his mind. He could only sneer and keep it coldly sustained. But it was very hard, indeed. Suddenly he remembered what he had seen Charley Horn do, and, shrugging his shoulders, he turned away and moved off slowly.

He went back to his own tent and began his cookery. He had hardly started when a footfall came near him. Looking up, he saw a little gray-whiskered man well on in later middle age, who stared grimly down at him.

"Carcajou," said the older man, "I dunno where you was raised or what you got behind you. But up here this far North every girl is a lady until she's proved otherwise. After that she's a lady all over again. Don't you forget it, son, or you'll find more trouble than even your hands can put away."

VI

The other moved away; Carcajou sat bewildered. He had been talked down to; he had been taught with a raised forefinger as though he were a child! Yet he did not feel like leaping up and starting trouble about this matter, because it occurred to him that there might be certain unwritten laws in this Northland about which he knew nothing. That little old chap would not have dared to speak as he had done unless he was aware that a vast weight of public opinion reinforced him.

It was a mystery to Carcajou, except that he was vaguely aware that there had been something admirable in the girl's behavior. She had courage, directness, everything that he expected to find only in brave, resourceful men of action. Yet he hated her with an emotion of sulky helplessness that he had not felt since his childhood. There was a tremor along his nerves and an aching in his heart. The world seemed a bitter place, and he wondered why he had come to this wild Northland to find refuge. Why should he not have gone, instead, to the Orient, where men are men and the women don't matter?

He gritted his teeth. American women were spoiled, he decided. Idle, uneducated, silly, proud, vain, useless creatures. Then he remembered how she had worked among those big, wolfish Huskies without fear, doing more than any man other than an expert dog puncher could have managed. No, all that he said to criticize American womanhood did not apply to her — only the pride, the self-confidence, the disdain of others. He looked back into his own heart. What were the qualities that endeared him most to himself? Why, they were pride, self-confidence, and disdain for the rest of the world. If he criticized her, he was criticizing himself. As he reached this point in his conclusions, he cursed between his teeth. The ache inside him grew worse, and there was a chill of fear along with it. He never had felt this way so long as he could remember. It was something like homesickness, a baffling disease of the mind.

A shadow sat down beside him. It was Charley Horn.

"Hello," said Carcajou, and then stared in

his own blank, lion-like way. He remembered suddenly, as the other spoke pleasantly enough in return, that there were duties of hospitality that he never would have thought of in the old days, but they were sacred according to the unwritten law of this northern land. Now he felt, whether he wanted to or not, he would have to pay attention to those traditional rules of the land of snow.

"Have some tea?" he asked. "There's another. . . ."

"No tea," said Charley Horn. "I dropped over here to talk business."

Carcajou nodded. He was not surprised to hear that Horn wanted to talk business. In fact, all of his dealings were with men of Horn's type.

"Business of what kind?" he asked.

"Day labor."

"Not interested."

"No?"

"No, not interested."

"I mean fifty dollars a day."

"What?" repeated Carcajou, lifting his brows. "Fifty a day?"

Horn grinned. "I wouldn't be offering your kind of a man pin money, would I?" he demanded, proud of the sensation that his offer had made.

Carcajou half closed his eyes. He knew perfectly well that Horn was a rascal, and that Jimmy Slade was another, but rascals were the only kind of men he was really familiar with. Again, the pair was up to some sort of sensational deviltry, and deviltry of that sort was what Carcajou liked. Usually he played a lone hand, but here in the North he was on ground so new that he would hardly know where to turn for employment. Finally, it would be amusing to learn that he had come this far into hiding at great expense, only to find that he had fallen upon his feet, and that other people intended to pay his expenses for him. This last item decided him.

"What's the job?" he asked.

"You'd consider it?"

"Yeah. I'll consider it."

"We've got a hard lot of work ahead of us. We're going down to Linderman and build a boat and cross the lakes. Then we hit the trail again. We want to build our boat fast, and we want to hit the trail fast."

"I'm no carpenter," said Carcajou.

"You can pull at your end of a saw, though," said the other. "I guess that you could do that as good as any three men boiled down and put into one skin."

"All right, go on," said Carcajou.

"That's all. We've got a good dog team. But we've got the blind old bat along with us, Old Tom, as they call him. He's got to be handled like so much dead weight of meat."

"How far do you let me in?" asked Carcajou.

The other hesitated, then lifted his eyes from the ground and stared straight at his companion. "We don't let you in at all. You're just a day laborer to us."

"Ah-hah," said Carcajou. He also considered. For he was offended by this suggestion, and yet, along with his offense, he felt the great temptation of attacking a mystery, stepping deeply into it.

"It's this way. We want help along the trail up to a certain point," said the other. "After that, we wanna pay you off and say good bye. We pick the point when we pay you off. It may be thirty days. It may be twenty . . . it may be fifty. We don't know."

"Fifty a day, eh?"

"That's our rate of pay. We'll give you twenty days' pay in advance to keep you interested."

"Oh, that's all right," murmured Carcajou. "I guess that I can trust you fellows not to cheat me when the time comes for paying off."

"Yeah, you can trust us for that."

"You want me, and you want my dogs, too?"

"We want your dogs, except Slaughter. You can shoot that brute, far as we're concerned."

"He stays with me," said Carcajou.

"We can't take you on, then."

"All right, then, you can't take me on," said Carcajou, relaxing. He glanced toward the great beast with redoubled hatred. Slaughter was separating him from an interesting adventure, but still he felt that there was more adventure in Slaughter than in the trio.

"Look," explained the other angrily, "the dog's no good. It'll tear somebody's throat out one day. You see if it don't. Whatcha want with that kind of a dog in your team, man?"

"Why, I like him," answered Carcajou.

"Blast it all, Carcajou, won't you come without him?"

"Not a step."

"We'll have to take him along, then, because we want you bad, and your sled and your team."

Carcajou said: "I'll tell you this . . . that dog will pull a whole sled's weight by himself. I won't let him do any killing in the team, if that's what you mean."

"All right," said Horn with a sigh. "We've got to have you, even if you've got Old Scratch himself along for a playmate."

"All right," said Carcajou. "When do you start?"

"In eight hours."

"I'll be ready. One thing more."

"Well?"

"Why are the others chasing you?"

Horn swore, but he added: "Questions are one thing that you forget to ask on this here trip."

Carcajou laughed softly. "All right," he said, "that goes with me, too. You let Slaughter go along and I keep my face shut."

VII

All that Carcajou remembered of the start, later on, was a voice that struck with a strange loudness out of the dimness of Sheep Camp: "Now that they're together, you take and try to pick out a meaner three than them, will you? And may heaven help poor Old Tom."

It was never the habit of Banner to take notice of offenses until they were offered directly to his face, and, although this was almost under his nose, he was perfectly willing to allow the affront to pass.

On that occasion Jimmy Slade said: "I got a mind to look up the gents that are talking like that."

"Why do that?" said Carcajou. "If we ever start in hunting for all the people that hate us, we'll have to kill most of the world, I guess."

Jimmy Slade looked at him with startled eyes, said nothing, and presently turned back to his work.

So they pulled out of Sheep Camp and started relaying the outfits to the summit. When that was finished, there was little trouble in getting over the nine miles to Lake Linderman, through a cañon bleak and barren, but frozen hard and offering good going for the sleds. From there on was the fine sledding of the lakes until they got to Tagish, where they would buy their boat, or build it, if necessary.

All of the first part of this trip was occupied with good hard work. While it lasted, Carcajou made his estimate of his two younger companions. They were both powerful men; they carried the extra burden of guns, and they knew perfectly how to use them; they had been in the Northland before and were experienced in handling dogs and sleds and building camps. Their tempers were fairly bright. They never dodged labor and worked well together at every task. It was only now and then that the murderous evil of their natures broke out in a glance, a few caustic or bitterly sneering words, or some expulsion of sudden temper. On the whole, they controlled themselves well, like men who have a great task in hand and are willing to put up with all sorts of troubles, including the presence of one another, in order to accomplish the end in view. But the evil that he saw in them did not offend Carcajou. It merely made him feel more at home. It warmed his spirit. It was a touch of that familiar characteristic that he knew best in life among other men. Moreover, he liked the physical vigor that they showed on all occasions. There was only one thing that displeased him and that was their attitude toward Old Tom. When he was in hearing, they were likely to express their actual thoughts in winks, gestures, a sign language, while their spoken words remained polite and gentle. It was plain that they did not dare to let the old man guess what they really were.

As for Old Tom, he was too much of a problem really to interest Carcajou. He did not matter, and, therefore, he was dismissed. It was clear that through him the pair hoped to attain some great end, but what that end might be was a mystery to Carcajou. As far as he could see, Old Tom was simply an excerpt from a fairy story. He was always gentle, never raised his voice, never spoke in haste, never complained of cold or wind, insisted on getting out and running behind the sled, holding onto a line, whenever the footing was at all possible, managing himself wonderfully well on his feet for a man of his age, totally blind. Indeed, in every imaginable way he was as little trouble about the camp as a blind man could well be. But blind he was, and why should a blind man attempt to reach the frozen heart of Alaska? What could he possibly gain there? Gold? But he could not even see the wealth he might be dreaming of. A friend? But what friend would wish to have this helpless burden placed upon his shoulders in such a land? Some familiar place connected with his past life? But in the howling wilderness there was no familiarity worth finding.

No, Old Tom was a great problem for Carcajou, but since the fellow was old, blind, and therefore unimportant, he did not give any time to the solution of the difficulty. He used to feel that the most interesting moment of all was when, in an interval of quiet brooding beside the campfire at night, he saw the face of Old Tom harden suddenly and swiftly into lines that looked to Carcajou like an expression of the most savage cruelty. Age and pain and the cruel affliction of the loss of sight were enough to embitter the spirit of the veteran, but it was only now and again, at long intervals, that he saw a glimpse, as through a frosted window, of the tormented soul.

The only incident of real importance on the way to Tagish was when Slaughter tore off his muzzle one day and killed three of the other dogs in the team in the few seconds before Carcajou got his hands on the beast. Carcajous's employers gave him black looks on this occasion, but they said nothing. There was another of the endless series of the battles between Carcajou and his dog, and the incident was closed.

When they got to Lake Tagish, Slaughter performed again, and this time with the most unexpected results. At Tagish they offered fantastic prices in their eagerness to get a ready-made boat, for it was feared that the thaw might come at any time. The frosty snow had disappeared from the face of the country; the limbs of the evergreens were no longer piled with white, and the river between the lakes was beginning to break up, the ice making noises that were anything from a cannon shot to a lion's roar. However, since the thaw was expected almost momentarily, no one was willing to sell a boat, completed or almost completed. Men who were that far into the interior of Alaska felt that golden fortune was just ahead of them. They were smelling and tasting the treasure, as it were. They felt that they would soon be at the heart of it.

So no one would sell, and the three had to set to work building. They had to build a scaffold, and on this they placed great green logs, from which ponderous planks were whipsawed, one man standing above and one man beneath. That is, this was the way that Horn and Slade labored, but Carcajou managed a saw all by himself, a little more clumsily because of the play that came in the saw blade after a wrong stroke, but, when he had mastered this, he cut by himself more planks than the other two put together. Men used to come and watch him, the ceaseless pedal motion of his body from the hips causing them to shake their heads with admiration and wonder. If the thaw came soon, it was clear that the two partners would never forget this giant in their employ.

Three days after them the girl arrived with Rush Taylor and Bud Garret. All three set to work boat-building, but it was apparent that they would soon be distanced; all their work on the trail would be useless if they were trying to keep up with Horn and Slade, unless the thaw on the lakes delayed longer than was expected. Yet the thaw did not come.

It was the night of that day when they had commenced to build the boat out of their green planks that Slaughter broke loose again. He was chained to the trunk of a tree, but broke the chain, and the light clanking noise of the breaking link of the chain was enough to awaken his master. Carcajou got up at once. There was enough twilight for him to see the gaunt, powerful form of Slaughter standing over the place where blind Old Tom was lying. He could see the glint of the fangs of the brute, bared by the lifting of the upper lip, but Slaughter was making no attempt to tear the throat of the veteran. One hand of the old man was raised, without real strain or effort, and laid on the head of the dog, and under the quiet touch of that hand Slaughter stood still. It was an amazing sight.

Gun in hand, Carcajou waited, but he heard the voice of Old Tom speaking gently, and his bewilderment grew intense when he saw the great dog lie down beside the man.

It staggered him utterly. He blinked and shook his head, told himself that he was a fool and seeing a dream, but there was the fact before him. He strode to the spot.

"What are you doing to Slaughter?" he demanded harshly.

The shaggy head turned like a snake's to regard the master with hatred. "Just talkin' to him, son," said Old Tom. "Ever try talkin' reason to dogs or men?"

Carcajou muttered a savage, nondescript answer and, seizing the brute by the neck, bore Slaughter off to the tree, where the broken chain was refastened. Then he went back to his own bunk and sat down in it.

Old Tom was propped up in his bunk, smoking. Carcajou had heard that blind men never smoke, but here was a proof to the contrary. More than once he had watched Old Tom working at his pipe with every sign of satisfaction, and here he was again, pulling calmly, serenely, no doubt, thinking over again the events of that evening and the way in which he had established his mastery over the huge mongrel. Carcajou slipped down into his sleeping bag with a gritting of his teeth. He looked up at the dim tops of the trees, all sharply pointing like spears that looked straight up to the sky. The sky itself was nearer, and the world beneath it more vast and confused and mysterious than the southern world that Carcajou knew, the world of cities.

He felt a sense of depression and helplessness, a childish sense of helplessness only to be equaled by what he had felt that day when he had faced Anne Kendal in Sheep Camp. But there was a different aftereffect this time. Before he had been amazed and down-hearted. Now he was swearing sternly to himself that he would penetrate the mystery and learn what it was all about. To him nothing was as strong as strength. He had lavished force in the training of Slaughter and made the dog more dangerous every day. How was it that a comparatively weak old man could subdue the brute with a quiet voice and the touch of his hand?

VIII

The thaw held off, unexpectedly, so that the very day it came, Taylor, Garret, and the girl launched their boat. It floated at the most a quarter of a mile from the boat of Horn and Slade, and the latter fell into a frightful tantrum, when he saw the craft. But Horn merely said: "You can't make your luck over. And those birds, they ain't come to the real pinch yet."

He was handling his rifle in a significant way when he said this, and it was not hard for Carcajou to guess that they meant murder when that *pinch* came.

"Luck? They've got the luck of Frosty Smith," said Slade in answer.

"Who's Frosty Smith?" asked Carcajou.

They both looked at him askance.

"You never heard of Frosty?" asked Horn.

"No."

"Listen, Painter," said Slade to Old Tom. "Here's a gent that never heard of Frosty Smith!"

"All the better for him," said Old Tom with his usual calm.

"Frosty Smith," said Horn finally to Banner, "is the king of the thugs in Alaska. Is that right, Painter?"

Old Tom nodded. "Nobody knows how many men have died because of him," said the blind man. "Or how many millions he's stole that other folks dug out of the ground. They used to say down in Circle City that we all did the work and Frosty had all the profit."

That name was to stick in the mind of Carcajou, and to good purpose, at another time in his life. In the meantime, they were hoisting their square sail, consisting of odds and ends, and making good time across the lakes. The third day they lost sight of the craft of Garret and Taylor, but that did not mean very much. In the open water their clumsy craft could not expect to gain very much on even a dishpan. So they reached, in due time, the end of the lakes and Miles Cañon.

Horn was for letting the unloaded boat down the rough water with a rope and packing the stuff around to them later on, but Slade was made of sterner stuff. He pointed out that this was the chance for them to gain on the others. Horn consented. He would run the rapids, and Carcajou shrugged his shoulders. It was a point of honor with him that he should accept any venture that any other man dared.

They bound big sweeps fore and aft, extending them on outriggers, and cast off from the shore a hundred yards above the mouth of Miles Cañon. Below lay the more open water, but the frightful rocks of the Squaw and the thunder of the White Horse Rapids were between. They would soon be swept through to safety, or else they would split and be overwhelmed by the terrible current.

What Carcajou remembered of that passage through the white water was nothing except the grand, calm face of Old Tom as he sat quietly, with the shaggy head of Slaughter on his knees. They never needed to chain the dog when Old Tom was with him. Slaughter closed his eyes and shuddered from head to foot while the spray dashed over the craft and the waters howled like a thousand fiends in the hollow cañon, but the face of Old Tom was unmoved.

Carcajou, because he had the strength of more than one man in his hands, handled the forward oar, trying to keep the prow centered. But now and again, glancing back as they shot through a less dangerous stretch, he could see Old Tom smiling faintly, contentedly with his head thrown back, and on his face the expression of one who listens to the most delightful music.

A dozen times Carcajou Banner knew that they were sliding from the piled-up waters in the center of the current, to be dashed to bits against the walls of the cañon, and a dozen times the rickety craft responded to desperate labor on the sweeps and continued safely on her way. These were miracles that were happening, and the miracles continued. They saw the end of Miles Cañon; they shot through the Squaw; they roared into the thunder of the White Horse, and so into the peace of the lower waters. They were safe.

As they unshipped the sweeps, the calm voice of Old Tom said: "Well done, lads. Well done. I've only been through twice before, but I've gotta say that going through with your eyes shut takes you a pile longer than going through with 'em open." He laughed a little, still softly.

"We'll never see a girl and two birds like Taylor and Garret run rapids like that," sneered Horn. "We can lay up to the bank and take things easy for a while, I got an idea."

They tied up to the bank and cooked and ate a meal. As they boarded the scow again and loosed her down the river, another boat shot from the spuming mouth of the White Horse. A faint cry reached them through the uproar of the waters, and, looking back as they made sail, Carcajou saw the craft of their trailers, with Rush Taylor laughing and waving at the bows.

Slade handled his rifle with a hungry look.

"Not here!" said Horn sharply. "We got too much light of day on us."

But it was plain that they both meant killing. That was nothing to Carcajou. Death was a small thing in this world, as far as he was concerned. What mattered far more to him was such a thing as the expression on the face of the blind man, looking with unseeing eyes down the river. The white North had left his heart clean. That was certain. For the thousandth time Carcajou wondered at him. There was a mystery deeper than anything Old Tom could guide his two villainous companions to; there was a secret of the soul that he possessed that they never could learn. Not that Carcajou himself greatly cared to change — he merely wondered what the heart of this man could be like. In all the years of his life, he had told himself that one man is not much better than another. As for those who pretended to honesty and humane qualities, it was because they felt that hypocrisy paid them in the long run. Of that he was sure. He never had seen one person who would not take all possible advantages once he had the upper hand. Only in Old Tom he felt an imponderable element that dashed his surety. On those about to die, it was said that a peculiar grace descended, and there was something as profound as that on the brow of the veteran.

Horn and Slade were in close consultation by this time. They had failed once more to shake off the bulldog tenacity of those who pursued. Now they must attempt another shift as soon as they were securely out of sight of the others. With the first dimness of twilight they would try to run the boat ashore, unload it, cache a portion of the load, and sink the scow in the shallows. Then they would pack in as much as they conveniently could and make for their ultimate destination.

So for two days they struggled down the swift, yellow currents of the great Yukon, making sail where they could, laboring with the sweeps night and day, straining every nerve to get ahead. Not until the second day, however, did they manage to get well out of sight of the other craft. Then, as that brief night, which could hardly be called night but rather a prolonged dusk, began, they beached the scow, unloaded her at once, sank her at the edge of the water, and hastily packed the goods inland. They dug a good deep trench and buried a quantity of provisions in it, covering it over with saplings crossed and re-crossed, so that even a bear would have had a great deal of trouble in opening up that cache.

What was left they packed on the backs of the dogs. There were fourteen of them now, including Slaughter, and they carried a stout burden, every one. Horn and Slade each took a heavy load; Carcajou, with equal ease, bore as much as both the others, and even Old Tom insisted on taking a burden of some forty pounds. With this he went along fairly easily. He was given a rope connected to the collar of Slaughter, and it was an amazing thing to see the dog lead the man. It might well be that Slaughter had in him an evil spirit, but Old Tom had managed to find the way to tame him. At any rate, there was never a moment when the beast was not ready to murder either dog or man in the rest of the party, but Old Tom he treated with more tenderness than a mother wolf would show to the youngest of her litter. When they came to an upward slope, he leaned forward and helped the veteran up. When they reached a deep rut in the ground, he paused until the staff of Old Tom touched him, and the man was warned to prepare for the obstacle in the way. Where a tree or a stump was ahead, he swung wide and steered Old Tom past the danger, and from morning to night Slaughter tended Tom Painter with unending devotion. It was not that he had learned how all at once, but during the three days they marched inland, steadily following the course of the Yukon but keeping it a mile or more to the right, he gradually picked up a hundred arts of conveying information to the blind and helpless old man.

Horn and Slade and Carcajou had fallen

behind on that third day and were watching Old Tom striding freely before them, when they commented on the strangeness of that performance.

"Dogs are just like safes," said Charley Horn. "All you gotta know is the combination to the dumb fools."

Slade turned his head at that moment and suddenly exclaimed: "By the black heart of a witch, look yonder!"

Over a swale of ground behind them, striding through a thin growth of small timber, they saw a man, erect, with the bulk of a pack on his shoulders. Behind him came dogs, carrying packs, also, and last of all another man and what might have been a boy — only it was not a boy. With one accord all three of them knew that it was Anne Kendal with her two companions.

"Carry on," said Slade through his teeth. "They've found the trail again, and now the fools are gonna learn what else they've found. Charley, they gotta be turned back, and the only way of turning 'em is to use guns. Carry on now, but tonight we'll turn back and give 'em a surprise."

"All right," said Carcajou, "and I'll do the surprising. I've got a grudge against one of 'em. And the whole three I'd like to show how. . . ."

IX

What would he show them? He hardly knew, except that he felt that he had been scorned by them all, and the proper answer for scorn is blasting wrath and the irresistible strength of a right hand. There were mysteries around him here in this Northland — the journey of Slade and Horn with the blind man they hated and pretended to feel an affection for, the boldness of Bud Garret in daring to affront him, the haughty bearing of the girl, the unknown goal toward which all of these people were striving. These made problems through which he could not look, but of one thing he was sure. That night he would attend to the affairs of at least one of those who traveled in pursuit.

His offer was readily accepted. Horn merely said: "We'll want you along, all right, Carcajou. But we'll be there, too."

"I'll go alone or not at all," said Carcajou calmly.

"Leave him be, you fool," said Slade to his partner with irritation. "What d'you want more than a chance to sleep sound and let somebody else do your work for you?"

Horn argued no longer.

When the twilight of the far North gathered, they increased their pace enough and marched long enough to leave the enemy behind them. Then they made their camp. Carcajou ate a hearty supper, rolled himself in his blankets, smoked a final cigarette, and went to sleep.

"You forgetting?" Horn muttered to him.

But Slade, more understanding, snapped impatiently: "Leave him be! You gonna try to teach Carcajou better tricks than what he knows already?"

Carcajou closed his eyes in sleep contentedly at this moment, and for three long hours he slumbered heavily. It was the time he had appointed for himself, and at the end of that time his eyes opened as though he had heard the ringing of an alarm bell. He did not need to yawn or shake himself into wakefulness. He was suddenly and completely alert, and, quickly dressing, he stood up in the icy chill of the night air.

It bit through his coat; it sank toward the bone like a cutting tooth, but he opened his lungs and inhaled a few deep breaths, and the strength of the cold fell away from him. A thin mist from the river had rolled over the land, rising to the top of the brush, but letting the trees stand up in little ragged islands here and there, with pools of paleness filling the hollows. It was a good night for such work as he had on hand, if only he could find the camp of the enemy.

He looked about him first and spotted Old Tom sleeping peacefully, his feet toward the embers of the almost dead fire, and the great dog Slaughter, curled into an immense circle beside him.

He stepped up to the pair and stood over them, while Slaughter raised his villainous head and favored him with a snarl. But it was a silent snarl, a mere voiceless convulsion of hatred, as though the savage brute did not wish to break in upon the slumber of the man he loved. Something of warmth touched the heart of Carcajou. Acts of thoughtful kindness were in his estimation the most absurd folly, and yet he found himself building up the fire again so that it could warm not those two rascals, Horn and Slade, but the old man whose face was so weary and so serene.

Then, as though ashamed of this act, as the flames began to catch in the wood and rise, crackling with dancing sparks, he strode hastily out from the camp and started on his journey. He had for weapons his Colt revolver, a good heavy hunting knife, and his hands. It should be enough in light like this, which made distant shooting impossible. But could he find the camp of the others?

It was amazingly simple. Not three miles back down the trail he heard a sudden clamor of dogs that led him better than a light, and then came a rush of savage Huskies about him. The biggest and strongest and bravest of the lot came first with enough of the wolf — or the watchdog — about it to take a running leap at his throat. More than one man has been killed by the rush of wolfish Huskies in a strange camp, but Carcajou laughed a little softly in the deep hollow of his throat, and picked the great dog like a ball out of the air.

He got in return a double slash that opened one sleeve of his coat from shoulder to elbow, and the other sleeve was torn straight across, just above the wrist. But that was the only damage done. He kneeled beside the struggling brute and throttled him quickly into submission, while the rest of the team dogs around him scattered back. Their howling and barking fell to a number of frightened, high-pitched yelps. They retreated into ghostly outlines in the distance.

Suddenly a voice not more than twenty feet from Carcajou said: "There's something out there."

The voice of Bud Garret answered: "Yeah. Likely a wolf prowling. Look at them coward dogs come sneakin' back. The mongrels, they don't like the looks of a full-size timber wolf. I tell you what I've seen . . . I've seen two real wolves chase a whole pack of sled dogs. Go back to sleep. I'm keeping watch."

"All right. You keep your eyes peeled, will you? Maybe I oughta be standing watch myself all this time."

"We argued that out. You've done your half of the shift. It'll be real daylight before long, and this mist'll clear. But I guess they won't try nothing on us tonight. Even three like them need time to get up their nerve for murder."

"Carcajou, he needs no time. He's always ready to kill," said the half-breed.

The talking ended, and Carcajou smiled to himself with a heart filled with delight. This, to him, was as great a tribute as he could expect. It showed that men feared him even in this wild Northland, and what more did he ask from the world than fear? As for what Old Tom got from Slaughter, well, that was another matter, a mystery that no ordinary man could hope to penetrate.

So he waited there on his knees for a full hour. Another man would have turned numb, and every nerve would have failed in

the extreme cold and in that cramped posi-
tion, but Carcajou had the patience of a
beast of prey, which must have patience if it
is to live in the wilderness. He would let
that camp settle down completely before he
moved again. In the meantime, the dog in
his hands did not move. It was not dead,
but it squatted on the ground with eyes
closed and with ears pressed back against
its neck in a frenzy of icy terror.

At last Carcajou stood up, released the
dog, and moved on. He glanced behind him
and saw that the Husky had not stirred, but
lay where he had put it, as though shot
through the brain. That sight pleased him,
also. Even dumb beasts could feel that there
was a deadly terror in him — in his touch a
fatal and cold magic.

He got down on the ground now. He saw
before him two or three red eyes, the glow
of a dying fire. Then there was the shadow
of a man sitting near the coals of the fire, a
black silhouette cutting through the night
mist and facing directly toward the hunter.
Carcajou moved inch by inch to the left,
inch by inch until he had come through the
half of a circle. He lay, finally, between the
sentinel and the fire behind him. Not a
sound did he make, and not a warning yip
came from the dog team. Perhaps they had

81

scattered too far and heard nothing.

He could see the girl in her sleeping bag on one side of the fire. He could see the half-breed on the other side. Then he rose behind Garret and gave him the blow that he himself had received in Steuermann's. He knew it perfectly. It was delivered with the edge of the palm, and it fell across the top of the neck and over the two big cords that run up to the skull. The head of Garret jerked back. He slumped sideways from the stump that he was sitting on. In one arm Carcajou received the falling rifle. In the other hand he received the body of the man, lifted him, and stepped slowly, soundlessly into the mist.

The trees thickened and blackened before him. He paused as his burden began to stir and mutter. So Carcajou put him face down on the ground, gagged him, and lashed his hands behind his back. He had plenty of cord for the purpose. It had been in his mind from the first.

Then he selected two trees a proper distance apart. He freed one of the man's hands and tied it well up the trunk of one of the saplings. Toward the other he stretched the right arm of Garret, and then drew the cord very tight. Before he had ended, Garret was strung in the air with his weight on his tensely drawn arms and with his toes barely touching the ground.

At present this was nothing, but after a time the weight of his body would wear out the strength of the arm and shoulder muscles. Then the full strain would come upon the tendons, and these, in turn, would begin to stretch. The real agony started at that moment. It would not take long. An hour or so of this would leave a man perfectly capable of walking, but his arms would not be fit for real service for a month.

Then Carcajou stepped close and said at the ear of Garret: "I was a murdering carrion-eater the other day to you, Garret, and now I've walked back here through the night to tell you that it's a bad business to call names. Don't call names, Garret. Kill your man if you have to, but don't call him names. You can stay here a while and think it over."

Then he turned and went off quietly through the night. The pleasure of his adventure filled him to the throat with joy. He wanted to burst into song.

X

When he got back to camp, the noise of dogs again showing him the way, he slipped back into his bed, and there he was found by the others when they awakened in the morning.

Horn said dubiously: "Well? What happened? Have a good sleep all night?"

"All except a funny dream," said Carcajou.

"What kind?"

"A kind that would make you laugh," said Carcajou. "I dreamed that I went back about three miles and found their camp, and Bud Garret was standing watch, or sitting watch, rather. And I dreamed that I got hold of him and snaked him away and said to myself that one helpless man would be a lot worse for the others to handle than a dead man. So I tied him between two trees with a gag between his teeth. I tied him so that his toes just touched the ground and the whole of his weight was pulling on his shoulders. By the time they find him, I've got an idea that he'll not be able to use his arms for a month or so . . . if he hasn't strangled to death trying to work against the gag and scream for help."

He chuckled as he said this. The other two grinned sympathetically.

"Got any sign that you really went into that camp and did all this?" asked Horn.

Carcajou looked narrowly, earnestly at Horn, without making a sound in reply. But

84

here Slade averted trouble, perhaps, by snatching up a rifle. "This here gun wasn't in our camp yesterday!" he exclaimed. "Look here, Carcajou! Did you bring away Garret's gun, along with him? A man in one hand and his gun in the other?"

Carcajou seemed to have lost interest in the conversation, but at this point Old Tom broke in: "D'you mean to tell me, Carcajou, that you tied up a man where he'll be tortured like that for hours, maybe?"

The voice of Carcajou was a mutter that sounded like a low growl. "How else would I do up a gent like Garret?" he asked. "Want me to ask him politely to turn back from our trail? Or would you like to have me kill him straight off, instead? I wouldn't have minded doing that, but one helpless man will tie up his partner as well. That was my idea."

Old Tom stood up straight and struck the ground with his staff. His empty eyes were turned under a depth of darkened brows toward Carcajou. "According to my lights," he said, "nobody but a mean hound and a low hound would do a thing like that."

Carcajou rose from his food with his face perfectly calm, except for the slight lifting of his upper lip. Opposite him, and in front of Old Tom, rose the monster, Slaughter, and stood with a frozen smile facing his real master. But suddenly it dawned upon Carcajou that ownership in the eyes of the law is a very small thing compared with ownership of honest and sincere affection.

Slade cut in at this point. "Carcajou is a rough man, Tom. You know that by this time. But he's all right. We had to turn 'em back, didn't we? They were gonna trail us right to the . . . spot, weren't they?"

The face of Old Tom was still stormy with wrath, but, fighting fiercely with himself, he controlled his speech. "We're far North . . . it's a hard country," was all he muttered, "and I'd rather lose all the gold in the world than put another man through torture before his time."

"Looks to me . . . ," began Slade angrily.

Horn exclaimed: "Jimmy, shut your mouth!"

He made a significant gesture toward Old Tom as he spoke. Slade controlled himself in turn. But all three were now glaring at Old Tom with a savage concentration. The same emotions that Carcajou felt, he could see clearly mirrored in the faces of his two employers. That did not altogether please him. They were a low cut, he knew, and it was far better to be like Old Tom than to be like either of the younger men.

It was a very sudden check, an odd shock to Carcajou, and it kept him in brooding silence for hours. It was not the first time that he had received a shock to the soul from the words and the behavior of Old Tom. It was not the first time that something in the dignity of the man overcame him with awe first, and with shame and hate later. He merely said, that day: "I've loaned you my dog these days, and you pay me back as a dog would. You can get on without Slaughter from now on."

So with his own hands he took Slaughter on the lead.

It was not a very convenient arrangement. It simply meant that either Slade or Horn had to walk in front of Old Tom that day, with a cord tied from the belt and running back to the hand of the veteran. But neither Slade nor Horn seemed to feel it strange that Carcajou had acted as he did. Neither of them appeared to bear the slightest resentment, and Slade actually said to Carcajou: "I don't blame you. We hate the old fool as much as you do, and after he's brought us to. . . . Well, listen to me, Carcajou. Me and Charley have been talking things over. If you've turned back the girl and her friends, it's a load off our minds. I'll tell you what . . . we ain't chasing this far North after any rainbow, brother. We're lookin' for the pot of gold. I guess you figgered that out a long time ago. And we want you to get a slice of the profits. Suppose we split the thing five ways. You get one way, me and Horn get the other four, because we had the idea first. Does that sound to you?"

Carcajou only answered: "I've got three wishes."

"What are they?" asked Slade.

"The first one is that Old Tom were just half his real age. The second is that he had his sight back. The third is that he should be forty pounds more of muscle."

Slade grinned brightly. "I know," he said. "You'd like to go at his throat, then? It's all right, son. Maybe you'll be even with him a long time before you think. Brother, me and Charley have pretty near choked over the old hound and his church talk."

They traveled on slowly that day, and yet there was never a sign of pursuit. Even when the air cleared of all mist and they reached a comparatively high knoll from which they could survey a great sweep of country, there was no trace of the train of pack dogs and people that had followed them the day before. The joy of Slade and Horn was great indeed. But Carcajou could feel no pleasure in the praises they heaped on him.

Watching Old Tom as that pioneer stumbled and staggered on his way, guided infinitely less by his human leader than by the dog on preceding days, a cold wave of shame swept over Carcajou. Shame had been a stranger to him before his journey to the Northland. Shame was a thing that one felt, according to his code, after one had shown the white feather, or had been outwitted or tricked or beaten by sheer force by other men. Shame was the emotion of the weakling, insufficient for the task in hand, and Carcajou never had been insufficient for the task in hand. But now he felt himself hemmed in and baffled and beaten in a strange way. He would have given more not to have taken the giant dog from Old Tom than to have undone any other act of his life. There were, indeed, few things that he would have wished to undo in his long career of successful crime. But this was different. As he watched the dog, constantly straining to get to the man he loved, it seemed to Carcajou, for the first time in his existence, that some all-seeing eyes must be fixed down upon the scene in judgment. What that judgment would be he could guess with much wretchedness.

They came to a creek, at midday, running down to the Yukon between steep, high banks.

"This ought to be the place," said Slade. "We've come about the right distance down the Yukon, Tom, according to your way of reckoning."

Old Tom stood on the edge of the bank and turned his empty eyes from side to side. With haunted faces, Horn and Slade watched him. It was clear to Carcajou that much hung upon this moment. Since he had been made a partner in their venture, he should have felt some excitement, also. Strangely enough, that was not the case. With a sort of melancholy disgust, he eyed the straight shoulders and the fine head of the old man.

"How does it come into the Yukon? About south, southwest?" asked Old Tom.

"Just that," said Slade eagerly.

"Is there a low bank on the north side, covered all over with brush and a few small trees?"

"No," groaned the other two in unison.

"A bank like that could be washed away any season, if a flood came down," said Old Tom. "Any fringing of trees on top of the bank across there?"

"Yes. There's a scattering of trees."

"I think that it's the place," said Old Tom. "Is there a big double bend of the bank off here to my left?"

"Yes, two big bends."

"It's the creek," said Old Tom. "It's Thunder Creek. And we're only a half day's march from the mine . . . ah, you told me not to use that word. I'm sorry."

"That's all right," said Slade. "Carcajou's in the partnership now."

"Carcajou?" exclaimed Old Tom.

He said no more, but the expression of his face was enough to fill the heart of Carcajou with a hot wave of wrath, and then an icy shock of this new shame went through him. He was beaten and depressed, but now his attention was taken up entirely by what followed. Old Tom had turned about and was saying: "I remember that the wind that day was just east of south, and, when I was lost in that fog, coming down the bank of the Yukon, I had to feel my way along till I got here to the mouth of Thunder Creek. When I got here, I felt that I could hit out the direction pretty well. I figgered that it would take me about four hours of steady marching. The fog was so thick, blowing down the wind, that I couldn't see two yards ahead of me. But I had to get back to the mine. I was nearly starved. You remember, it'd been two days since I'd eaten. And marching along all of that time. Well, I knew that wind prevailed out of the south, or a point east of south. I got the feel of it on my face and my hand and marched for four hours. I crossed about half a dozen creeks, got through a tangle of trees, and at the end of the four hours I started to cut in circles." He paused and shook his head.

"Go on!" urged Slade eagerly.

"Why," said Old Tom, "just as I was about to cut for sign in circles that fog lifted a mite, and the willows around me had a kind of familiar look. And all at once I understood. I'd been lucky enough to walk plumb onto the old mine. But I've told you boys this before."

"I could hear it a million times more," said Slade. "Now, you think that you could walk blind to that same spot?"

"If somebody can give me south by east, a point or two, I'll try to make it. Mind you, the map ain't as clear in my mind now as it used to be. I guess I'm stepping a little shorter, too, since I've lost my eyes. Suppose we make it five hours of marching and then stop and look around? But if we don't come out close on the spot, you'll have to start searching that swamp from head to heels, and that's no joke, I reckon. If I can't bring you right on the place, maybe you'll never find it in a life of searching. But I've warned you before. There's a hundred of those creeks, and every one of 'em the same, and every one of 'em with the landmarks washin' out and fillin' in every year, y'understand? It's a regular labyrinth. You'll see, pretty soon. Head on, then, and give me the direction, and I'll try to measure out the right distance once more. Oh, for some luck. The folks back home certainly need it."

XI

Money for its own sake was a small thing to Carcajou, and yet he could not help being stirred by the possibilities that might be ahead. As they trekked across the rolling miles in the hours that followed, he found occasion to say to Slade: "If the split is in five parts, one for me and four for you and Horn, where does Old Tom come in?"

"Why should he come in anywhere?" snapped Slade with an oath. "Ain't he old enough to die?"

He sneered as he said it, his eyes flashing, and John Banner looked straight before him, seeing the future and amazed because he did not relish it. It seemed to him as though a mist lay over his spirit, through which he saw all things dimly. He felt that he could not criticize Horn and Slade without criticizing himself, and he had never learned to sit in judgment upon himself.

They came, now, to a district shrouded in dark trees, all small and rarely growing closely together, but with heavy brush between. As they climbed a knoll, they could look forward upon the gleaming face of a swamp that was cut by the waters of scores of twisting creeks. It was such a tangle that even a compass seemed of little use in guiding one across.

But Old Tom was going confidently on, feeling his way a little with his staff, when Slade looked back and exclaimed: "There! By all the demons below!"

Looking back, the other two saw four Huskies come through a thicket not half a mile from them, and after the Huskies a small stripling, carrying a pack. It was the girl, then?

The brain of Carcajou spun into a dark mist. He had the explanation easily at hand. The disabling of Garret had been enough to make the half-breed see that this trail was no longer practicable. Even Garret and Taylor together might have a hard enough time in facing the dangers before them, but those dangers were impossible for a man to combat single-handed. So Taylor had turned back, taking his companion with him, but the girl, dauntlessly, had gone forward. For there she was, trudging steadily on toward trouble.

"Go back and turn her around and start her toward the Yukon," said Horn to Carcajou. "Throw her into Thunder Creek and let it carry her into the Yukon, for all that we care."

"I'll handle her," said Carcajou. He turned and hurried back with long, swift strides. The affront that she had put upon him long before still rankled in his very flesh like a poisoned barb, and it seemed to him a pleasant thing to stand before her on this day as master. The others disappeared behind him into the brush; he went rapidly on, down a small hollow, and over the next swale he stepped fairly out before her.

She stopped, closed her eyes, drew away from him, and then pulled herself together with a mighty effort. The four dogs crowded about her feet, snarling at the intruder, and Carcajou laughed with a sound like an animal's snarl.

"What were you gonna get out of this?" he asked. "Walking straight ahead, what were you going to get out of this? Tell me that, Miss Kendal?"

He heard the catch of her breath. She was looking at him as at a nightmare. "I kept on because I'd gone too far to turn back," she said. "That's why I kept on trailing you."

"You can turn around and follow your own trail back into the Yukon, then," he said.

She made no answer to this, but eyed him gravely.

He waved his hands. One of the dogs jumped far to the side and yelped. "Start going!" commanded Carcajou. Still she did not move. He laughed brutally, saying: "I gotta force you, do I?"

Her eyes were as steady as they had been back there at Sheep Camp, where there had been plenty of people around to support her, and at this he chiefly wondered, seeing the dismal emptiness of the landscape about them and hearing the growling of the currents in Thunder Creek, not far away. He walked up close and towered over her.

"Start moving," he repeated.

Nothing that he had ever seen in his life amazed him like what he saw now — for she was actually smiling up at him, although rather faintly.

"You can't do it," she said.

"I can't do it?" echoed Carcajou, still more astonished.

"You could torture Garret till he was half mad," she said, "but you can't touch me."

"Oh, I can't, eh?" muttered Carcajou. "You tell me why, will you?"

"People are made that way," said the girl. "A man who can take another man as you took big Bud Garret couldn't lay a hand on a woman."

He stared at her. It never had occurred to him that Garret was particularly big. A six-footer, to be sure, and with plenty of shoulders about him, but that was all. Bigger men than Garret, by far, had been as fragile reeds in his hands long before this.

"You're trying to now, but you can't," said Anne Kendal confidently.

"Why, you talk like a fool!" he broke out, and strove to rouse his anger at her assurance, but anger was a cold, dead thing in him.

"I may be a fool, but you're not the demon people make you out," said this strangest of women, nodding at him. "I guessed it the first time I saw you and heard your name. You're more man than carcajou. I'd be a thousand times more afraid if Horn or Slade stood in your boots just now."

"There's a short cut to the Yukon, and that's Thunder Creek that's muttering over there," he said.

"Meaning that you could carry me over there and throw me in?"

"Well?" he said.

She put her hands side-by-side and turned them palms up and looked down at them. "I suppose you could," she said. "But you won't."

"I've taken a job on my hands," he said. "D'you think that I'll come short of it because of you? What started you on this crazy trail, anyway? Your partners have turned back. If they're beaten, you're beaten."

"They're beaten, but I'm not beaten," she insisted.

"Talk some more," said Carcajou. "Because I'm interested. I like to hear you. Talk some more, and tell me how you can carry on without a man to help you."

"Perhaps I'm not without a man," said the girl.

"No?" He swept the horizon with his eye. "Where's any man?" asked Carcajou.

"In your own boots," she amazed him by answering.

"In my boots?" said Carcajou with a snarl.

"That's what I mean," she replied.

"I'm listening," he said. "There's a joke behind all this, I suppose. What's your idea?"

"My idea is that murdering hounds like Slade and Horn couldn't buy as much of a man as you are."

"They couldn't?"

"No, nor a scoundrel and hypocrite like Old Tom."

He started. "He's not a scoundrel, and he's not a hypocrite," said Carcajou.

It was surprising to him that he felt sure of what he was saying as of nothing else in the world — the virtues of Old Tom, who he detested so.

"He's both things," said the girl. "You're merely pretending that you don't know it."

"I'd like to hear your proof about Old Tom before you start on the back trail along with me," he said.

"What sort of proof do you want?" she asked. "When a man lets down his partner and breaks his word, isn't that enough?"

Carcajou shook his head. "Old Tom never did that, never could do that," he said.

"I *know* he did," said the girl.

"How do you know?"

"The partner he let down was the husband of my sister."

"Then he lied," said Carcajou brutally.

"Dead men don't lie," answered the girl. "He was dying when I heard him say it for the last time."

XII

It is true that death seems to brush away falsehood. Carcajou sobered, listened, and looked, hard and deep, into her eyes. Suddenly it seemed to him that in this world of lies it would be almost as hard to doubt her as to doubt Old Tom himself. Yet a lie must have existed somewhere between the two of them. His eyes turned small with suspicious doubt.

"Well, go on and tell your yarn," he said.

"Jimmy Dinsmore was my brother-in-law," said the girl. "He came up into Alaska four years ago for the first time. Then he went away and came back two years ago. He'd made a good stake the first time. He wanted to make a bigger one, because there were a wife and two children to be supported. So he came back last year. When he came home, he had a hundred pounds in gold dust. That's over thirty thousand dollars, you know. But he talked as though that were nothing, as though he had millions in his pocket to spend, if he cared to, and the story he told was this. He'd heard an Indian tale about following down the Yukon and up Thunder Creek, a little tributary of the big stream. He went on this particular trail, and there he struck a huge marsh. While he prospected in it here and there, he ran out of provisions and he could get at no game. He was close to starving when he happened to run across the camp of an old sourdough who had heard that same Indian legend and had beaten him to the spot. The Indian yarn was true. Jimmy Dinsmore saw the sourdough wash three hundred dollars out of one pan!"

"Hold on," muttered Carcajou. "Three hundred dollars out of one pan?"

"Yes. Just that. Oh, you could trust Jimmy if you'd known him. He was the soul of honor. He stayed with that prospector for a few days, and the old man took care of him. Jimmy was half dead, and he gave him food and treated him like a father. He was absolutely square with him. Then one day the sourdough tried a shot at some birds near the diggings, and the shotgun exploded." She raised her hand to her face, which had twisted with pain. "He wasn't killed," she said. "But both eyes were put out."

"Old Tom?" exclaimed Carcajou, immensely interested.

"Old Tom," she said.

He shrugged his shoulders. "This doesn't prove that Old Tom was a hound," he said.

"Not yet. You'll hear," said the girl. "The

next thing was to get him out of Alaska, or far enough south to find a good doctor. It was the worst season of the year, but they had plenty of good dogs and enough provisions to make the try, so they pulled out. It was a terrible march going out, but Jimmy was an iron man. He had to handle himself, and he had to handle Old Tom as well. It was a frightful trip. They had two dogs left when they mushed the last mile down to the sea. They got a boat and went to Seattle. Jimmy took Old Tom to a doctor, and the doctor said that nothing could be done. It was a hopeless case. There and then Old Tom swore that he would reward Jimmy for sticking by him on the long trek out. He said that he would give Jimmy a half interest in the mine and let him go back and clean out the placer. It was a rich find. There was no doubt of that. One man could wash out a fortune in a single summer. Jimmy was for turning about and going back straight into Alaska, but about that time he got a telegram from my sister in Portland, Oregon, telling him that their little boy was terribly ill. So down he came with a rush. Old Tom was to make out the legal papers and send them after him, giving him his share of the mine. Then, on the way down, in a steam-heated train, he caught a cold that turned into pneumonia. He was a mighty sick man when he arrived. I know, because I met him at the train."

Carcajou, focusing his eyes beneath a frown, continued to stare at her. "Go on!" he commanded harshly.

"I got him home," said Anne Kendal. "The next day he was delirious. The day after, he seemed a lot better. He told us all about Old Tom, and we began to watch the mails for the letter that was to come from Jimmy's partner. But the letter didn't come. Two weeks later Jimmy was well enough to sit up. The next day he had a relapse, and died in less than a week. And there was never a sign of a letter from Old Tom. I knew then that Jimmy was being cheated. He had saved the life of that old sourdough, I knew . . . and I knew, also, that half of the mine was no more than his by right. So, finally, with everything going worse and worse at my sister's home, I went to Seattle to look up Old Tom. It wasn't easy to trace him. But finally I located him, trailed him, and found him walking up a gangplank on board a boat bound for Juneau. Well, I followed him. He had two men with him that looked like criminals. They were your friends, Horn and Slade. If you call them your friends. I took the next boat for Juneau, found the three getting an outfit there for the inside, and I decided that I would do the same thing. I had enough money to stake one try. Everybody recommended Garret. Through him I got Taylor, the better man of the pair. They bought the dogs and the outfit, and we loaded onto the same boat that carried the others to Dyea. Since then we've hardly had them out of sight. If there had been only the two of them, I would have won, too. But they came across you. That was their good luck. They persuaded you to join them. Otherwise, right now I'd have Taylor and Garret beside me, and their guns would clear the road if the road needed clearing. That's the story. I've finished."

He cleared his throat and said: "Either you're a liar, or your brother-in-law lied to you, or else Old Tom is the greatest faker in the history of the world."

"What d'you believe?" asked the girl.

He closed his eyes and thought. It was hard to doubt her and her straight-glancing eyes. But it was still harder to doubt the man who had conquered Slaughter with a touch of his hand. "Old Tom is not a faker," he said finally, shaking his head.

"Good for you," murmured the girl.

He was surprised to see her eyes shining.

"You like him, and you stick up for him," she explained. "There's nothing better than that. I knew you were the right stuff, even if they call you Carcajou. I know you'll do right by me."

"What would doing right by you mean?" he asked.

"Let me stand in front of Old Tom and tell my story, and see if even a blind face can keep from admitting the truth!" she exclaimed.

Carcajou started. It seemed, at first glance, a quick and too simple a defeat for him. On the other hand, he was tempted by the thought of seeing the two of them face to face, the girl and Old Tom, both, apparently, so dauntlessly devoted to the truth. The thought made him smile. He had always felt that honesty is only a mask that some people are able to wear more effectively than others. He was sure of it now, in looking forward to that encounter. Either the girl lied, or Old Tom was a consummate cheat. To be sure, he had half the value of an incalculably rich mine to influence him. But the girl had the same idea to influence her. Should he believe the man or the woman? He hesitated and shrugged his shoulders.

When he looked at her again, he saw that

she was smiling, and she explained: "I wanted to see you blasted off the face of the earth when we found poor Bud Garret tied between the trees that morning. Then I started hating Bud when he begged Rush Taylor to turn back with him and not to go on when there was such a thing as Carcajou ahead of them. But now it seems to me as though the whole thing were planned out for me by a good genie, because I can see Carcajou will give poor Molly better justice than both Garret and Taylor put together."

"And who's Molly?" snapped Carcajou.

"Why, Molly's my sister," said the girl with an air of surprise.

Carcajou frowned. It was all too simple and virtuous. "Nothing for you to gain yourself in making this long march?" he asked.

"Except to see Molly well fixed. No."

"Bah!" grunted Carcajou in disgust.

She shrugged her shoulders, and then looked straight back into his face.

"You're smiling at me. You're mocking me right now," he said angrily.

"I'm smiling," she said, "because I know that you'll help. Brave men are never wrong. They're always on the right side."

He glanced back through the annals of his life — with its scent of gunsmoke in the nostrils and the sickening odor of red blood spilling all the way across a table. Brave men are always on the right side? Well, he could have told her a few little incidents in which they had been on the side of death and destruction for its own savage sake. But he merely said: "You think that I'll go with you on that trail and catch up with 'em?"

She nodded.

He drew in a quick breath. He wanted to swear, but his tongue was tied. "If I put you in front of Old Tom," he said, "will you promise to tell the same story that you've told me?"

"Promise? I'll swear!" she exclaimed. "Do you think that I've made it up? Oh, if there were light in his eyes, I'd make him blench."

He looked around him at the gloomy rolling landscape. Even where there were trees, there was little green along the boughs, as though life feared to show itself openly to so cold a world. Then he shrugged his powerful shoulders again.

"Come on with me," he said. "I may be a fool, but I want to see which of two honest people is the liar."

XIII

It was not hard, of course, to trail Old Tom and the other two men. If there had been any difficulty, it was removed by a sudden outcry not far ahead, a wild and wailing sound that, nevertheless, was not one of lament, but rather of maddening joy.

"They've found the place," said the girl. "Although how a blind man could lead them. . . ."

"I've heard of things like that," said Carcajou. "And blind men able to find things in houses they haven't been in for half a lifetime, too," he added.

They hurried on. To the voices of the men was added the howling of the dogs, and the pack of Huskies of Anne Kendal began to yelp as though they were on a wet blood trail. Presently they broke out from the trees into pandemonium. It was only a small clearing that extended from the edge of the creek over a low hummock, with the remains of a shelter hut on the top of it. Over that hill the dogs were racing or rolling to get off their packs, some of them leaping up and down or sitting to point their noses at the sky, some bristling their neck fur and howling with a melancholy abandon. Their frenzy was nothing compared with that of

Slade and Horn. Staggering drunkenly back and forth, they shrieked and howled. It was as inarticulate as the yelling of the dogs. They clapped one another on the back. They laughed till they cried. They flung up one hand and brandished clutching fingers as though they were trying to tear the blue out of the sky. But each kept one hand close to his breast, palm up, and from time to time they stared down at the contents of that hand.

Carcajou, approaching the clearing, had stepped out a little ahead of the girl. When the pair saw him, they did not pause to ask how he had managed with the girl. They simply rushed at him, babbling madness and joy. They thrust out their hands, and he saw the gleam of yellow dust in the hollows of their hands.

Horn raised his own few grains of treasure and flung them far, drunkenly laughing. "You dunno what it means, Carcajou!" he yelled. "It means that the yarn was true. The stuff is here. Whoever in the world seen a lay like this? Gold that ain't behind a steel door with a combination lock, but gold that's salted away through the ground like so much grit. Look, man! Look, look!"

He dragged Carcajou to the edge of the running water, tore up a bit of the peaty soil, put it to the hand of the other, and forced him to hold the clod in the running water. As the ground disintegrated, the yellow stain of it floating down the current, there remained in the hand of Carcajou two or three pinches of bright, glittering gold dust. He had handled plenty of money before, in large sums, too, but never had it had such an effect upon him. Money was a social product, along with jails and the other tools of the law. Money was a thing to be desired, but for which one had to pay either with labor or with crime, or with both. But this was different. Here was gold that the bare hands could take from the earth; here was gold growing, as it were, out of the headwaters of the river of happiness and prosperity.

Then a strange aftermath of emotion overwhelmed Carcajou, and he looked up with sullenly savage eyes, like a dog that had found food and is ready to defend it from the rest of the pack. They had offered him one-fifth share in this, had they? And he had accomplished the great feat that baffled the others — turning back Bud Garret and Rush Taylor? He would see these partners of his in perdition if he did not get a larger share!

Ordinarily Horn forced himself to a decent

attitude toward Old Tom. Now, however, he lunged for the old sourdough, shook him by the arm with a mighty grasp, and into his hand pressed the particles of gold he was holding.

"You don't need your dog-gone' eyes now!" shouted Horn. "There's something that you can buy new eyes with. There's something that will buy you everything you want most in the world. Except youth, Painter. It won't buy you that. You're that much closer to the infernal regions, but you can brighten up the rest of the way downhill."

Old Tom lifted his face and the dark hollows of his eyes turned up like the glance of a statue, in vain. There was trouble in him, not pleasure. "When I hear you yammerin' like this, Charley," he said, "I don't hardly recognize your voice. It's like a wild howlin'. It's like murder. I've heard men yell before they started to shoot. They sounded the way you sound now. I remember that it made me pretty giddy and sick, too, when I found that stuff. I got more'n four hundred dollars in one pan. I got more than a pound of gold in one pan. Not average, mind you, of course, but in one pan I picked up more than a pound. That's worth a day's work, lads, I guess?"

He laughed a little as he said this, but he was not overwhelmed by his emotions. Instead, he was as calm as could be and at ease. He merely smiled at the frantic excitement of the other men, which had driven even the dogs into a frenzy.

A thunderclap came in the brain of Carcajou as he asked himself what Old Tom had that was worth so much that he could actually despise a vast fortune in new gold? No, Painter did not despise the money. He had worked hard years before getting to it. But it was an end subordinate to other ends more important in the life of the sourdough. What ends might those be?

Carcajou shook his head and sighed a little. He let the gold dust spill out of his hand. He almost forgot the water behind him, the world about him, for the sake of staring at the illumined face of the blind man. For there was a secret, Carcajou knew, worth far more than gold or diamonds.

A yell came from Horn: "Look! There she is! Carcajou, I thought you was gonna either turn her back or throw her into Thunder Creek!"

She was coming slowly down the slope from the edge of the woods toward the rushing water.

"Carcajou, what's the meaning of this?"

roared Slade in turn. "I'll handle her!"

"Hold on, boys! Hold on!" exclaimed Old Tom, fumbling vainly in the air before him, as though trying to find the cause of the trouble. "What's wrong? If it's a girl, don't yell at her like that."

"Back up from her, Jimmy," said Carcajou to Slade.

He had only delayed long enough to watch her manner of encountering a man like Slade when the latter was simply an hysterical animal. Now he saw, and he was filled with admiration. She was not afraid, it seemed. She merely stood still and faced the rush of Slade.

"Come back here, Slade!" shouted Carcajou.

Slade yelled over his shoulder: "I'll come back when I've taught her the way to start back for . . . !"

He grabbed her by both arms. His head was wavering from side to side in the excess of beastly joy and triumph.

"You'd foller us, would you?" shouted Slade. "I'll teach you to foller. I'm gonna make you turn back, Annie, my dear, and if. . . ."

Carcajou took him by the nape of the neck and squeezed. It was not a pleasant trick. Nerves were crushed against strong tendons, and tendons against the neck bone. Once, when he was a boy, a grown man with a powerful grip had done the same thing to Carcajou, and he had practiced all his life to gain a grip so strong that it would cause white, shooting flames of agony to dart up through the brain and cause a paralysis downward through the body when he tried the same maneuver.

Jimmy Slade gurgled in his throat and fell on his knees, with both hands raised to thrust away the remorseless pressure of that strong hand. Carcajou sneered down at him with a brutal complacency.

"Don't go grabbing people, Slade," he said. "Because this is how it feels sometimes." He released Slade. Then he said to the girl: "Now you explain what you meant by calling Old Tom a traitor and a crook that didn't keep his word, will you?"

Savagely she faced the old sourdough, and Old Tom was now coming slowly toward them, fumbling with his staff and resting his left hand on the lofty, powerful shoulders of Slaughter, for the dog had been given back into his hand when he started up Thunder Creek to find the mine if possible. A very odd picture he made as he came with trouble expressed on his face.

The girl said: "If you're Tom Painter,

you've done everything I say. You've cheated a man who might have let you rot in the snows right here."

"Cheated?" said Old Tom in distress. "Cheated, did you say, ma'am?"

His eager humility did something queer to the heart of Carcajou. He pinched his lips together and stood there, searching their faces, looking from the face of the girl to Old Tom. One of them lied, of course. Both of them seemed perfectly brave and fearless in their integrity, but the very point of their debate proved that one of them had lied and was still lying. Which could it be?

Charley Horn rushed up, shouting loudly: "Don't talk to her, Tom! Don't say a word to her. Don't believe her. She's crazy. She's a crook!"

But Slade chimed in: "Aw, let them have their confab, anyway. What difference does that make to us?" But he added: "Unless he turns crooked on us, and tries to help 'em out."

"He's not a fool," said Horn.

"Who are you?" Old Tom was asking the girl.

"I'm the sister of Jimmy Dinsmore's wife."

"By thunder!" cried Old Tom, and came toward her, stretching out his hand. "Are you really?"

"You detestable hypocrite, keep away from me!" she screamed, and he stopped, stunned by what he had heard.

XIV

"If you're Jimmy Dinsmore's sister-in-law," said Old Tom, "you've got no right to speak mean to me, I guess."

"No?" she asked, savage with anger.

"If Jimmy were here . . . ," began Old Tom.

"You know well that he can't be here," she interrupted. "You know well that he's dead and in his grave."

Old Tom caught his long staff with both hands and leaned upon it. "Jimmy Dinsmore dead?"

"Ah," cried the girl, "he loved you! He was never finished talking about you and the fortune that you were going to make with him. And you left him to die, his wife and youngsters stripped of everything, except a little saved from what he brought home. Why did you do it?"

"Why did I do it?" exclaimed Old Tom. "Are you Anne Kendal that he was always telling me about?"

"That's my name. Poor Jimmy."

"I wrote to Jimmy . . . I wired to Jimmy. Why didn't he ever send me an answer? Did he die then right after he got back, my poor partner?"

"What address did he give you?" asked the girl, her voice sharpened by hostility.

"He gave me number Seven Fourteen North Shore Drive."

"That's the right address," said Anne Kendal.

"But wasn't he there to get the letters or nothing?"

"I was there," said Anne Kendal, "either my sister or myself. Never a word came from you. Why do you pretend? Why don't you admit that your greed made you go back on him?"

He sighed, murmuring: "Poor Jimmy Dinsmore . . . dead. Poor old Jimmy." Then he added: "How am I cheating Jimmy?"

"By throwing him off and running away to locate the mine with other men!" she challenged.

Still Carcajou looked eagerly back and forth from one of them to the other. Before long now the truth would come out in its ugly nakedness, and one of them would go down — Old Tom, no doubt, unless all the fire of this girl was the merest pretense. A savage excitement possessed Carcajou. It was better to him than watching a fight to the death between two fierce men. Whatever the result, it would prove to him that one of them was a scoundrel. Of the two only honest people in the world, only one would remain. The rest, all the rest, were wretches like himself, criminal wretches, too, if they simply had the strength to turn desire and conviction into acts. They were all like Carcajou — all the rest. That was the grimness of his satisfaction as he watched this debate. From one face to the other, the mask was now about to be stripped.

Old Tom had paused to consider her last remark. The length of the pause convinced Carcajou that the blind man was the villain. Men do not have to pause so long, he said to himself, when they have free consciences and open hearts.

"Jimmy Dinsmore," said the sourdough, "was the last man I ever knew with my eyes as well as my ears. I depended on eyes, Anne Kendal, after all those years of prospecting. Slade and Horn had stuck by me through thick and thin, but you tell me why I would throw over Jimmy Dinsmore and give a half share to these two, will you, if I could have got in touch with him?"

"Nothing but diabolical spite," said the angry girl.

"Were you in town all last year?" he asked her suddenly.

"Yes, all the time."

"If you didn't get any letters, any telegrams . . . and that I don't understand . . . how come, then, that my advertising in every morning and evening newspaper didn't get to your eye? Big, black-letter print, asking for information about Jimmy Dinsmore, describing him, and offering a reward?"

"How can you say such things?" asked the girl, more and more indignant. "A thousand people knew Jimmy. One advertisement would have been enough."

"Charley," said the old man, shaking his bewildered head, "you know how many letters I dictated to you, how many telegrams you wrote out for me, and wasn't the bill for the advertising more'n fifteen hundred dollars?"

Charley Horn scowled at the face of the blind man, his upper lip curling. He answered nothing at all.

"You can give 'em your word that I've told the truth, Charley, eh, boy?" said Old Tom.

Carcajou, catching a new idea at last, whirled sharply around and glared at Horn.

Then Jimmy Slade cut in: "Why, you old fool, you were sold out from the start. D'you think that we weren't playing you for a long chance? Why else would we've trailed up here with you? You simply led us to the right spot, but dog-gone' little good you'll ever get out of it, you half-wit."

Old Tom freshened his grip on the staff on which he was leaning. The great dog, Slaughter, looked suddenly up and licked those weather-browned hands. Understanding rushed on Carcajou, on the girl, on Old Tom in a single instant.

Then Anne Kendal said: "I see what happened, Old Tom. When Jimmy Dinsmore lay there dying, groaning, cursing his luck because he had to leave his wife and the youngsters behind him unprovided for . . . all that while, all those terrible days, he might have been at ease. Is that it? But this . . . this Charley Horn was lying to you all the while?"

"Charley, the chills that I've had up my spine about you now and then, they were the truth, weren't they?" asked Old Tom.

"You've talked enough," said Charley Horn. He turned to Banner. "Now, Carcajou," he said, "you and Slade and me had better step aside and talk this here thing over. We've got a pair of 'em on our hands. There might have been only one, if you'd done your job and turned the girl back. It was a fool thing to let her come through. Now there's two of them that've got to be handled. We'll have a sit and talk it over."

"We don't need to talk," said Carcajou.

"You got a bright idea already?" asked Slade eagerly. He ran his eyes curiously over their hired man, as though finding and admiring infinite possibilities.

Carcajou took from his pouch a thin, sausage-shaped canvas bag filled with the gold dust that was his advance pay, and threw it at the feet of Slade. "I've made up my mind," he said. "There's your share in me. You can have it back. I stand with the girl and Old Tom. I've done my share of hard things, and crooked things, old son, but it seems to me that I'm stopping short of the pair of you."

Horn gasped. "Hey, Carcajou, you're crazy. You dunno what a placer like this means. Millions, likely, millions, man. D'you hear me?"

"Why, sure," said Carcajou, "I hear you well enough. I've heard dogs bark before. I've heard them growl, too." He made a gesture, while they gaped at him in astonishment. His gesture indicated the girl, who was standing petrified with amazement at the side of Old Tom, her two hands affectionately clasped about his arm. "They're honest, Slade. It's the first straight up-and-up pair that I ever drew at one deal in my whole life, and I'm not going to play out your hand with them."

"It ain't really possible," said Slade.

"He thinks that he can slide us out of the picture, the fool!" shouted Horn. "He thinks that, and then he'll try to pass them out of the picture after us, and have the whole caboodle for himself. But the fool don't think that we. . . ."

He went for his gun as he spoke. It was not clear of leather before his hand stopped, and he stared bitterly at the blue-black length of the Colt that glistened from the fingers of Carcajou. The latter held the gun carelessly, a little above the height of his hip, and thrusting forward half the length of his arm. His thumb had raised the hammer of the weapon and held it with familiar ease. He made no effort to glance down the sights. By touch and the instinct of long practice he would do his shooting, if shooting there had to be.

Both Slade and Horn stood frozen before him. "Old Tom, I've got 'em on the draw," said Carcajou. "I've got 'em stopped. Now you tell me what to do with 'em, will you?"

Old Tom broke in: "Carcajou, I've been thinkin' that you was a pretty mean, rough customer. But I dunno but I'm the greatest fool in the world when it comes to readin' character ever since I gone and lost my eyesight. What to do with Charley and Jim Slade? Dog-gone it, Carcajou, I don't know. If they're what they seem to be, if we turn 'em loose, they'll try to knife us from the bush. If we don't turn 'em loose, we've got to watch and guard 'em here, and that would be a pretty hard job, Carcajou. I dunno what to say."

"Disarm them," said the girl, "and then let 'em go. If they try to come back, we have enough dogs about to spot 'em."

"Take their guns, then," said Carcajou briefly to the girl. "Take their guns and let 'em go. I might have known that would be your way with the pair of 'em. But they were aiming straight at murder, and I'd give them what they wanted to give Old Tom . . . a bullet through the brain. But go get their guns while I cover 'em. You fan them, will you?" He added sharply: "Turn around, the pair of you, and keep your hands up. Keep trying to touch the sky, will you?"

One revolver apiece was all that she took from them.

"Keep your hands up and now start for that brush," said Carcajou. "Faster, faster!"

He began to shoot rapidly. The bullets struck the ground at their heels, driving stinging volleys of grit against their legs.

Suddenly, capering, bounding, they rushed with a loud yelling into the shadowy bushes and disappeared.

XV

Seven days followed before the end, and they meant, to Carcajou, seven steps toward a strange heaven. He learned a number of things with mysterious speed. In the first place, in a single moment, by one act, he had destroyed the suspicion and disgust with which Old Tom and the girl had looked upon him. In the second place, once they accepted him, they opened their hearts and minds to him. That was the way to the new heaven for Carcajou. He had not known before what it was to talk freely with another human being. There were always doubt and hesitation. Contact with other people had been always war, a war of wits, craft, or savage strength. He had won many a battle, and now he hardly knew how to adapt himself to the society of people who accepted his naked word as through it were gospel. He responded as one entranced.

They worked hard and through long hours. The plan was to gather what they could in a month, and then take the out trail. Now that they had the bearings of the mine accurately taken, they could send in a crowd of hired laborers. So Carcajou was always toiling. The girl did the cooking. In between meals she came down and helped in the washing of the dirt. They began to take out three, four, five thousand dollars a day. Wealth of incredible proportions began to loom before their eyes.

They had to labor, moreover, with all of their attention alert. It was true that Slade and Horn had been driven off, but they were not very far from the Yukon, and boats were many on the great river at this season. It would be strange if they could not get new weapons and perhaps return with reinforcements.

That was still in the minds of all three of them when they sat down outside the shelter hut for the second meal of that seventh day. They finished eating, and sat about drinking cups of steaming, strong coffee. Slaughter, lying across the feet of the blind man, was sleeping, and suddenly Carcajou leaned and laid his hand on the dog's head.

Slaughter wakened like the wild thing that he was. A twist of that snaky head and he had the forearm of Carcajou in his jaws. One crunch of his teeth would ruin that arm forever. The girl sat frozen. Old Tom, unaware of anything, was continuing calmly in a yarn of the early days. So Carcajou waited, looking steadily into the eyes of the dog.

Little by little the green gleaming disappeared from the eyes of Slaughter. At last he relaxed his grip. Head high, ready for a spring, he silently showed his long white fangs to the man. But Carcajou reached out again and laid his hand once more on the ugly head. The head sank down. Carcajou patted it gently, drew back his hand, and for a long moment he and Slaughter stared at one another.

The story of Old Tom halted suddenly. "Ah, something's happening," he said. "I kind of feel it in the air."

"John and Slaughter have made up," said the girl. "He let Slaughter take his arm in his teeth. Why, John, that's pretty brave. Look there. Slaughter's wagging his tail a bit."

"You trust a dog or a man . . . it seems to do something to 'em," muttered Carcajou. He stood up. "I've got to be getting back to work."

"Wait a minute," answered Old Tom. "I've been talking things over with Anne, here. We both think, and we both know that you ought to have a share in this mine. A fair share. Does a third sound right to you,

Carcajou?"

"I don't like that name," said the girl.

"Nor me, neither," said Old Tom. "Does a third of the thing seem right to you, John?"

John Banner shrugged his thick shoulders. There was a puzzled look in his face. "I was working for Horn and Slade for fifty dollars a day," he said. "That's plenty for me. I didn't come inside to try to find gold. I came to keep low for a while. That was all. I'll take wages, not a share in the gold we wash."

Old Tom cried out in husky protest: "You're washing forty days' wages every day! We can't cheat you, son."

"We'd have nothing, nothing at all," said the girl. "Except for John Banner, we'd both be dead, I suppose."

"You'll take a third. You oughta have a half," said Old Tom.

Dimly, like the voice of a stranger speaking far off, Carcajou heard himself saying: "I stick by what I've said. I don't want a dead man's share of this, or yours, Tom, or yours, Anne. I'm a day laborer, that's all."

He had turned from the shack down the slope toward the creek when a scattering sound and a clamor of dogs broke out in the brush. As he stopped, staring, Anne

Kendal said: "They're after a rabbit again."

"No, they're scared of something," interpreted Old Tom.

Then there rang out from the bushes the unforgettable voice of Bill Roads, that patient hound of the law, yelling exultantly: "Shove up your hands, Carcajou, because I've got you covered over the heart! Shove 'em up!"

What Carcajou might have done would have been hard to tell, for on the heel of the call of Bill Roads a rifle rang in the ambush, and Carcajou felt a hammer blow on his left leg. It turned numb, and he slumped heavily to the ground. He had drawn his revolver in falling, but it spilled from his hand as he tried to break the shock of the fall with his arms. It rolled half a dozen feet away down the slope.

"Don't do that!" shouted the voice of Roads. "You hound, that's murder. That ain't the law."

The voice of Horn answered: "You take chances with him and you're a fool. I wish I'd got him through the heart, but I got buck fever and shot too low, I guess."

They came hurrying from the shrubbery, Roads first, with Horn and Slade behind him, rifles in their hands. Old Tom, feeling before him, found the fallen man and gripped him. "Are you hurt bad, son?" he asked the wounded man.

"I'm only scratched," said Carcajou calmly. "But if I had . . . Anne, throw me a gun and I'll show 'em. . . ."

Anne Kendal, he saw, had snatched up a rifle and stood on guard.

"Stop where you are!" she called to the trio.

"Look out, Roads!" exclaimed Slade. "She's as sandy as they make 'em, and she can shoot."

"Lady," said Bill Roads, "I've brought the law with me."

He showed her the badge inside the flap of his coat. The strength for resistance wilted out of the erect body of the girl. Roads came striding up to her.

"It's straight law," he told her. "Don't you doubt me. This bird goes back with me to look a jury in the eye. That's where he goes. At last! Three years' work wound up." He dropped to one knee beside Carcajou. "Where did you get it?" he asked.

"Through the leg," said Carcajou without emotion. "It'd be all right in a few days. It didn't get the bone, I'm sure."

"Good for you," said Roads. "It was a long trail, Banner. But it was worth it! You don't mind if I fan you?" He was searching the fallen man as he spoke.

"There's nothing else on me. Not even a penknife," said Carcajou.

"Are you trying to let him bleed to death?" exclaimed Anne Kendal.

"Bleed to death?" said Roads happily. "I tell you, no one bullet could make a hole big enough to let out the life of this man, lady. We'll tie him up, though."

He rolled the trouser leg as he spoke and exposed the wound, wonderfully small where the bullet had entered, but with blood streaming from the back of the leg where the bullet had torn its way out of the flesh.

"Get some hot water. Some of that coffee would be better still," said Bill Roads. "We'll wash the blood away and pack a bandage around it. I've got bandages in my shoulder pack. I never take Banner's trail without a first-aid kit along. But it's last aid that I've been nearer needing a pile of times." He talked cheerfully in this manner as he went about the bandaging of the wound, with the girl helping skillfully.

Horn and Slade were equally exultant for different reasons. Horn had found the canvas sack in which the washed dust had been stored. He weighed the ponderous burden with his hand and shouted with glee. "They been doing our work for us, Slade!" he cried. "We just been having a little vacation while they worked for us!"

"You fool," said Slade to Carcajou, "did you think that we wouldn't come back? But it was luck that ran us into Bill Roads, I got to admit. Still we'd've been back, anyway. It ain't the gold, only. It's your scalp that we wanted mostly, you sneaking traitor."

Old Tom said: "If one of you is a policeman, which is it?" He was standing, grasping his staff with both hands, leaning upon it, a favorite attitude of his, as though he were braced to receive a shock from any direction.

"I've got the warrant and all," answered Bill Roads. "You're Old Tom, I guess? You've got a reputation up here, Tom. How d'you come to be trying to beat Horn and Slade out of their mine?"

"Their mine?" exclaimed Old Tom. "Who said that it was their mine?"

"He can lie, too, old and blind as he is. He can see his way to the telling of a pretty good lie," said Slade. "Don't be wasting your time on the old fool, Roads."

The bandaging was finished. Roads stood up. He shrugged his shoulders. "What do I care about the infernal mine?" he said. He pointed to the prostrate form of Carcajou.

131

"There's my gold mine," he said, "and my diamond mine, too."

XVI

"That's right, Roads, but you're going to get a slice out of this from us, too," said Slade. "You just herd the girl and the old man off along with Carcajou. Just clean 'em off the claim for us, and. . . ."

At that moment Anne Kendal spoke up: "He's honest, John? Is this man honest?"

Carcajou nodded. "Bill Roads is one of the honest men, I guess, or an honest bloodhound. Call him whichever you please. But he will shoot at a man from behind. That's his style."

"It was a bad play I made there in Steuermann's," admitted Roads. "I'm sorry about that, and I got what was coming to me for it. I went sort of crazy, I think, when I saw you at last, after the long hunt, Banner. Something went crash in my head. I wanted to see you dead, that was all."

"You intend to take us away from the claim and then turn it over to Horn and Slade?" the girl asked Roads.

"That's what I intend to do," said Bill Roads. "They've helped me to turn the best trick. . . ."

"Will you listen to our side of the story?" she asked.

"Hey, Bill, don't be a fool," said Charley Horn. "She's the slickest little liar that ever stepped in a shoe."

Bill Roads frowned. "Down in Texas," he said, "we don't call any woman a liar. Go on, lady, and let's hear what you have to say."

It did not take long. She told the entire story in a hundred words, hardly more. But truth weighted every phrase that she uttered. She reached the death of Dinsmore, the attempts of Old Tom to locate his young partner, how those attempts had been blocked by the knavery of Horn.

Then Bill Roads broke in: "Horn, this sounds pretty straight and pretty black to me."

"Look, Bill," said Charley Horn. "You ain't simple enough to believe what a girl says . . . this far North, are you?" Laying a friendly hand on the shoulder of Bill Roads, he patted that shoulder familiarly and laughed a little. Therein he made a vital error, because the laughter had no ring of conviction in it.

Bill Roads stepped back from under the caressing hand and shook his head. "This here," he pronounced, "is no case that I can settle out of hand. No, sir, it's gotta be done according to a court of law. You can arrange for a hearing when you get back outside. Maybe the best thing is for the whole lot of you to come back outside with me, and then the law'll say what's what. Old Tom, here, has a pretty good name. I've heard a hundred men talk about him, and never an accusatory word."

"Wait a minute, Bill," pleaded Slade, "you mean that you're gonna make us waste our time? Is that what you mean? Make us mush all the way back to get the cursed law to . . . ?"

"Don't curse the law, brother," said Bill Roads, growing colder and colder. "Maybe you're all right, you two. But if Horn double-crossed a blind man, while another man was dying, then Horn oughta be burned alive, and maybe you alongside of him. That's what it looks like to me."

While Roads was speaking to Slade, the latter gave one hard, bright look to Horn, and the latter stepped instantly behind the man of the law. Now, with a very faint and cruel smile pulling at the corners of his mouth, Slade raised his pistol.

"Take it, you!" gasped Horn, crashing the barrel of his revolver against the skull of Bill Roads.

The man of the law made one stumbling step forward, stretching a hand toward the ground to save himself from the inevitable fall, with the other hand tugging at his revolver. But blackness was in his brain, and, as the revolver came forth, it fell to the ground, with its owner beside it. Not uselessly did it fall, however, for Carcajou, giving his body a sudden pivotal movement, came up on his good knee and one hand. His other hand held the Colt.

It was a twin brother of the gun he himself had lost the moment before. There were no sights. They had been filed away like the trigger. There would be only five shots in that gun. No one would have a cartridge under the hammer that was controlled by such a delicate spring as this that operated in the old-fashioned, single-action Colt. To the grasp of Carcajou, nothing could have been more welcome. He was ready to shoot as Slade yelled: "Behind you, Charley! For God's sake, Carcajou!"

Slade's own gun was out. Charley Horn raised his revolver and spun toward Carcajou, shooting as he turned. One bullet struck the ground and knocked a handful of turf into the face of Carcajou, but the latter was not perturbed. Without haste and without delay, he fired. Charley Horn promptly turned his back, raised his face toward the sky, to which he seemed babbling a wordless complaint. Then he fell on his back, dead.

His partner, Slade, had seen that bullet strike. He had heard the dull, heavy, pounding stroke of it as it went home, and the spirit went out of him. He had an idea of what Carcajou could do with a gun. He had seen him shoot birds out of trees. The heart of Jimmy Slade collapsed. The big Colt in his own hand became a mere encumbrance. He cast it far from him. He screamed as he turned and fled, and threw out his arms as if to grasp at safety.

Carcajou raised his gun.

"No, no, John!" cried the girl.

He looked across at her. The evil went out of his heart, and he dropped his hand. Jimmy Slade disappeared into the brush.

They were left alone, suddenly, with the senseless body of Roads on the ground, and the groaning, curious voice of Old Tom murmuring: "What's happened? Somebody tell me. Anne, John, somebody tell me."

Carcajou barely heard the question. What mattered was the shining eyes of the girl, as she answered: "John has saved us all again. That's all. It's the same old story, with one dead man added. I don't think that Roads is badly hurt."

Roads, in fact, was on his feet in five minutes. For another five he sat staring about him, before he spoke.

"You could have tagged me while I was down and out, Banner," he remarked.

"That's all right, Roads," Carcajou said. "They don't play the old game that way up here, this far North."

"I'm gonna take a walk and think things over," muttered the man of the law. He picked himself up and strode off into the brush, his head bent forward, his whole attitude one of thought.

"He won't come back," said the girl, looking toward Carcajou.

"He won't come back," agreed Old Tom. "That leaves a blind man, a wounded man, and a girl. Can we beat the game?"

"We can beat the game," said Carcajou. "I'll be on my feet again in a couple of weeks."

"Ah, man," muttered Old Tom. "How can we reward you?"

"There's only one reward that I'm going to try for," said Carcajou, staring.

Anne Kendal met the glance steadily, unabashed, unblushing, and she smiled her answer.

"Only," said Carcajou, "I'd still need a lot

of teaching, and a lot of remaking, and all I know is that I want to learn. Slaughter and I can learn at the same time."

"You know, John," said the girl, "this far North the days are pretty long. We could learn a great deal together." She stopped.

A harsh, metallic calling came faintly to them out of the air, and, looking up, Carcajou saw a scattering wedge of wild geese flying toward the north. Let them go, he felt, for he, John Banner, had reached the bourne of all his journeying.

■ ■ ■ ■

SEÑOR BILLY

■ ■ ■ ■

Although Faust continued to write for Street & Smith's *Western Story Magazine* through 1935, by 1933 his output was appearing in a variety of publications. "*Señor* Billy" was published in the January 7, 1933 issue of *Western Story Magazine*, appearing under Faust's George Owen Baxter byline. Bill Jeffers, the "*Señor* Billy" of the story, is a selfless hero who is willing to sacrifice everything, including his freedom, to bring happiness to the woman he loves. This is the first time this story has appeared since its original publication.

I

He was the bulldog type, looking almost fat with strength, but with his features well thumbed out like those of an athlete in good training. He had not a handsome face, but rather one built to stand a battering; only the brow was deep, and the gray eyes were set well in under it. Otherwise he was a fellow who could have melted easily into a crowd, unless he were known. As a matter of fact, the whole range knew Bill Jeffers and understood that he was worthy of the most careful attention.

He presented many contrasts now. His clothes, from his gray-checked flannel shirt to his leather chaps and high-heeled boots, were new; the wrinkles were not yet worked into the outfit. His very saddle was new, and so was the bridle on his horse. Furthermore, his face was rather pink than brown, a thing seldom seen on the range except in a tenderfoot. But on the other hand, he sat his horse like a master wrangler. When the mustang chose to shy at a white stump and begin pitching, he indulged that pony in enough bucking to loosen all the kinks in its system; then he straightened it out in flawless style and continued on his way up the valley.

It was a shallow, twisting valley, with a high bank of hills on either side and twisting cattle trails that wound down here and there toward the water of the creek. The cattle themselves appeared as tawny patches or bits of red; now and then one loomed against the skyline, looking supernaturally huge, and always the sound of lowing kept a melancholy undercurrent in the air. It was not sad to the ear of Bill Jeffers, however, for he had a cattleman's interest in beef, and therefore the booming voices, far and near, were music to him. They represented the blossom and the fruit of the great range.

The cows had wintered well, and, although it was only the early spring, their coats were not staring, their backs were not humped. He passed only one carcass, with three coyotes scurrying away from the spot. Bill Jeffers tried four shots with his Colt revolver. He missed, and shook his head. It was almost the same as shooting at tawny bits of mist blowing down a gale, but Jeffers was disappointed by the failure. He looked down at the gun and shook his head. He frowned, as one who is determined to fit his work to a proper standard.

When he glanced up again, he saw a woman ride over the right-hand range of hills. She sent her horse sweeping down the slope, drove it unfalteringly at a point where the banks of the creek drew close together, and jumped the gap with a shout.

Bill Jeffers, galloping hard to overtake her, gave a ringing echo to that cry. She looked about, then turned her horse. He overhauled her rapidly, taking off his hat, letting the wind blow his hair into a tangle. One hand was stretched out as he came up to her.

"Hey, Anne!" he called.

"Hey, Bill!"

His hand on hers was less firm than the grip of his eyes as they laid hold on her.

"You're grown up, Anne," he said. "By thunder, who'd think that half a year would make such a difference?"

"Am I changed a lot?" she asked. "You look as pale as prison. But am I changed a lot?"

"You're still a kind of a rangy steer, Anne," he told her. "But your face has smoothed out, and there's not so much devil in your eyes. The wind has still got some pink in the end of your nose, though."

She touched her nose with the back of her hand and her eyes shone over the edge of it. "Well, have you been in jail in Philadelphia, and New York, and Pittsburgh, and Chicago, and all the other places you've written to me from? Have you been changing jails all the time? You're pale enough, Bill . . . and, all the while, you never would tell me a word about what your business was."

"I wasn't in jail," said Bill Jeffers. "Knowing me so well, of course that surprises you a lot, but I wasn't even inside a jail once, all the time that I was away."

"Honestly?" said the girl.

"Say," said Bill Jeffers, "don't talk that way, Anne. You bet I wasn't inside a jail all the while."

"That must be a record for you, then," she said. "These six months must stand out in your life like a nose on a face . . . a regular high spot, Billy."

He was angered, and he looked sternly at her, and sourly, with a smile breaking gradually in spite of himself. She pulled off a glove and smoothed her hair with a slender hand. All her pretty face and body was flushed with the knowledge that Bill Jeffers was in the palm of that hand.

"You're going to kiss me for that," said Jeffers.

"All right," said the girl. She put one arm around his shoulders as he leaned above her from his higher saddle. She pouted her lips for him, but he hesitated, feeling the coolness of her eyes drift over his face.

"You're not so excited about seeing me again, are you?" said Jeffers. "You're controlling yourself pretty well, I'd say."

She smiled again. It had a strange effect on him to see her so calm, and her eyes so quietly studious, close to his own. He straightened again in the saddle, and gave his hat a jerk onto his head.

"Well, what's the matter?" she asked.

"Nothing's the matter. You're just so blame cool about it. Just so kind of professional. I'd as soon kiss your picture. I'd rather kiss your picture, the way I've been doing for six months. Quit shining your eyes at me, too, will you? You make me nervous."

He pulled up his belt a notch with another jerk.

"This is the old way," she commented. "I hardly see you, when you begin to quarrel before you've even told me what took away the tan. Come on. I'm late."

"This is Sunday. What are you late for?"

"A fellow from the Circle Eighteen said

that he'd drop over to see me this afternoon."

"What fellow?"

"Quit it, Bill."

He rode along at her side, the horses walking, touching noses with foolish looks of surprise.

"I want to show you something," he said.

He pulled out a thick wallet and passed it to her. She opened it and counted the contents of the sheaf of bills.

"Five thousand dollars!" she exclaimed. "Five thousand. . . ." She handed the wallet back to him, and flushed suddenly.

"You know what you said," he remarked. "That you thought people ought to have three or four thousand dollars before they tried to settle down and marry. Well, there's the capital. What about the marrying and settling down?"

She was full of haste and shame. "I never gave you a real promise about it," she told him. "I never did, Bill."

He stuffed the wallet back inside a pocket, looking grimly down at the ground that was passing underfoot.

"No," he admitted. "It wasn't in words exactly. You can dodge it."

"It wasn't a promise at all," she insisted. "Only . . . we were talking, and I spoke about the money."

"Well, don't be nervous," said Jeffers. "Don't act so scared of me. What's the matter? I'm not going to kidnap you."

"I didn't make a real promise," she appealed to him.

"There's somebody else, I suppose?" he said.

"Wait a minute. You're all white. And there's a red scar standing out over your eye. How did that happen? And what did you do to make all of this money in six months?"

"Guess," he demanded gloomily.

"Cards?" she suggested.

He shook his head.

"I don't know," she gave up. "Did you ride herd on the Chicago and New York herds?"

He touched the scar over his eye, saying: "I was fighting in the ring."

"Prize fighting? Bill!"

"Well, that's not murder," he said gruffly.

"Standing up and beating other men, naked, in front of a crowd . . . and . . . Billy, did you fight those frightful brutes? Oh, Bill, what have you done?"

"Gone and disgraced myself, I see," said Jeffers. "And made five thousand dollars. I thought . . . well, never mind. I didn't fight any frightful brutes, if that makes a difference to you."

"Would you have fought them?" she demanded breathlessly.

"I would have fought the devil," he answered in his abrupt way, "if I thought that it would give me a chance to . . . well, let that slip."

"And that's why you're pale?"

"Gymnasiums and indoor training. That's all."

"But the cut over your eye. Who did that?"

"The first fellow . . . the first fight I had. It was four rounds. It seemed like forty. He hammered me over the eye in the fourth round, and put me to sleep."

"Bill!"

"The bell saved me from a knockout," Jeffers told her, looking straight before him, and never at her face. "It only went down as a decision. But I was licked, all right." He drew in a quick, short breath.

"I don't believe it!" she exclaimed. "I don't believe that anybody could beat you."

"You don't, eh?" he said. "Well, you're wrong. A whole lot of fellows can beat me. Some of 'em are smaller than I am," he added, pouring poison into his own wounded pride.

"I don't believe it. Nobody on the range ever dared to stand up to you. Nobody ever will." Some sort of local pride made her flush. She doubled up her fists. "I don't believe that anybody ever beat you fair and square!" she cried.

"Don't you? I wish that you'd seen Dago Elder then, when he was ghosting around the ring, and dropping trip hammers on my face every second or so through eight rounds."

"But how did you make your money?" she asked. "They don't pay so much to losers, do they?"

"I began to improve. I had the fat knocked out of my head and some boxing beaten into it. And I started betting on myself. That doubled up the money. And that's enough about me. You talk turkey to me, will you? When I left you six months ago, I was in a class by myself, and had an inside track. Now I'm on the outside. Who's the new fellow? Or are there half a dozen of *hims?*"

"Don't sneer at me," said the girl.

"I'm not sneering. I'm asking. When I put that five thousand into that wallet, I thought I was putting you away among the greenbacks. I came out here practically a married man. Now I'm outside the door, and I have a right to know who's put me there."

"It isn't that," she insisted. "I'm as fond of you as ever."

"In a sisterly way. I know that kind of bunk."

"Billy," she pleaded, "my father and mother always told me that it never would do. You're too wild and free. You never would stay settled down. You never have, all your life. You know. . . ."

"Well, how old am I?"

"Why, you're twenty-seven or eight."

"I'm twenty-six."

"Think of that. Twenty-six, and you've never settled down. And you know, Billy, that a girl wants to feel some sort of surety . . . she wants to have children that won't be dragged all over the world, from pillar to post. My father says. . . ."

"That's enough," said Jeffers. "That's too much, too. Tell me the name of the other fellow."

"Even if there were one, I wouldn't dare."

"D'you think I'm a crazy Indian? D'you think that I'd go and take his scalp?"

"Well," she said, "there isn't anybody, really. Except there's one fellow that Father and Mother think a lot of. I like him, too. And he's quiet and steady, Billy. You're grand. I know that. But this fellow's the sort that could be depended on to. . . ."

"I know. He's one of these home builders, eh? What's his name?"

"Give me your hand first, Billy." Reluctantly he gave her his hand. "Look me in the eye," she insisted. Slowly he turned his glance and let the weight of it bear down on her.

"It's Dixie Trimble," she said, "and you're sworn not to harm a hair on his head."

"All right," said Jeffers, controlling his very breathing even. "Who's Dixie Trimble? One of the first families?"

"He's not been on the range long. His folks have a ranch in New Mexico. He's punching cows for experience, at the Circle Eighteen."

"And he rates ace-high with you?"

"He's gentle, and he's kind, and he's decent," said the girl. "But I don't know whether or not he's . . . well, I don't know how much of a man he is."

"You're not all burned up to a wisp of smoke about him?" said Jeffers. "Well, I'm going to go to the Circle Eighteen and look him up."

"You've promised . . . ," she began.

"I'm not going to eat him. I just want to take a look at the fine young man. Besides, I need a job, and the Circle Eighteen might as well give me one." He halted his horse. "So long," he said.

"You mean that you're not coming to the

151

house?" she exclaimed. "You're not going to see Father and Mother or. . . ."

"They want steady young men around, with ranches in New Mexico," he said bitterly. "I won't bother them."

He pulled his horse around sullenly. The instant he had done so, he regretted it. He knew that he was appearing in the rôle of a sulky child, and that she was looking calmly and rather contemptuously after him. Her voice called out. He would not turn, but spurred savagely down the valley.

II

The Circle 18 ran cattle over twenty thousand-odd fenced acres and a great deal more of free range. It was a big outfit, and it was run in a big way. Dave Walsh was the head of it. He was famous because he had bought four thousand yearlings at $10 a head in '88, after the terrible season of '87, and those yearlings he sold four years later at a net profit of $55 a head. It was a sweeping stroke of fortune that came on the heels of the '86 and '87 disaster and made Dave Walsh a celebrity and the Circle 18 a familiar brand all over the range. Dave Walsh was a silver-haired old fox now, and he had a hard-fisted foreman, Alec Reynard, who did most of the active managing of the ranch.

It was Alec Reynard who Jeffers interviewed, as the foreman sat his horse and bossed a job of fence building. A cold wind came off the snows in gusts and made the grazing cattle turn tail to it, and set the cowpunchers shuddering in spite of their coats and their labor. But Jeffers was comfortable in his shirt sleeves, for he was very warm-blooded, and his body was sleeked over with fat, like the body of a fine swimmer — just enough for protection and not enough to poison the muscles. That same wind sometimes flicked the end of Reynard's saber-shaped mustache into his mouth as he roared an order. Now and then he fired a question at Jeffers.

"How much experience have you had?"

"Six or seven years."

"That's not much."

"It's all I've had time for."

Reynard glanced aside at him. "Not enough experience," he said. "Tell me, are you a good cowpuncher?"

"I can do the handwork, all right," said Jeffers. "And I can pick up some of the brain work from the older men . . . if you have any that know the business."

"You look green and you sound fresh,"

said Reynard. "I don't want you." He roared another command at the fence builders. They were tamping in the earth around a set of heavy posts.

Jeffers waited patiently. He was not a man to be turned off by one rebuff.

"You still here?" asked Reynard presently. "What do you want now that you can't get a job?"

"I want to look over some of the fellows you have here. They don't look so big to me."

"They may not look big, but they are big. I'll tell you what," said Reynard, grinning, "I'll give you a job if you can lick any one of the lot."

"You're in the lot, aren't you?" asked Jeffers.

"Me? What you want? To fight me?"

There were six feet and four inches of Alec Reynard. His big body had been trained in fighting in Canadian lumber camps, and he had been educated on the range in the science of rough and tumble.

"I'd as soon fight you as any of the rest," said Jeffers.

"By thunder, stranger," said Alec Reynard, "I don't want to believe my ears."

"I've been in the ring," said Jeffers. "I ought to warn you of that."

"You been in the ring, have you? I'll make you wish you were back in it again," said Reynard. "You ain't the first plug-ugly that I've bit in two."

"Come over the edge of the hill, where the others can't see you drop," suggested Jeffers. And he led the way.

The foreman, after staring an instant, followed with a rush. Both men disappeared from the gaze of the working gang. At the end of three minutes, they hove in view again. They were exactly as they had been before, except that there was a small crimson spot on the side of Reynard's jaw.

"You get the job," he was saying to Jeffers. "You been in the ring, all right. But wasn't that a blackjack that you shook out of your sleeve and socked me with?"

Jeffers smiled.

"It turned the hills into a merry-go-round," said Reynard, who had fought enough to know how to take defeat. He rubbed the sore spot on his jaw, and added: "What do you weigh?"

"A hundred and fifty," said Jeffers.

"A hundred of it is in your hands," said Reynard. "There's going to be a lot of soreheads in the bunkhouse. Those fellows are a tough lot. They have three pairs of boxing gloves already, and Chuck Wilson thinks he's going to be the next heavyweight champion of the world. You'll fit into that gang like a hornet into a Sunday-school picnic. Join that gang and go to work."

So Jeffers went to work in his new clothes for the Circle 18. Some of the men knew him, and particularly Bunty Graham, a long, lean rope of a man, as tough as rawhide. He worked at the side of Jeffers until it was time to return to the house that evening, then he rode in with Jeffers and gave him some useful information. The Circle 18, he said, was composed of hand-picked tough ones.

"Somebody'll try to take a fall out of you before you've been a day on the ranch," said Bunty Graham. "Some of this crowd have heard of you. They know that you've used a gun now and then. But guns are no good on this place, and they're ruled out. Guns are hung up on the wall when we get in, and, if there's any arguing, it's done with the fists. Are you any good with your hands?"

"I've been spending a few months in the ring," said Jeffers. "That ought to help."

"In the ring!" exclaimed Bunty. "Sure it will help. How did you come out?"

"A little more than fifty percent," said Jeffers, smiling a little. He did not mention that all his reverses had come in the first few weeks. He would not have mentioned the ring at all, except that he wanted to enjoy no secret advantage.

"Well," said Bunty, "most of the boys will lay off you, when they find that out, but some of them are going to get ambitious as soon as they know. A couple of 'em would fight a grizzly bear, even if it started roaring in their faces, and there's only one down-right peaceable gent on the place."

"Who's that?" asked Jeffers.

"A young gent from New Mexico, by name of Dixie Trimble. His old man has a ranch out yonder, and the kid is picking up experience by punching cows for a while in this part of the world. He's as quiet as a lamb, and the boys have been laying off him because he's in with the old man. But his time is coming. They want to see the color of his inside lining, and they're surely going to find out."

"What sort of a fellow is this Trimble?" asked Jeffers indifferently.

"He's a fine-looking young gent," said Bunty. "Six feet of beautifulness, and husky, too. But his nerve . . . well, I dunno about that."

It was not until suppertime and dusk that

157

Dixie Trimble appeared. Jeffers knew him at once. Bitterly he scanned the handsome face, the smiling blue eyes, and the six feet of huskiness that went to the making of the rancher's son. It was no wonder that Anne Calhoun had lost at least half her heart to him. But the matter of nerve? Well, that was another thing. Grimly, hopefully Jeffers made that reservation. He did not know that that very night the nerve of Trimble was to be tested.

III

It had looked to Jeffers, when the men retired from the dining room to the lantern-lighted bunk room, as though he himself would receive the testing. Dixie Trimble had retired to the end of the room, at once, where he sat on his bunk and scribbled a letter. But Jeffers was picked up by the keen eye and the loud voice of Chuck Wilson.

The foreman had said that Chuck aspired to be heavyweight champion, in time, and he looked fit for the part. He had one of those huge, blunt faces that are made to withstand shocks; his great shoulders and arms were ideally built for delivering them. Now he pushed his hair out of his eyes, and said: "Hey, you! You new man."

"Jeffers is my name," said Bill Jeffers.

"The kind of a name that lasts, on this ranch, is the name that you get on it," said Chuck Wilson. "I hear you been in the ring?"

Jeffers nodded.

"How far did you get?" asked Chuck.

"I got as far as the Circle Eighteen," said Jeffers, smiling.

There was a laugh at this, and most of the men relaxed their expectation of trouble. It seemed plain that Jeffers would dodge a fight.

"You learn a lot from the trainers and the pugs?" asked Chuck Wilson.

"I learned never to pick a fight," said Jeffers.

"We got some gloves here. They're five ounces, too," said Chuck Wilson. "I'd like to put 'em on with you and get some lessons." He could not help grinning savagely as he used the last word.

"You need to box somebody with a reach as long as your own," said Jeffers.

"Well, where would I find somebody? There's Bunty Graham, there, that's as long as me, but he's too light. Hold on. There's Dixie Trimble that's pretty near to my size. Hey, Trimble! Come on and put on the gloves."

Trimble looked up with a start. His body stiffened. "Oh, I'm afraid that I'm no good with the gloves," he said.

"You ain't, eh?" said Chuck Wilson. "That don't matter. You gotta learn some time, and now's as good as any. Get up and take a pair of gloves."

There was a pause. It did not last many seconds, but while it endured, it had much meaning. For his own part, staring with a savage exultation down the lantern-lighted length of the big room, Jeffers made out that Trimble had turned pale. But the brutal invitation of Chuck Wilson could not be refused. Trimble had to stand up, and, when he did so, he looked to Jeffers like a brittle statue that would break at the first blow.

Over the face of Chuck Wilson spread a leer of satisfaction. His big hands closed and opened, once or twice, and he reached suddenly for the gloves, where they dangled in big, clumsy bunches from the wall.

Trimble came slowly forward. He was afraid. His face glistened. He was white, and his lips were pinched together. Yet he was forcing himself forward to what? To disgrace, shame, and a beating.

Jeffers saw it. He saw, furthermore, the animal gloating in the face of Chuck Wilson. And suddenly Jeffers was on his feet.

160

"Trimble can give you your real work-out, Wilson," he said. "I'll show you what I know, to begin with."

"You will? Oh, all right. We're going to have a chance to see a real professional now, boys," said Wilson. "Here! Here's some gloves, brother."

He flung a pair in the face of Jeffers, who let them strike him, and who then drew them on. There was an instant scuffling. It was plainly not the first time that this bunk room had been cleared for action. The center table was run into a corner. The four lanterns were arranged to illumine the central space. And while Bunty Graham tied on the gloves of Jeffers, the latter picked out Trimble, and saw a world of relief sweep over him, though his eyes remained big.

"Watch out for him, Bill," said Bunty Graham to Jeffers. "He's got a right uppercut that ought to make him rich, someday. And he can hit with both hands. He's got a shift that's a beauty. He's a tough *hombre,* too, and he won't fall the first time you nail him."

Jeffers paid careful heed. He knew the advantage of professional training. But he knew, also, the importance of seventy pounds pull in the weights when that pull belonged to a savage like Chuck Wilson. A

161

moment later, they were putting up their hands, the bright little eyes of Wilson roving the body of his antagonist to pick out vital spots. The cowpunchers stood about, grinning. Only big Dixie Trimble remained in the background, with a sick look still in his face.

Was he a coward, or was he simply inexperienced? Fear may be in the best of men, as Jeffers knew, before a fellow has proved his strength, and before he discovers that victory is not a crown of gold, and defeat is not an icy ignominy, never to be lived down. He, Bill Jeffers, was no coward, and yet he knew the chilly weakness that comes over a man when the gong sounds and the crowd goes silent, the savage crowd that wants to see blood.

Big Alec Reynard strode into the room, saw what was going on, and took charge.

"I'll put five dollars on Jeffers," he said. "Who'll take me?"

There was a roar from the voices of those who eagerly accepted. In half a minute, a dozen of those $5 bets had been placed.

"All right," said Reynard. "You fellows break clean. Outside of that, raise dust and let's see what settles to the floor." He stepped back and slapped his hands together.

Big Chuck Wilson came in with a good long left and followed with an excellent right cross. But he hurt nothing but the air. Jeffers moved very slightly, but enough. His feet and his swaying body kept him out of harm's way, and both hands were ready for use. So, sliding in under the guard of Wilson, he caught the big fellow off balance and jammed a short right to the jaw.

Wilson went back on his heels, staggering. The thing had to be finished quickly, Jeffers knew that. Once Wilson became accustomed to the style of his opponent, his weight and reach and power would tell at once. So Jeffers never let him get set. He went dancing in, measuring his man, hitting with beautiful precision. Those blows made the hair lift on the shaggy head of Wilson. And every one of them brought a yip from the watching cowpunchers.

Wilson, striking out with all his might, gallant though baffled, could never regain his balance. A rib roaster made him drop his guard; a solid right clicked the end of his chin and caused his knees to sag. But the man seemed to be full of spring that supported him, though falling. Twice more, Jeffers found the button with all his might. And then, at last, Chuck Wilson eased forward, slumped, and struck face downward on the floor. His big body whacked the boards so hard that puffs of dust shot upward from the cracks.

There was one deep roar of amazement. Then they carried Wilson to a bunk and stretched him out. It was five minutes before his eyes began to roll with returning consciousness. Another object than Wilson was in the mind of Jeffers, however. It was the white face of big Dixie Trimble.

The man could be shamed, broken, ruined, and there was nothing that Jeffers wanted more than to have him swept from the consideration of Anne Calhoun. But that was not all. There was something else in Jeffers's mind, a compassion and a pity that amazed him, and a sort of sick disgust at the thought that such a magnificent engine as belonged to Trimble should be ruined by a lack of spirit. If that man could be helped, suddenly Jeffers decided that the help should be given, though in a strange way.

"All right, boys," said Jeffers, as Wilson was carried away, and as the foreman, laughing grimly, received the payment of the bets he had won. "Now I'm warmed up . . . who else will have a few rounds with me? How about you, Trimble? You're big enough. Step up and we'll box."

Two or three of the men laughed loudly. Trimble sent a shuddering look at the prostrate hulk of Wilson, but he had to come forward. With a set face, he allowed the gloves to be tied on his hands.

"Who's betting?" asked someone.

"Who's fool enough to bet on a cold horse?" answered another.

The lips of Trimble twitched as the insult stung him. He was sensitive enough to feel shame to the quick. If ever the proper courage wakened in him, what a bright flame it would be, thought Jeffers.

Every man in that bunkhouse had seen the fear in Trimble. Not a one of them but despised him now. Well, if the plan of Jeffers worked, they would change their opinions shortly.

The instant Alec Reynard gave the signal, Jeffers was in at Trimble. Purposely he missed with his left, letting it graze the cheek of the big fellow. Then he clinched, wrestling here and there a helpless bulk that seemed ready to melt out of his grasp and fall to the floor. Fear had made Trimble a mere shaking jelly.

The cowpunchers shouted.

"Wake up and sock him, Dixie!" they yelled, and then laughed, one to the other.

Jeffers broke from the clinch and danced

away. He saw a scowl on the marble-white face of Trimble. It was merely the agony of terror that caused the contraction of the muscles. The man was limp and loose. Feebly he struck out — and Jeffers deliberately swerved his head into the path of the punch. The instant it landed, he dropped to one knee, and remained there an instant, shaking his head.

A huge yell of incredulity and amazement roared out of the throats of the cowpunchers.

Jeffers got to his feet, and backed cautiously away.

"What's this . . . a fake?" shouted Alec Reynard.

"You don't know what a left he packs," said Jeffers, still shaking his head as though to clear his brain. "It's a natural, and it's poison. Did you see the hook on the end of that punch?"

As Jeffers backed away, big Trimble followed slowly. Bewilderment was in his face, but a faint flame of joy was in his eyes, also, and a spot of color was in his cheeks.

He came in skillfully enough. Plainly he had been taught boxing, but no doubt he never had engaged in fisticuffs with any except a boxing teacher. The strain of battle for the sake of battle had never been his.

But livening up, as hope and sudden confidence poured through him, he tried his left again. It went like a well-oiled piston, this time. And again Jeffers gave his head to it, and let it thump him. This time he dropped flat.

Someone was counting over him. "One . . . two . . . three . . . four . . . five . . . six. . . ."

He got feebly to one knee. The place was in a pandemonium. Then a pair of padded hands took him beneath the armpits, and he was lifted. It was Dixie Trimble, who was saying: "I'm sorry I hit out so hard that time, Jeffers. I forgot that I'm a lot bigger than you are. I hope I didn't hurt you."

Yes, it was Dixie Trimble, but now he was a man transformed, his face flushed, a bright confidence and courage in his eyes.

"I'm all right," said Jeffers.

"We'd better stop," said Trimble. "I'm a lot heavier. I'm sorry, Jeffers."

"Yeah. We'd better stop," said Jeffers. "I'm not getting paid for taking this licking, after all." And he laughed a little, carelessly.

But huge Chuck Wilson had come lurching from his bunk, and now he roared: "It ain't right! It's a fake! That last punch wouldn't've dented an eggshell. It's a damn' fake!"

"If it's a fake," said Trimble quickly, "put on the gloves with me yourself, Wilson. Or . . . if you'd like it better . . . we can have a go with bare fists."

Jeffers caught his breath. This was the crisis, and all his fine work might be undone suddenly by the bruising, iron fists of Chuck Wilson.

But Chuck shook his head. "I'm still seeing double," he said. "I hit that floor hard enough to drive nails. But I'll take you on tomorrow."

That was not true, and Jeffers knew it. Neither Wilson nor any other of that hard-boiled outfit would ever challenge Dixie Trimble in the future. For they had seen, or thought that they had seen, the handiwork of an invincible fighter on that night.

"That's a beautiful left," said Jeffers to Trimble.

The big fellow dropped a hand on the shoulder of Jeffers. "I just had a bit of luck," he said. "If you'd hit me first, it all might have been different."

Aye, thought Jeffers, how very different, indeed. He had gained his point. He had made Dixie Trimble a man. And now came the cruelly bitter result — that Anne Calhoun, hearing of this clash, would be lost to Jeffers finally and forever.

IV

To Jeffers, there was no point in remaining on the ranch, now that he had made Dixie Trimble into a man — and thereby lost what was dearest in the world to him. But he remained day after day, until the end of the month came, torturing himself perversely by the sight of Trimble, and by guessing at the happiness that lay ahead of Trimble in the future.

One Sunday evening, Dixie Trimble came back from a visit to Calhouns' and slapped the shoulder of Jeffers. "Why didn't you tell me that you knew Anne?" he demanded. "What a girl she is, Jeffers, eh? What a wonderful girl! You'll think that I'm the luckiest devil in the world, and I am, for she's wearing a ring of mine now."

"Is she?" said Jeffers, in a dead voice. "You're engaged to her?"

"Yes. I can hardly keep my feet on the earth. I could walk on the air, Bill. She's mine, old son. You know her so well that I don't mind telling you, though . . . telling you that she's mighty cool about it. You'd think that life was a problem in mathematics, and that she simply seemed to think that I'm the right answer, just now. All I could touch was the tip of a cold hand. But she's wearing the ring, and that's what counts. She gave me a letter for you."

Jeffers took that letter to a secluded corner and read it.

Dear Billy:

The talk is all over the range; I didn't have it from Dixie Trimble. But everyone knows how you beat that hulking brute of a Chuck Wilson — and how afterward you tried to beat Dixie himself — and how you failed. I can't trust myself to words when I think of how you attempted to hurt him — you, a trained pugilist! I know what was in your mind. I had told you that I was fond of him. And straightway you decided to go to the Circle 18 outfit and beat him! That was your way of finding out whether or not he is a man. I'm sick at heart when I think of such detestable meanness. Poor Dixie has such a big, generous, forgiving heart that he suspects nothing. And you'll feel less nervous if I assure you that I shall never tell him.

Oh, Billy, once I loved you in spite of my better judgment. And even now I feel as though I'd discovered my brother in the midst of some treachery. Even if I could forgive you, could you forgive yourself?

Anne Calhoun

He read the letter through twice. It was in his memory, then, never to be dislodged. So he touched a match to the corner of the paper and allowed it to flame up, and as he abandoned the last corner from the tips of his fingers, the wind blew away the final sparks of fire and crumbled the sere black ash in the air.

The "big, generous, forgiving" Dixie Trimble suspected nothing, she had said. Yes, how very little Trimble suspected of the bitter truth. How very little, indeed!

It made Jeffers want to do a murder. He sat with a blackness over his mind, and that shadow did not lift during the days that followed before the end of the month. She had loved him in spite of her better judgment, and now he was no more than a detested memory.

The month ended, of course, with a pay day, and Trimble sought out Jeffers. It was one of the peculiar ironies of the situation that Dixie Trimble had picked out Jeffers as his special friend. Whenever possible, he was with the smaller, older man. There were only three years between them, and yet Trimble always seemed no more than a boy to Jeffers.

"Now that we've got a pocketful of pay," said Trimble, "let's go into Benton Creek and throw up our heels. You'll be going to the dance tonight, anyway, I suppose? Anne is going to drive in with her folks, and I'm to meet her there at eight-thirty. You'll be coming along, won't you?"

"I'm not dancing," said Jeffers. "But I'll go to town with you. I might even throw up a heel or two."

They swept into Benton Creek together, that evening. The day had been hot, and it was still warm when they rode through the purple dust of the twilight into the town. They passed through the Mexican half of the village to get to the bridge that spanned the creek and led to the American section beyond the water. In the Mexican quarter, the dust lay deep enough to silence the hoofs of the horses. Playing children and dogs in pursuit of them ran through the dim shafts of lamplight, and in the doorways sat the men, smoking cigarettes. The women were still at work inside the houses.

"Billy!" called a voice as they rode through a bit of lamplight.

Jeffers checked his horse, big Dixie Trimble halted his mustang close by, and out of the shadows appeared a girl with a lace mantilla framing her face like a picture. There was a flash of jewels from her hand,

and the glimmer of silver work about her head and dress.

"Billy, you've been back all this time," said the girl, "and you haven't come to see me!"

"You didn't miss me till you saw me, Dolores," said Jeffers. "What are you doing?"

"I sing at the restaurant still," said the girl. "I'm on the way there now. I sing at the restaurant, Billy, and wait for you. And I always sing the high notes to your empty chair, Billy."

"You're a little Mexican liar, Dolores," said Jeffers. "But I'm coming to see you, one of these nights. Will you dance with me?"

"I'll walk with you, dance with you, run with you. I'll run away with you, or dance away with you, someday, if I can," said Dolores.

Jeffers had swung down from the horse to talk to her.

"You can ride with me, now, Dolores," he said, and, picking her up, he swung her as high as the saddle. She sat sidewise in it, as the horse went forward. She was laughing and chattering down at Jeffers, and he said: "You know how it is, Dolores. It's a lot of fun to see you again, but it's a pretty dangerous pleasure. How many of your caballeros are watching me out of the shadows and fingering their knives?"

"Not one," said the girl. "You always mock me, Billy. I am a poor, sad girl, but I laugh when I see you."

"I know I have a funny face, Dolores," said Jeffers.

She turned to Dixie Trimble in appeal. "You hear him?" she said. "Why should I break my heart for such a man, who will not understand? Here is the place."

They had come to the restaurant on the bank of the creek, with trees standing before it, and small tables set about under the trees. The waiters hurried back and forth from the building. Somewhere a guitar was strumming.

"They're playing for me now," said Dolores. "That music is to call me, Billy. Will you come soon?"

"Of course I'll come soon," he promised.

"Are you glad to see me?" she insisted.

"Of course I am."

"I mean, does your heart spring, and is there a tingling in you?"

"Like an alarm clock, Dolores," he said.

She made a moaning sound in her throat, and a pathetic gesture.

"Quit it, Dolores," said Jeffers. "Twenty of your Mexican friends can see you going through those motions. And, oh, how I do hate knife work."

"Then I tell you the truth," she said. "You don't care for me. I can see that. I've been true to you, and waiting for you, like a little fool. But tonight I shall throw my heart away."

She hurried from them toward the restaurant. As she passed under the trees, voices called out eagerly to her. She began to make curtsies and throw kisses to her admirers on every side, as Jeffers mounted and rode on beside Trimble, who still was looking back.

"She's marvelous. She's a little beauty," said Trimble. "What a girl she is. Bill, how can you treat her that way?"

"What way?" said Jeffers. "She doesn't mean a word she says. Everybody in the county has been in love with her, and she shies her hat a little harder than usual at me simply because I've kept on the sidelines. Flirting is a fine art with Dolores, but I'd rather see the picture than be a part of it."

"You're cold-blooded, Bill," said Trimble. "If she said such things to me, I'd be tingling, I can tell you, and not like an alarm clock, either."

"You keep away from the fire, old son, and you won't burn your fingers," said Jeffers. "Twenty of those young Mexican bucks are crazy to marry her. They'd knife the first

175

gringo that she got serious about. Believe me, I know what I'm saying."

"Listen . . . ," said Trimble eagerly. "Is that her voice? Is that she, singing now?"

"That's Dolores," said Jeffers.

The voice rose like the pure, rounded notes of a flute, and pursued them.

Trimble stopped his horse.

"Afterward she'll dance, and that's her best trick of all," said Jeffers, making a cigarette expertly in the dark.

"What's the song about? Great Scott, what a lot of heart she's throwing into it! As if she'd die of the song, Bill. I don't know Spanish. What's she singing?"

"Oh, it's an old song," said Jeffers, lighting his cigarette.

"I know, but . . . what does it mean?"

"That part . . . now. It goes like this . . . 'The day is most beautiful at the moment of its departing, and you, oh, my love, are most dear to my sad heart as you say farewell.' "

"She's singing for you, man," said Trimble. "How can you keep away? What a voice . . . and what a heart in it. She loves you, Bill, and you treat her like a dog."

"Not at all," said Jeffers. "It's just a game with her, and I don't want to be it."

They rode on, Trimble with his head bowed.

"Tonight she's going to throw her heart away," muttered Trimble. "Well, there'll be some lucky dog, I suppose. . . ." He broke off, exclaiming violently: "Let's have a drink. I'm dry. I never was so dry in my life."

"All right," said Jeffers. "Here's Maury's Saloon."

They tied their horses and entered. The swinging doors swished in rapid vibration behind them. They stepped into an atmosphere silvery with smoke and pungent with the smell of liquor.

"Whiskey!" called Trimble loudly. "Whiskey for the crowd, bartender. And bottoms up!"

Jeffers stood beside him, and studied the face of Trimble with a sardonic smile.

V

There were three rounds in rapid succession. The cheek and the eye of Trimble were flaming now, when a new group of thirsty men, entering and finding the bar lined two deep all down its length, formed a flying wedge and crashed through to the front. Jeffers, seeing the trouble coming, had drawn aside, but the burly fellow with long, flying hair, who made the point of that wedge, crashed full against Trimble, and spilled the fourth drink out of his glass.

He turned, without a word, and, as he pivoted on his heel, he brought the long left that Jeffers had complimented flush against the jaw of the stranger. There was skill and nice timing in that blow; there was the weight of Trimble's strong body, also, and the long-haired man staggered back, struck a chair, and crashed to the floor.

He was drawing a gun, even as he toppled. His first bullet plowed up the floor. His second smashed the mirror. Before he could fire a third time, the ready Colt in the hand of Jeffers was about to speak. But he heard another weapon boom, and the long-haired man suddenly twisted up in a knot of pain.

It was Trimble who held the smoking revolver that had fired the final shot. He strode across the room and stood over the victim. "You're a murdering rat," he said, "and I wish that I'd shot your lights out, instead of shooting you through the legs."

Then the swarming of the crowd shut Trimble out of the view of Jeffers.

Jeffers himself managed to get to the wounded fellow. The long-haired man lay very still now, his blue eyes patiently enduring the pain. Blood oozed from the wounds in both legs, between knee and hip. It was Jeffers who got him onto the table in the back room, and there cared for him until the doctor came. It was an hour before he set about looking for Trimble, and found that his man had disappeared from the saloon long ago.

There was the dance, however. Of course Trimble must be at the dance.

Sheriff Jim Rainey entered the saloon and went straight up to Jeffers. His cold gray eye was colder than ever. "You were in the middle of this, Jeffers," he said. "Where's young Trimble?"

"I don't know," said Jeffers.

"You mean to say . . . ," began the sheriff, his voice ringing out quite loudly.

"Steady, Jim," said Bill Jeffers. "You're the sheriff, but that's all you are. Keep your big words in your pockets. The small change will be enough for me."

The sheriff swelled with anger, but he checked his tongue somewhat. "You've raised enough hell around here, Jeffers, at one time or another," he said. "You ought to stay in the prize ring, and get enough fighting to satisfy you. Young Trimble is a decent fellow, or he was decent, till you turned him into a drunkard and a gunfighter."

"I turned him into that, eh?"

"You did," declared the sheriff. "The most peaceable on the range, till you started him on the wrong path."

Peaceable enough to be a coward. I waked him up, and now he runs wild, and that's my fault, thought Jeffers.

"Dixie Trimble's probably at the dance," he told the sheriff. "You have nothing on him. This was straight self-defense. A fellow smashes into him at the bar and spills his drink. Trimble knocks the chap down, and he pulls a gat and fires twice before Trimble sinks a chunk of lead into him."

"I may not have anything on him," agreed the sheriff, "but he's going to learn what the decent people of this county think of boozing and gunfighting. And what they think of his friend Jeffers, most of all."

The sheriff left the saloon. Jeffers went out more slowly. There was a bitterness in him that congealed, moment by moment, until his heart was cold steel.

He went down the street to the flare of light that extended over the door of the dance hall. At the ticket window, he bought a ticket and entered the great barn-like room. The feet of the dancers filled the air with whisperings; the orchestra blared; the slide trombone was braying; the silly waltz tune jigged up and down in the ear of Jeffers. The whole scene seemed tawdry to him, and worthless and lifeless, from the twisted streamers of bunting that drooped under the rafters to the girls in cheap dresses of pink and blue who whirled in the arms of the cowpunchers. Their hands were sun-blackened and their arms were white.

He looked everywhere for Trimble, and found Anne Calhoun, instead, listening with a downward head to the laughing recital of Harry Wilmerding, who went off as Jeffers came up. He would have avoided the girl, but she came straight up to him. It seemed to him that she was not like the others. She had both more dignity and more beauty. She was not tall, but anger made her imposing now.

"You've come here to gloat, I suppose," she said. "You've turned Dixie into a hoodlum, a fist-fighting, man-killing drunkard. The whole town knows that he's across the river making a fool of himself over that poisonous little Mexican snake, Dolores. And you've come here to gloat. But I tell you, Bill, that for every step he takes down, I despise you more and more. I've thought you were the finest fellow in the world, and you're nothing but a traitor, a. . . ."

"All right," said Jeffers. "I won't stay and bother you. I wasn't here to hunt for you, but for. . . ." He stopped himself.

"Billy," she cried, with a sudden change of tone, "won't you say one word to explain yourself? Is there no explanation?"

"Listen to me," said Jeffers. "Friends of mine don't have to offer me explanations, when they do something queer. I don't chuck away their friendship in a moment. Your way is not my way, thank God. I thought that I'd never be cured of caring about you, but, when I hear you talk like this, I'm just about cured on the spot. You don't know a thing. You're on the outside. Still you talk as if you could read the smallest print of the smallest ideas in my mind. I don't call you a gold-digger because you're going to marry the son of a rich rancher when you don't really give a rap about him. Why don't you try to be as fair to me as I am to you?"

He turned on his heel and left her, but something made him look back, before he had gone far, and he saw half a dozen young fellows off the range surrounding her with their laughter, but it seemed to Jeffers that she looked pale and still and remote from all the merriment. Something melted in him then. He wanted to hurry back to her, but he knew that there was a better way to serve her.

There was Trimble, probably a little dizzy with liquor by this time, and still dizzier with the beauty and the wiles of Dolores across the creek.

He stepped out again onto the street. The sight of the stars made his heart ache. How he had watched them from the window of the train, on the last night when he was returning West with the money in his pocket, and the girl in his mind. Happiness had moved with every pulse of his blood then. But now he felt alone in the world.

He climbed onto his horse and headed grimly for the Mexican quarter of the town.

VI

When Jeffers reached the Mexican restaurant again, he found it far more gay and noisy. The crowd had gathered. The tables were filled almost entirely by Mexicans, but here and there appeared a small group of white men. The dance floor was a circular flagged space in the center, and the music came from the verandah of the building, where the orchestra played as from a dais. It was not a roaring and whooping band as at the American dance in the other section of the town, but rather subdued, with the violins singing loudest of all and the thrumming of guitars and the trembling of mandolins keeping the accompaniment.

Jeffers, from the shadow of a tree, in the circle of the watchers who could only envy this entertainment without joining in it, observed that Dolores sat at the table of Trimble, at the edge of the dance floor, where all could see them. No wonder that the report had gone over Benton Creek that Trimble was making a fool of himself about the pretty Mexican entertainer. Literally she seemed to be throwing her heart at the feet of the American with every flashing gesture of her hands, and Trimble watched her, pale with enchantment.

Jeffers shrugged his shoulders and turned back to the hitch rack where he had tethered his bay pony. He was not, after all, his brother's keeper. Those sinister, dark Mexican eyes that watched Trimble meant mischief, of course. But Trimble had been warned, and therefore he could look after himself. He had both a good pair of hands, and a gun.

But when Jeffers reached his horse, he heard the voice of Dolores rising in a song. He turned and saw her dancing as she sang. Every Mexican in the throng was swaying with the quick rhythm, but all the song and all the wooing of the gestures as she danced were for Trimble, who sat like a stone, too far entranced to stir hand or head.

Jeffers cursed softly under his breath. For another moment, he hesitated. Then he went back around the open-air portion of the restaurant and into the interior. He passed through the bar, where the bartender called to him: "Welcome, *Señor* Bill!"

Jeffers waved to him, and went on into a small, dim-lighted room behind the bar. Here sat the proprietor, Alvarez, with a cornucopia-shaped cigarette in his mouth, and on the table before him a scattering of ashes and a small glass of brandy. Every night he sat there growing fatter and whiter and more soggy of face, and brighter and keener of eye. Few people came near him, and yet Alvarez seemed to know every gesture, every word of what happened in his restaurant both outside and indoors. It was as though an invisible nervous system extended from his brain through the place. With intangible ganglia he touched every part of it.

Jeffers he greeted with a wave of the hand and an attempt to rise. But Jeffers forestalled him by slipping quickly into the chair that stood opposite him at the little table.

"What shall I do for you, *Señor* Bill?" asked Alvarez. "Juan!"

The bartender came on swift feet, and placed the brandy bottle and another small glass on the table.

Alvarez filled the glass. "Welcome to my house again, my son," he said. "We have missed you for a long time. The men have asked for you, and the women have sighed for you, *Señor* Bill."

Jeffers smiled a little. For a long time, he had not heard the soft Mexican tongue pouring out its flatteries. He raised his glass. "I have thought of them all, but mostly of you, Alvarez," he said. "I drink to your honor."

Alvarez bowed as far as the depth of his fat chest permitted. "I drink to you, my son," he said. "And I thank you."

They swallowed the liquor.

"Last night was the night of Miguel Santos again, and he came here and entertained his friends, and we all stood up from the table and drank to your honor."

"Miguel Santos?" said Jeffers, frowning. "Miguel Santos? I don't remember him."

"No?" exclaimed Alvarez.

A waiter glided out of the shadows, whispered a few words at the ear of Alvarez, and went silently out again. Alvarez resumed:

"You forget the young Mexican boy who took a horse that was not his off the range, because his feet were tired, and how the cowboys chased him, and how they found him in this town, and how they would have lynched him, and how you defended him, and took him away from the crowd?"

"No, no! I remember now, of course," said Jeffers.

"So does his father," said Alvarez, with emotion. "And every year when the day comes again, he comes here to eat with his friends and to drink your health, your happiness, and your long life, *Señor* Bill, and damnation to the other. . . ."

He stopped himself, and began to drum the fat tips of his fingers against the edge of the table.

"And damnation to the other *gringos?*" queried Jeffers.

"*Señor* Bill, your glass is empty," said Alvarez, filling the glass promptly from the bottle. He added: "You are not dancing, or watching the dancers, tonight?"

"You know, Alvarez," said Jeffers, "that when a man grows older, he likes to sit and listen to wiser men talk. That's why I've come here to talk to you."

"Ah?" said Alvarez. He lifted his brows. All the lines of his face lifted, also, into a whimsical inquisition.

"Tell me the news of tonight," said Jeffers. "You know all that's happening about the restaurant. You know everything that is going to happen, too. Talk to me about that."

Alvarez smiled slowly. His keen eyes watched his guest critically. "When you speak, *Señor* Bill," he said, "your words say two things at once. What will happen? For a little while, all the voices will grow louder and happier. After a while, some of the people will go away. Many of them will call the waiters robbers. Many of them will swear that they will not come again to this place. And that is true. They will not return until pay day of the next month. Little by little, the crowd will disappear. And there will be a moment when the orchestra members begin to put covers on their instruments. The night will be old. The dawn will commence before I close my eyes, of course." Vast weariness crept into his voice.

Another waiter entered, whispered softly at the ear of the proprietor, and vanished.

"Other things may happen," said Jeffers. "But you can't tell the fortunes of this night until your palm has been crossed, Alvarez." He drew out a $100 bill and slid it across the table.

Alvarez covered it with the flat of his hand.

He grew paler, and his eyes brighter. "Words are easily bought," said Alvarez.

"Not true ones," said Jeffers. "I know the fortune-tellers who talk about the whole future of a man's life, *amigo.* They do it for fifty cents or a dollar. But it takes a great deal more skill to foretell what is to happen in this night, the happiness that may come out of it, or the blood that may be shed."

Alvarez slid the $100 bill back across the table. But Jeffers covered it with a second hundred and shoved the two back.

"Bloodshed?" said Alvarez, putting the tip of a finger on the edges of the bills. "You are as safe with us, *Señor* Bill, as if you were in your own home."

"Not having a home, I suppose I am," said Jeffers. "But what about that fellow out there . . . the big one . . . called Trimble?"

"I know nothing about him," said Alvarez calmly. "Each of us has his fate. I am not a fortune-teller, *Señor* Bill."

"Of course not," said Jeffers, and pushed another $100 bill across the table. "I only ask you to guess what may happen, Alvarez."

The face of the Mexican shone, as a fine perspiration broke out on it. Suddenly he picked up the money and stuffed it into his coat pocket. He leaned his thick elbows on the edge of the table.

"What is it that you want to know?" he asked.

Jeffers was equally direct. "Trimble is monopolizing Dolores," he said. "And some of her Mexican friends don't like it. A few of 'em are likely to use knives or guns. Which are the dangerous ones?"

Alvarez took out a silk handkerchief, spread it across his hand, and wiped his face with care. But the sweat still poured. He put his hand into his coat pocket.

"This is yours, also," said Jeffers, and pushed the fourth hundred across the table.

Alvarez picked up the banknote with a sigh and put it away with the others. He spread his big hands on the table and looked studiously down at them. His voice was the merest whisper as he murmured: "There is the big man with the mustache . . . Muntaner . . . there is the little man with the pockmarks on his face . . . Oñate. Those two are dangerous. And now my own throat is in peril."

"Will they try to kill him, or simply knock him out of the way?" asked Jeffers.

The hands of Alvarez contracted. "Kill," he said.

Jeffers stood up. "That brandy is the best I've ever had here, Alvarez," he said. And he went out to the verandah and looked out on the dancers.

Dolores was no longer at the table of Trimble. Her silk cloak lay over the back of the chair opposite that of the American, but she herself was sweeping through a waltz in the arms of a big, yellow-skinned Mexican whose upper lip was stained black by a short mustache. He danced well, almost as a professional might have danced. But at every turn the glance of Dolores sought the pale, dreaming face of Trimble.

Jeffers went around the edge of the dance floor and paused beside Trimble. "Dixie," he said, "you're wanted."

Trimble looked up at him. "Hello," he muttered. "Oh, hello, Bill. Sit down a minute. Here." He pulled up a third chair.

Jeffers disregarded it. "You're wanted," he repeated.

"Who wants me?" asked Trimble.

"Anne Calhoun. She's at the dance. You were to be there at nine. It's long after ten. It's nearing eleven now."

Trimble stirred impatiently. "Did she send you after me?" he asked, frowning.

"No," said Jeffers. "I simply thought I'd better come and let you know how the time's slipping along." He passed his hand across his face, as he spoke, and let the tips

191

of his fingers linger for an instant on the scar above his eye.

"It's too late now," said Trimble almost angrily. "She has her folks with her. She'll go home with them, anyway . . . and . . . don't worry about Anne. I'll be able to handle her, all right."

"Will you?" said Jeffers.

"Yes. Of course I will. Why not?" He stared straight at Jeffers, with a challenge.

"All right," answered Jeffers in disgust. "I simply wanted to know. And there's another thing . . . you've been paying a lot of attention to Dolores, here. The town's talking about it, Dixie."

"The town can be damned, for all I care," said Trimble. "She's the most wonderful. . . . What's the matter, Bill? Want her for yourself?"

As though a whiplash had flicked him, Jeffers trembled. He grew so pale that the scar above his eye was a streak of red.

"I've got one more thing I'd like to tell you," said Jeffers. "Want to hear it?"

"I don't know," answered Trimble. "Suit yourself."

"It's this," said Jeffers, breathing with difficulty. "Some of these Mexicans, as I told you before, have knives, and they know how to use them. You're riding for a fall. To put it another way, you're getting ready for a knife in the back."

"A pack of greasers?" said Trimble.

"Call them what you want," replied Jeffers. "Their ways are not our ways, in some particulars, yet I've known Mexicans as good as anybody north of the Río Grande. But some of 'em are ready to kill for the sake of a woman."

"Herd with 'em, then," said Trimble, snapping his fingers. "But if you're afraid of them, I'm not."

VII

Out of the crowd walked Jeffers toward his horse, but, as the music of the dance ended, he turned in time to see Dolores sitting down again at Trimble's table, giving him her most radiant smile, holding her head back a little, half closing her eyes with invitation.

And Jeffers walked up and down the street, as far as the bridge over the creek, and back again, several times. Still he cursed as he walked, and turned in his mind various alternatives. It seemed to him that he had spent plenty of time, money, and effort on Trimble. Every gesture he made in behalf of the man redounded to his own discredit.

It was like an infection; the best way to escape it was to let Trimble go his own way. Even the sheriff of the town, to say nothing of Anne Calhoun, considered him the guilty influence in the life of Trimble.

How far that might be, he himself could not tell. Yonder in the bunkhouse of the Circle 18 there had been a timorous but a safe young man, when Jeffers appeared on the scene, a man who shuddered at the thought of so much as a boxing contest. But on that night he had been awakened, aroused, filled with a sense of his own power, and now he was going blithely on his way even when threats of murder were in the air.

Jeffers could not leave him. So he went back into the crowd and found a little empty table where his back could be against a tree. He got a small black coffee and drank it. He needed a clear brain, and the coffee might help. Dolores was singing again, moving around the restaurant, dancing through the crowd that laughed joyously and threw her glittering coins that she caught out of the air with her flashing hands.

She lingered for a moment in front of Jeffers's table, and he recognized the singular throb of appeal that came into her voice, but he looked straight before him, trying to find his plan.

It was not until he heard a waltz begin, shortly afterward, that his mind cleared suddenly. He went to the table where Dolores sat with Trimble and said: "May I steal Dolores for this dance, Dixie?"

Trimble looked up from his dream coldly. "That's as she pleases," he said.

But Dolores was already rising, and presently she was dancing with Jeffers in the sweep of the crowd on the floor. He moved slowly, keeping just within the beat of the music.

"You, Billy," she whispered, "are the only dancer. All the others, they jump and run like rabbits."

"Except Muntaner?" said Jeffers.

"Muntaner? Oh, I pay no attention to him."

"He pays enough to you, my dear."

"Have you been watching? Are you jealous, Billy?" she asked him anxiously, eagerly.

He did not answer, but asked in turn: "That fellow Trimble . . . what do you want with him? He's spending a lot of money over there with you. All of Alvarez's best wine. What do you want with him, Dolores?"

"Well, do you know what he has?" she demanded.

"A ranch in New Mexico," he said.

"And six thousand beeves on it! If every steer were a pearl, there would be enough jewels for poor little Dolores, eh?"

"You're going to marry him, are you?"

"Why not?"

"He's already engaged, Dolores. You're wasting your time. He's half drunk, tonight. Tomorrow he'll be sober again."

"Do you think so?" said the girl. "Ah, but I know. I can tell when it is only the wine in them that loves me, and when it is their hearts. And he is in love with poor little Dolores." She began to laugh.

"Stop it," said Jeffers.

"Yes," she answered. But still she laughed. "Are you jealous, Billy? Are you a little jealous? Do you care for me at all?"

"You're such a pretty little cat, Dolores, that I'd always like to have you around," he told her. "How many men are engaged to you now?"

"Engaged? Nobody. Only *Señor* Trimble, before the evening is over. That will be all."

"You've promised to marry Muntaner," said Jeffers.

"He? Oh, he is nothing."

"And little Oñate, with the pockmarked face. You've promised to marry him, also?"

She pushed herself a little away from him,

to look up into his face. "Have you been reading minds, Billy?" she asked. "Have you been talking to a fortune-teller, wonderful Billy?"

"Listen to me, Dolores."

"As if you were my father confessor."

"If you want that ranch in New Mexico, the thing for you to do is to get him safely out of here. Muntaner and Oñate are watching him like wildcats, while you sit with Trimble. Muntaner and Oñate are together now, and it's plain that they want the heart out of Trimble. They'll have it, too. He can't guard himself against the pair of 'em. If you want the ranch, Dolores, get Trimble out of here at once."

"Will you stay, if I send him away?" she asked quickly.

"I'd have to go along to take care of him. He's too full of liquor and too excited. There'd be trouble."

"Let him stay and take his chances then," said the girl, with a shrug of her shoulders. "After all, he's only a. . . ." She paused.

"A *gringo,*" said Jeffers. "And so am I."

"No, no! You are *Señor* Billy. Everyone knows that. Tell me again, Billy, that I am pretty . . . and a cat . . . and you want to have me with you. If you want to keep him from trouble, I'll send him away, and you can take care of the great simpleton. But swear that as soon as he's safe, you'll come back to me here. Swear that you'll come, Billy, and take me away with you, somewhere."

"When you say that, smile," said Jeffers. "Trimble is watching you like a hawk, and you look too serious."

"Trimble? He's nothing. What do I care for him? Nothing at all. I'll handle him. But you, Billy. If you'll take me away, I know how to make you happy. I'll make you so happy that you'll sing all day long."

"You would, Dolores," he told her. "Nobody in the world could make me happier, I suppose. But there's trouble, around here, that keeps me in Benton Creek. I can't go, for a while."

"It's the girl with the blonde hair and the blue eyes. Her name is Anne Calhoun. Oh, I heard about her, and I saw her. *Bah!*"

"Where did you see her, Dolores?"

"A year ago, when you stopped coming here, I asked a few questions and heard about her, and I rode all the way out to the Calhoun Ranch. You call me a cat, Billy? Well, I climbed like a cat, that night, and I found the window of her room, and looked in at her. Why do you care about her? She is nothing. She has no color. She is a poor, pale thing. She is not like me, Billy."

"She's engaged to Trimble," said Jeffers. "So let him have her, Dolores."

"Is it because of her that you must stay here?" she asked.

He thought for a moment. "No," he said. "Not because of her."

"*Señor* Billy never lies," said the girl. "Even the little children in the streets know that. They say . . . 'As true as *Señor* Billy.' So you are not lying to Dolores?"

"No," said Jeffers. "Anne Calhoun doesn't care a rap about me, my dear. She despises me, in fact."

"Oh, the fool, the fool," said the Mexican girl. "But I'm glad. Tell me why you won't go away with me, Billy? Tell me why you must stay here?"

"Because of him . . . because of Trimble," he said.

"Why, he's not your brother . . . he doesn't owe you money . . . why should you care about him?"

He tried to think out the problem. He had tried to think it out before. "I don't know," he said at last, "unless it's a question of honor, Dolores."

"Honor? *Bah!* Look at me, and see if I'm not worth more than silly honor. I could love you so that the angels would envy us.

You care about me a little. You told me so, there . . . when we sat under the tree with the broken limb . . . that was the glorious moment out of my life. And if you cared once, I could make you care again. I could make the fire bigger and bigger every day until you shone with happiness. Now your eyes are lighting a little. Now you're beginning to wonder if it could be true. Speak quickly, before the thought dies away. Say you'll go with me."

The music drew to an end with a long, dying fall.

"You've got my brain whirling," he told her. "But I know that I can't go, Dolores."

"Do you know why?" she gasped. "Because you're just a . . . damned . . . *gringo!*"

And she slipped away from him into the crowd. He followed her vaguely toward the table of Trimble, who was saying: "You had a pretty serious talk with Jeffers, Dolores."

"He stepped on my foot, the great, clumsy creature," she answered. "I was dying with the pain. How could I laugh, Dixie?"

Jeffers went by, with the dark look of Trimble trailing after him.

Taking his place at his small, round iron table, Jeffers drank more coffee, and turned the situation grimly in his mind. He felt that he had tried every artifice of which he was capable. Everything had failed, and yonder were Oñate and Muntaner, looking more than ever like two sinister beasts of prey, crouching over their table, and getting ready for the kill.

They rose, a moment later, and disappeared into the building. Yet a moment more, and all the gaiety of that scene was blotted out as the electric current that kept the globes burning inside the Japanese lanterns was switched off, and the whole outdoors circle was blanketed with velvet blackness, through which dim figures went stumbling and crying out in peals of laughter or of alarm.

But Jeffers, coming out of his chair with a bound, ran straight for the table of Dixie Trimble, for he guessed that it was not chance that had caused the darkness, and he feared to find a dead man, when the current flowed through the bulbs again.

VIII

He identified Trimble not only by his table, but by the height and the big shoulders of the figure that stood beside it, bending over a smaller form. That was Dolores, perhaps, and he was kissing her under the cover of the darkness?

A whirl of people came toward them, floundering through the darkness. One of them sprang from the rest with the dull gleam of metal in his hand. He was a tall fellow, and a smaller companion ran at his side. Jeffers would stake his life that it was Muntaner and Oñate. And he hurled himself forward, flinging his body sidewise at their knees.

Heavy and floundering weights crashed down on him. He rolled from beneath and came to his feet with a gun in his hand. The tall man was gone, stumbling off in flight. The smaller fellow leaped at Jeffers like a wildcat, and received the heavy barrel of a Colt laid along the side of his head.

"What's up? What the devil's happening?" called the voice of Trimble.

But Jeffers was already melting away into the darkness. He was at a considerable distance, and the gun already put up under his coat, when the lights flashed on again, in the midst of a roar of relief. Then it was seen that at the feet of big Dixie Trimble lay Oñate, blood trickling down the side of his head, and a long knife lying beside his outstretched hands.

It was enough to end the party for that night, this obvious attempt at murder. And as the people broke away from the tables and paid their bills, Jeffers heard Trimble protesting that he knew nothing about the attack. He had merely heard a scuffling close to him, that was all.

As for Dolores, she had disappeared utterly; there was no trace of the cause and incentive toward this attack in the darkness. Jeffers, observing this, smiled faintly and without mirth.

More trouble followed for Trimble. When his bill was presented, it appeared that his money had been gone long before. He declared that his pocket had been picked. He was sure $30 had been in it. But even $30 would not have gone far toward settling a bill for $75.

How could it be so much?

"Well, if the *señor* will drink nothing but the finest wines, and offer them to everyone. . . ."

Jeffers appeared at the side of the argument.

"I'll pay the bill for you, Dixie," he said. "I have plenty of money."

But Trimble turned a grim eye upon him. "Your money is no good to me," he declared. "You're too deep in this sort of a game to please me, Jeffers. By thunder, I've half a mind to take some change out of your skin, if only I knew. . . ."

He actually made a step toward Jeffers, but two waiters caught his arms at once.

"¡Señor!" they cried at him. "It is *Señor* Billy! What are you about to do? Do you wish to throw yourself away?"

"You know when murder's coming because your methods are that way, eh?" demanded Trimble. "You could read the greaser mind by your own. Is that it? Jeffers, no matter what *Señor* Billy may be, I'm going to have an accounting with Bill Jeffers, one of these days. And it may be an accounting that you'll remember."

"I won't run away. You'll be able to find me when you want me," said Jeffers. "But use your brain, man. This is a bad spot for you. You owe this money, and, if you don't get it from me, you'll have to telegraph to your father for it. That'll simply bring the whole deal to his attention. He won't be too pleased about a scene in a Mexican restaurant, a wine bill, a girl, a brawl, and an attempted murder. Use your wits, Trimble, and take a little of my money on loan."

"I want to know one thing," said Trimble. "Did you try to get Dolores away from me? Did you swear that you'd marry her and take her away on a wonderful wedding trip?"

"Did she tell you that?" asked Jeffers.

"Are you daring to say that she lied?"

exclaimed Trimble.

"I never say that a woman lies," said Jeffers.

"And I say," said Trimble, "that I'd rather take poison than use the money of a sneaking, treacherous hound. Jeffers, you're the worst snake in the world!" He turned to the waiters, saying: "I'll spend the night here. I need to think things over. Don't worry about your money. I'll have enough of it here to pay you, sometime tomorrow. To-morrow's Sunday, and I can stay here."

That was all Jeffers heard as he went out to the street. For the third or fourth time he was tempted to let Trimble stay and stew in his own juice, but the picture of the contorted face of Oñate as he was led away, the hate and the malignity of those pockmarked features, made Jeffers take his horse straight back to the stable behind the restaurant and give it, there, to the yawning boy.

Then he hunted up Alvarez, who was drawing up accounts for the evening in his little room, half hidden behind the silver wreaths of the cigarette smoke.

"*Señor* Billy, *Señor* Billy," said the fat Mexican, grinning. "You have done something again, and no one knows. Only Dolores and Alvarez."

"Does Dolores know?" asked Jeffers.

"She can see in the dark," said Alvarez. "She is a cat."

"She is," said Jeffers. He felt very old, very tired. There was a throbbing at the base of his brain, and an ache that pulsed with the blood.

He poured out a small glass of brandy, and sipped it, letting the strength of the fumes come up into his nose, letting the burn of the alcohol pass slowly over the roots of his tongue.

"You look angry, *Señor* Billy," said Alvarez. "Is it Dolores? She is in her room, crying. Shall I send for her?"

"How many men have died on account of her?" asked Jeffers.

"Ah, as to that . . . ," said Alvarez.

"Does she care?" asked Jeffers.

"No more," said Alvarez, "than a man-eating tiger."

"Has she ever loved a man in all her life . . . really loved one?" asked Jeffers. "I mean, with her whole heart and soul?"

"Yes," said Alvarez. "One."

"I don't believe that," said Jeffers.

"Not a very big man, not a rich man, not a handsome man," said Alvarez thoughtfully.

"No," said Jeffers. "One of those grim devils, with brows that meet in a line, and a sneer on his lips. Some knife expert and dancing master, I suppose?"

"Well," said Alvarez, "he dances very well. She likes his dancing better than the dancing of any other man, in fact. But knives are not what he loves. Guns are more to his taste. He's not a black-browed fellow, either, but blond."

"That surprises me," answered Jeffers. "But nothing ought to. Nothing about her ought to surprise any man. Not a dark man, eh? It's her opposite that she takes to, then? But you speak as though he were still alive."

"He is, *Señor* Billy. For how long, I don't know, but he's still alive. He is a quiet man. All the people here love him."

"I haven't seen him, have I?" asked Jeffers.

"Yes, yes. You've seen a great deal of him."

"That baffles me," said Jeffers.

"He's been away for a long time," answered Alvarez. "You'll know him by his eye. He has an eye that people never forget, pale and bright. And there's a new scar, just over his eye."

Jeffers straightened. Automatically his hand rose to touch the scar. He stared at Alvarez, who shrugged.

"I tell you the truth," said Alvarez.

"We'll talk of something else," said Jeffers coldly, angrily. "Where is Trimble sleeping?"

207

"In the corner room, at the back of the second story."

"That room has too many windows. Move him into another. Move him into the next room."

"He'll be very angry, *Señor* Billy."

"Let him be angry. The corner room has too many windows . . . and Muntaner and Oñate are still afoot. I'll take the corner room myself."

"Suppose that they try to visit you in the night?"

"Do they think I'm the fellow who got in the way?"

"They can suspect. There is only one *Señor* Billy."

"Well," said Jeffers, "I've had so much trouble in one day that a little more won't make any difference. Change his room, Alvarez."

Alvarez spoke, not loudly. A man appeared. The message was sent.

The two sat for a long time in silence.

"You are sad, *Señor* Billy," said the Mexican softly.

"Sad? No, but sleepy," said Jeffers.

Straightway he went upstairs, and down the hall to the corner room. It had two sets of windows — two overlooking a side lane, and two opening above the little courtyard to the rear, where Alvarez tried to make a garden thrive in an ungrateful soil.

Jeffers went to bed by the simple method of pulling off his boots and wrapping a quilt around him. He allowed all his body, all his senses to relax, except the sense of hearing. And this he kept on the verge of consciousness with a special effort of the will.

Hours went by, and still his condition did not change, for his will was fixed irrevocably to hold his attention at a certain point.

That was why he heard a whispering sound come down the hall. He heard his door opened with a delicate caution. Only the faint draft that blew into the room and cooled his face gave real notice that the door was wide.

"Billy," whispered a voice.

He lowered the gun that he had raised. "Yes," he whispered in return. "Dolores?" She came to the side of the bed. He could feel rather than see that she leaned above him.

"Am I a wicked devil, Billy?"

"Yes," said Jeffers.

"Someday, can you forgive me?"

"If you start sobbing, Dolores, I'll throttle you," said Jeffers. He brushed the drop of water from his face.

"Someday, can you forgive me?" she repeated.

"Yes," said Jeffers.

She found his hand, kissed it, and was gone. The draft no longer entered the room; the door had been closed.

IX

Hardly ten minutes went by, after that, before he heard another series of noises, very subdued, and seeming to come from the next room. He got up from the bed, moving with care for fear of the squeaking of springs. To the windows he stalked, first on one side of the room, and then on the other. Nothing that he could see moved outside of them.

But now he made sure that the door of the next room was being slowly opened. The faint, groaning noise of the rusted hinges was what made him sure.

He pulled on his boots with two jerks, opened the door of his own room, and made out a form disappearing down the hall.

What would young Trimble be doing at this time of the night? He followed to make sure. Down the hall, down the stairs, moving furtively from corner to corner, crouching low, he trailed his man to the back door of the inn. The chains that held it jingled like little silver bells as they were unfastened. The bolt was pushed back with a dull, muffled clank.

Then the door opened, and the wide shoulders of Trimble appeared against the starlight beyond. Jeffers, moving forward, slipped a trifle. His foot made an infinitesimal sound against the floor, but it caused Trimble to whirl instantly, gun gleaming in his hand. There he waited, crouching low, scanning the darkness. He came back three steps, and stood within touching distance of the point where Jeffers lay almost prostrate. For half a long-drawn minute, the pause continued. Then Trimble drew a breath and moved back to the door, and passed through it. He closed it behind him.

Jeffers, following, went first to the nearest window and looked out. Gun in hand, Trimble was waiting beside the door. But he seemed to feel that his alarm had been causeless, for, after a moment, he went on toward the stable.

And this was the quiet, timid fellow who Jeffers had brought to life, and to such a life as this. More than ever a sense of deep responsibility drove home into the heart of Jeffers.

He followed through the doorway, stalked

forward to the barn, and, after listening to the sound of creaking leather, worked his way through the open door and crouched close against the manger. The horses nearest him rose, with a grunting and scraping. Then, directly past him, came the moving silhouette of Trimble, leading a saddled horse.

Was this his way — to slip away in the darkness rather than remain till the morning and face his bill?

He hardly had left the stable, before Jeffers was at work. Going down the line to find his bay mustang, he quickly discovered that it was gone. And he was amazed. Why should Trimble have taken Jeffers's horse when he had a perfectly good one of his own?

The first horse at hand would serve the purpose of Jeffers, however. He picked a saddle off a peg, threw it on the back of the nearest mount, and shortly he, too, had led a horse out of the stable and into the open of the street.

There was no sight of a living, moving thing. Only on the dust of the street the starlight fell as though on the pallor of water.

Which way should he go?

He turned to the right, running forward, the horse jogging behind him. Presently he felt he was far enough away from the inn to risk the creaking of saddle leather, and swung onto the back of the horse. He put the mustang to a canter, and so, sweeping out of the town, he saw before him, moving up the ridge of a sandhill against the stars, the black silhouette of another rider.

It must be Trimble.

He followed on, cautiously. The rolling ground grew into larger hills. Still he had glimpses of Trimble passing before him in the distance — or of the rider that he took to be Trimble.

As he crossed a low ridge, not more than four miles from the town, he saw the road from Hallet Junction winding like a dull, pale ribbon through the valley. And beneath him, the rider of the night was dismounting, then taking his horse into a small thicket.

Again the man appeared, and finally took cover in some shrubbery near the edge of the road.

Something that was expected down the road was the man's goal, beyond any question. Jeffers had dismounted in turn. He tethered his borrowed mustang, and stretched himself out on the ground behind a projecting rock; he waited comfortably, scanning all the dull, starlit scene below him.

Still the mystery tingled in his mind and in his blood. What could be the possible goal of Trimble, on such an excursion as this?

The light seemed to grow dimmer; the hills blackened; the stars near the horizon disappeared as though a mist had covered them from sight. It was, he knew, the coming of the dawn. Presently it brightened to a clear gray. The hidden brush, the rocks, the trees began to loom. Every moment the light increased, until now the first faint pink of the morning showed over the eastern horizon.

It was from the west, however, that a sound of thudding and of thumping approached. It came clearer, with distinct metallic rattling sounds, and suddenly a coach drawn by six fast-trotting horses swung around the next curve and went rushing on toward the spot where Trimble lay concealed.

The meaning grew suddenly clear to Jeffers. It brought him to his knees, exclaiming: "The poor fool! The fool!"

And then, as the coach swayed over a bump in the road, the figure of Trimble jumped up before the horses. His face was made blank by a mask. He fired a shot into the air as the driver pulled the lead horses back on their haunches. Jeffers clearly heard the screeching of the brakes, and then a rapid mumbling of voices. He was very near, and yet he was much too far away to be of the slightest help. If only he could have read the mind of the foolish fellow. . . .

There was no semblance of resistance, except when the guard, for half a moment, started to lift his scatter-gun. But he thought better of that, and climbed down from the box, along with the driver.

Five people got down from the night coach from Hallet Junction. They stood in a shallow semicircle, with their hands raised, while Trimble, disregarding them, went to the boot.

Was there a special prize in the stage? And if so, how had Trimble heard of it? He stepped back, presently, with a heavy sack over his arm. He had to sway his body against the weight of it.

That was not all. Presently — no doubt at the direction of Trimble — the wheels were taken off the stage, one by one, all the passengers joining in the effort. Finally it lay a flat, unwieldy box on the ground. And Dixie Trimble backed into the brush.

He was hardly there before a shout came

roaring up the slope of the hill toward the ears of Jeffers. All of those men who had been so easily overawed by Trimble now sprang into action as soon as the direct menace of his gun was removed. A rifle appeared here, revolvers there. The guard sent two rounds out of his riot gun toward the spot where Trimble had disappeared. Others rushed for the horses, which were whipped out of harness, and mounted bareback. In a few moments, as Trimble fled up the hollow toward Jeffers, six mounted men, hungry for revenge, all the more savage because they had been shamed, swept after the thief, Dixie Trimble, rich man's son, and stage robber!

They came with such an earnest rush that it seemed they had more than an equal chance of overtaking him, and the spirit of the devil seemed to enter the bay gelding as it neared its real master, for it began to buck as it ran, and almost pitched Trimble out of the saddle.

Jeffers pulled a revolver and commenced to shoot. He did not shoot to kill, and yet he never had fired with such accuracy in all the days of his life. He literally brushed the sombrero of the stage driver, who was leading the hunt. He knocked up the dust and the gravel under the nose of the next rider.

In a moment, he had caused that sweeping troop to scatter to the right and to the left, diving off the bare backs of their horses to get shelter where they could.

And Trimble passed to safety over the crown of the ridge. Jeffers, also, mounting in haste, was soon in pursuit, and he found Trimble waiting for him beyond the next sweep of the hills.

Trimble was laughing cheerfully. "I never had such a lark in my life!" he shouted to Jeffers. "Did you see the whole game? As easy as making mud pies. Just holler and they line up like so many calves. But that was a near thing when they came after me in a rush. I hadn't thought about the stage horses. Otherwise, I would have brought 'em along with me for a ways. However, you were there to fill the breach, though how the devil you happened to be there, I don't know."

"You nearly fell over me in the hall of the inn," said Jeffers.

"Were you there? You lay as still as a mouse then. Or you would have been salted away. What brought you out, Jeffers? By the way, I was damned short with you, last night. The girl . . . I mean . . . well, it seems all sort of foolish, now. But what a beauty she is, Bill. What brought you out after me, anyway?"

"I wonder," said Jeffers, "if you realize that you're riding my horse?"

"Am I? Well, so I am. I didn't want to take my own. I was afraid that they'd spot the trail of me, that way."

He swung from the saddle, and they exchanged mounts.

"Stage robbery is apt to mean fourteen or fifteen years. Understand that?" remarked Jeffers.

"I understand, I suppose. They'll never follow me, though. It's a clean job, and not a drop of blood spilled." He laughed again, adding: "What did bring you out after me? Well, you smelled money, I suppose, and you're certainly going to get your split. Half or a third? Which have you earned, Bill? I'll tell you what . . . that gun of yours sounded good to me, when you made the rear guard stand. Why didn't you come up before, and let me know that there were two to turn the trick?"

"I don't want the money," said Jeffers coldly. "And the only reason that I followed you was because your mangy hide seems to be worth something, in the eyes of Anne. Why, I can't say."

"That's a parcel of strong talk, Jeffers!" exclaimed Trimble angrily.

"It's the last time that I dirty my hands on account of you," said Jeffers. "Understand that. You may go to the devil, for all of me. But I'll tell you this . . . if this stage robbery business is brought home to my door, you're going to confess. Is that clear? You're going to clean up the slate. I won't go to jail for you, Trimble. And if you try to let the thing slide, I'll come and take it out of your hide . . . with a gun. Now good bye, and be damned to you."

He turned his horse and his back on the astonished Trimble, and cantered at a brisk pace toward distant Benton Creek.

X

Trimble was only a moment behind Jeffers in reaching the stable behind the inn of Alvarez. He peeled the saddle from his horse and would have left, in haste, carrying the weighty sack across his arm, but Jeffers exclaimed: "Rub down that horse, you fool! D'you want them to find it sweating? Take some twists of hay and rub it down. Hard!"

Trimble went back silently, to obey, while Jeffers worked as long as he dared over the bay. When he was forced to call a halt, owing to the near approach of sunrise, he shook his head, for the sweat was still rising through the hair on the sleek-coated gelding.

He hurried through the back door with Trimble, and replaced chains and bolts to make all secure. Then he went up into the upper hall, and there saw Trimble confronting a slender figure in white. As Jeffers approached, Trimble jingled the contents of the sack that he still carried.

Jeffers heard him say: "Why wait twenty years for the ranch? Here's ten thousand dollars in hard cash. And yonder's Mexico, a step across the line. Come along with me, Dolores. Here's the stuff this sack is filled with." He handed something to her.

She glanced down at it, and then backed away. "I can't go, Dixie," she said.

"You can't go?" he exclaimed. "Why not? You're as free as the air. So am I, with this coin. So will we both be, the instant that we're across the line. You've told me about the life down there. It was meant for me. I'm sick of drudging, and being the honest man. What does it buy except more hard days to come? Here's some easy money. When it goes, there are a lot more sheep waiting to be sheared. And we'll collect the wool when we need it."

She shook her head, and laid her hand on the knob of her door.

Trimble caught her roughly by the shoulders. "Were you just stringing me along, last night?" he demanded.

"Billy!" gasped the girl.

"You've made your own bed. Now lie in it!" said Jeffers.

"Billy . . . he's hurting me!" gasped Dolores.

"Take your hands off her," said Jeffers, "or I'll break your head for you, you whelp."

"You'll do what?" exclaimed Trimble, turning.

In that instant the girl was through her door, and the lock clicked.

"Go to bed. Peel your clothes off and get into bed," directed Jeffers. "They may follow the horses. Get into that bed and pretend that you haven't waked up all night long. What a fool you are for carrying that sack into the house. Stow it out of sight and play 'possum. They'll be on your trail before long, or I'm a liar."

The directness and the assurance of these words seemed to impress Trimble. He turned, muttering, and disappeared into his room, while Jeffers, already undressing, was entering his own.

There he stripped off his clothes and slid in between the sheets. Mentally, physically he relaxed bit by bit, his arms thrown upward above his head, his eyes closed, making his breathing perfectly smooth and regular.

Trouble, he felt in his bones, was coming, and he would have to meet it as one just wakened from a long sleep.

He was not in the least surprised when a sound of horses came beating up the street and paused in front of the inn. Then came a banging upon doors. Voices called out inside the place. Footfalls ran here and there, and the rosy light of the rising sun streamed through the two eastern windows of the room and painted the opposite wall with red gold. The noise of many steps, many voices, flowed through the house, spilled out into the court toward the barn, and there arose a shouting. Had they found the two sweating horses?

He gritted his teeth, then made himself relax again.

The sounds of the moving men now flowed back rapidly into the tavern. He heard the voice of Alvarez protesting loudly, swearing that *Señor* Billy could not have left the place during the night. There was some mistake. If his horse had been used, another man must have used it.

That river of noise poured up to his door;

there was a beating on it. Then it was cast open.

Jeffers did not stir. "Hey, hello!" he called, and yawned enormously. "Time to turn out?"

The sheriff stood over him, with a gun in his hand. Those men from the robbed stage had made sure of bringing the law with them, when they hunted for their quarry, it seemed.

"Yeah," said the sheriff, "it's time to turn out, and, afterward, maybe it'll be time for you to turn into a place where you'll be kept good and quiet for about twenty years. Get up, Jeffers! You've raised the last hell you're going to raise this side of the grave."

"That's a lot of talk and doesn't mean a thing," said Jeffers, sitting up in the bed. He looked around him at the grim faces of the men. Some of them were from the stage, of course, but there were others. There were ten of them, outside of the sheriff, and more seemed to be in the hall.

"What are you driving at?" asked Jeffers. "Are you pinching me, stupid?"

"I'm stupid, am I? I'm a fool, am I?" said the sheriff savagely. "You'll spend a little while in jail, thinking what a great fool you are. Where have you been riding to-night?"

"In the sky," said Jeffers, grinning. "What's the matter, deacon?"

"I'll deacon you!" said the angry sheriff. "You're going to make a joke out of this, are you? Your horse is in the stable, sweating. He's been rubbed down to take the sweat off. I could see the bits of broken hay. I found the twists of hay that had been used to cool him off and dry him out, too. But it wasn't any good. He's still sweating. Where did you ride him last night?"

"From the Circle Eighteen to Benton Creek, your honor," said Jeffers, and lay back in the bed again, yawning once more.

But all the while his wits were working rapidly behind his dim, half-closed eyes. He was studying the set faces of the men from the stage. He felt that he could pick them out from the others, the ones who carried the personal grudge with them.

"Rode in from the ranch, and where did you ride after that?" asked the sheriff.

"Up to a saloon. Had a couple of drinks. Went on to the dance. Stayed there a minute, and then back here. I sat around and wasted some coffee and brandy. Then I pulled out and came to bed. And after a while, the sheriff himself came to call on me with a lot of his chums. How's that for a story of the night . . . leaving out all the sweet dreams."

"One of the dreams that you leave out," said the sheriff, "is about how you got out of the bed, in the middle of the night, and saddled up your horse, and then tore away across country and waited for the stage from Hallet Junction. Remember how you stuck up that stage and grabbed the gold shipment?"

"I'd like to remember that," said Jeffers. "Go on, brother, and tell me some more good news."

The door down the hall opened. The voice of Dixie Trimble, a voice as big as the man, exclaimed loudly: "What's all the noise and trouble?"

Someone told him briefly.

"Well, that's his business, not mine," said Trimble, and strode off down the hall. His step was heavy. No doubt he carried the sack of loot under a coat or slicker over his arm.

"I'd say one thing," remarked a man with very gray hair and very black eyebrows. "I'd say that this *hombre* don't foot up the inches of him that stuck up the stage."

"A man always looks bigger when he's got you covered with a gun," answered the sheriff.

"Maybe so. But his voice don't seem the

same, neither," said the passenger from the coach.

"A voice behind a gun always sounds different, too," said the sheriff. "This is the boy for the picture, the way I see it. If there's any hell to raise, Jeffers will raise it. But this time he's gone too far. Jeffers, you might as well talk out. Where'd you put the gold?"

"In my left-hand trouser pocket," said Jeffers.

"This ain't the man," said another passenger, who had been staring intently at Jeffers. "We're wasting time. Maybe Jeffers's horse made the tracks that we followed, and maybe Jeffers wasn't on board of it. But this ain't the man, I'd say and I'd swear. He ain't got the inches, and he ain't got the voice. Let's spread out and try to pick up the real trail of that skunk that stuck us up."

No matter what the conviction of the sheriff, the passengers from the coach spoke with too much surety to be denied. Furthermore, they acted on the last suggestion, and hurried out of the room to carry their hunt farther. Somewhere about that inn was the man who had robbed the coach. That much seemed fairly certain, even if Jeffers were not the guilty fellow.

But the sheriff lingered, as Jeffers began

to dress.

"You hypnotize 'em first, and then rob 'em afterward," said the sheriff, "and then. . . ." He paused, fascinated, as Jeffers pulled on his boots. Then, stepping forward, the sheriff touched the inside of the right trouser leg of Jeffers, near the knee. It was wet with sweat, where it had rubbed against the hot shoulder of the bay.

With his left hand, the sheriff touched that moist place, and, with his right hand, he jerked at the revolver that he had just slid into a holster, but he found a cold length of gray-blue steel already shining in front of his eyes.

"Stop petting that Colt of yours," advised Jeffers. "Turn your face to the wall. And put your hands behind your back." He kicked the door shut, as he spoke.

"It *was* you, then," groaned the sheriff. "And the fools had to walk out on me after I'd cornered you. It was you that rode the bay horse . . . and the sweat of that horse is still wet on the knee of your trousers. Jeffers, you've got no chance to get away. Don't try any funny tricks on me, when I'm bound to be top dog in a minute."

Jeffers, glancing out the window, saw big Dixie Trimble leading out his horse from the mouth of the stable.

"Saddle up my horse, Dixie, will you?" he said. "I'm in a hurry to pull out of here."

Trimble hesitated, then waved his hand in assent, as he turned back into the barn.

Footfalls swept down the hallway. "Hey, Sheriff!" called several voices.

"Keep them off!" commanded Jeffers.

"Keep out, boys!" yelled the sheriff loudly. "I'm having a private talk with Jeffers."

XI

The noise of the men receded. Jeffers was lashing the hands of the sheriff behind his back, then tying the lashings to the ankles of the man of the law. The sheriff moaned and cursed.

"The queer part of this job," said Jeffers, "is that I didn't take the coin from the stage, after all. You've got enough stuff on me to put me on the run, old boy, but one of these days the truth may come to life."

"You're making a fool of me, Jeffers," said the sheriff. "You're making such a fool of me that I'll be the laughingstock of the county. But I'm going to be on your trail till I've worn my hands and my feet to the bone. I'm going to nail you sooner or later, Jeffers, and I hope I see you swing. And as for your not doing this. . . ."

228

His voice stopped, because a wadded handkerchief had been thrust in a hard knot into his mouth. He struggled, but could not eject it with his tongue before Jeffers had fastened the gag in place with another string.

The efforts of the sheriff left him wriggling and writhing helplessly on the floor, while Jeffers walked out of the inn. He passed the slender figure of Dolores on the stairs. She looked very pale, and her face was set.

"Billy," she said, "are you getting a split of that stuff, or shall I turn Trimble in?"

He paused.

"I saw the sack in his hands," she said. "And I have one of the coins that he gave me. I can put him in jail in two minutes."

"I'm getting a split," said Jeffers. "Leave him alone."

Her face darkened. "If you're afraid to work alone, these days, why don't you find a real man for a partner?" she demanded softly and fiercely.

Jeffers went past her into the stable yard. There were more than a score of men swarming about as he mounted the bay that Trimble had saddled for him, and rode off at the side of the other. A faint, continuous jingling came out of one of the saddlebags tied to the saddle of Trimble, when they reached the street and struck out at a trot.

As they came out of the town, Trimble turned and thrust out his hand. "That was a near thing, and you took all the shocks. You were the lightning rod, Bill!" he exclaimed. "What a cool devil you are."

Jeffers overlooked the hand that was extended. "You were walking out and leaving me, Dixie," he said. "How does that sit on your mind?"

Slowly the proffered hand of Trimble fell. "What could I do?" he muttered. "I knew that you'd trick them, some way. That is, I knew that was the only way out. But you don't want to see things my way. You're simply against me, Bill."

"Your way is a queer way, old son," said Jeffers. "I want to ask you about another thing."

"Well?" growled Trimble.

"This coin. What about it?"

"We'll make a fifty-fifty split," said Trimble. "I'm square, Jeffers. I won't beat you out of your cut."

"You planned to rob the stage just to get enough to pay your bill that you owed to Alvarez. Isn't that right?"

"Well, maybe that was all I had in mind," said Trimble. "It was a tight place for me.

The old man would have had a fit if I wired him for seventy-five bucks to pay a bill for liquor in a Mexican dive. What the devil could I do? I was sore at you, Bill. I didn't feel that I could take your money. I didn't know anybody else well enough to ask for the coin. It was pretty black for me."

Jeffers nodded. "Then," he said, "you paid Alvarez this morning?"

"Yes. Of course."

"Out of that sack?"

"How else could I do it?"

"People might start putting two and two together . . . the coach is robbed . . . a lot of freshly minted gold is stolen . . . and a fellow who's broke at night pays a bill with newly coined gold in the morning. How does that sound to you?"

Trimble blanched, for an instant. Then a gleam came in his eye. "Perhaps I happened to ask the thief for a loan, not dreaming that he was the thief. That's all. And he gave me the money not to help me out, but because he hoped to plant the job on my shoulders." He laughed. "Not that I'd talk that way, Jeffers. But it just shows how many ways there are around a bad spot."

"Yeah," muttered Bill Jeffers. "There are a lot of ways to jail."

"What d'you mean by that?" asked

231

Trimble. "You don't think that I'll be fool enough to make a habit of this sort of thing, do you?"

"Not till the next time you get into a pinch," answered Jeffers. "But you'll have some expensive habits, old son, before you finish spending all that stuff."

"I have a good time coming to me," answered Trimble. "The old man has always kept me on a short rope. Too damned short. Now I'm going to cut loose and have a party. I'm ready for a party, too. Jeffers, tell me something. How have you hypnotized that little devil of a beauty, that Dolores?"

"How have you hypnotized Anne Calhoun?" countered Jeffers.

Trimble laughed. "Because I'm such a good boy," he said. "And she doesn't like the shifty fellows. She wants to know where a man stands. What she wants is a home builder, a father of a family, somebody she can count on. That's the only reason she looks at Dixie Trimble."

Jeffers set his teeth and snarled through them, a wordless sound.

They had come into a waste of sand studded with ugly lumps and bristling stalks of cacti. Their horses were scattering the gravel of a hard-bottomed draw, and the heat of the sun blazed and gathered about them.

"I'm saying good bye to you, Trimble," said Jeffers. "We have to stay on the Circle Eighteen Ranch for a while, I suppose. It won't do for anyone to disappear suddenly from this neck of the woods. But this is good bye, because, from now on, I never want to speak to you, if I can dodge it."

"I'm not good enough for you. Is that it?" demanded Trimble.

Jeffers regarded him with an almost painful diligence, sweeping him up and down. "I don't want to be rash," he said. "I don't want to be hasty. But when I think you over, Trimble, and see what you are and what your chances have been, I think you're about the lowest hound I know."

Trimble brought up his horse with a jerk. A white mask was fitted tightly over his mouth. "You've done some pretty big things for me lately," he said. "I ought to be grateful, and I am grateful. But I won't take talk like that. In a couple of minutes, I'll forget that I'm a bigger man than you are, Jeffers."

"Will you?" said Jeffers slowly. "Will you forget how big you are? Listen to me . . . turn the head of your horse for the Calhoun Ranch. Anne may be feeling a little cross about you, brother. Go out there and explain yourself. Make your peace with her. And take yourself out of my sight before I dress you down like a green hide."

"Before you what?" asked Trimble. Suddenly he flung himself to the ground and caught the reins of the bay horse. "Get out of that saddle before I pull you out, Jeffers. I'm going to spoil that mug of yours so that even Dolores won't be able to look at it without laughing," said Trimble. "And don't make a move for a gun. I'm covering you, Jeffers!"

In fact, he held a gun hip-high, the muzzle unwaveringly fixed toward the body of Jeffers.

As for Jeffers, he regarded Trimble and the gun, both, for a moment. "Are you going to beat me up with your fists, Dixie?" he asked.

"I'm going to pound your face to a beefsteak," said Trimble. A savage joy got hold of him and made him shudder.

Jeffers swung one leg over the pommel of the saddle and, with his hands raised shoulder-high, slipped to the ground.

"Shell out your gun, and drop it," commanded Trimble.

The thing was done patiently. The faint shining of the eyes of Jeffers was not noticed by the larger man. Trimble unbuckled his own gun belt and let his gun drop. Then he stepped forward, flexing his hands into fists.

"You're going to get what you earned last night, when you knifed in between me and Dolores," said Trimble. "You wanted her to take a trip with you? I'll fix you so you'll need a trip to a hospital, Jeffers. Put up your hands!"

He rushed as he spoke. That beautiful long left that Jeffers had praised so highly shot out like a piston with the weight of the big, charging body behind it. The head of Jeffers tipped to one side. The long arm shot over his shoulder, and into the body of Trimble he drove a lifting punch. It doubled Trimble up. Staggering, with feet braced wide, with his face gray and contorted, he tried to keep up his guard.

"I ought to cut you to pieces," said Jeffers. "But Anne still wants you, I suppose. Let her have you, then, with just one trademark on you."

His right hand snaked through Trimble's guard and thudded on the end of the chin. Trimble slid into a loose heap, with his arms flung out around his feet. He was both stunned and winded. He began to struggle for air, gasping.

Jeffers regarded him with a bland satisfaction. Then he went to Trimble's saddle, untied the heavy saddlebag, and fastened it on the bay gelding. He took Trimble's gun, broke it, emptied it of shells, dropped the cartridges into his pocket, and flung the gun back on the ground, still open. Then he mounted, as Trimble got to uncertain feet.

"Are you going to rob me?" gasped Trimble. "Bill, are you going to take all that swag? Are you going to . . . ?"

"You'll find your way to more of it," said Jeffers. "You want it badly enough, and you'll find a way to get more of it. Go marry Anne Calhoun. She wants you . . . heaven knows why. But this swag isn't for me, brother. I'm not so young or such a fool. A man can't get something for nothing, and I know it. This coin goes back to the stage company, brother. Then, if they catch me, they'll hardly know what to hold me for. So long, Trimble."

"Wait a minute!" exclaimed Trimble. "Back there in the bunkhouse . . . did you simply let me beat you that night?"

"Yes," said Jeffers. "I thought there might be a man inside the hulk of you. But it turned out to be half hound and half crook."

Then he turned the bay and departed.

XII

Now that he had the money, Jeffers nevertheless realized that it would not be a simple matter to return it to the stage coach company. His best plan, he felt, would be to cut back toward the brush along Benton Creek, and try to find a good hiding place for the gold until night. Then he could return, during the hours of darkness, and attempt to replace the coin with its owners. When that was done, the wrath of the sheriff, presumably, would either disappear or become a very dim and light matter.

So he headed up out of the draw, and, as he straightened the mustang away for the creek, he saw a large dust cloud rolling up against the wind. Then figures of horsemen issued from the upward twisting column.

He put the bay gelding to a sharp trot, and then to a steady lope. Behind him, he saw the riders cross the draw and drive straight on toward him. There were a dozen or fifteen of them; some of them rode with rifles balanced across the pommels of the saddles, and there was not the slightest doubt that this was a posse of men from Benton Creek. It was not strange that they had ridden out, of course. It was only strange that, hitting aimlessly across country without picking up a trail, they had so unexpectedly come into view of the quarry that they wanted.

He quickened the pace of the bay mustang

to a full gallop. In half a mile the good horse was laboring. The weight of that gold made up a burden like two riders, and one of them a dead poundage.

Something sang overhead like a wasp blown down the wind. A moment later, a report followed, a sound as if two hammer faces had been brought together in the distance.

He looked back. They were in fact close enough for shooting. They had spread out in fan-shaped formation, the leaders evenly matched in horseflesh, it seemed, and the slower mounts trailing off to the rear like the tail of a kite.

Plainly he dared not keep the burden of the money with him. But if he were seen to throw it down, the guilt would be fastened on him forever. He could only take a chance, and a crude one.

He loosened the fastening of the saddlebag as he rode, bending forward. Over the side of a draw he shot the bay. In the bottom of it were great patches of broad-leaved cactus. Into one of these he tossed the bag, saw it smash its way deep into the thorny green arms, and groaned as he made sure that even the most casual eye would probably detect the spot in passing.

Then he turned his lightened mustang

down the harder bottom of the draw, and made it fly. Looking back, he saw the van of the posse sweep over the rim of the draw and rush down into it. Anxiously he watched. But they came roaring on, past the cactus patch that contained the treasure.

There were still other chances of detection from the laggards in the race. One by one he watched them whipping their way, or spurring hard to catch up. The last man of all sped past the danger mark. And Jeffers groaned with relief.

There were good riders and good horses in that outfit, and they rode as if for life or death. But it was not for nothing that he had picked the bay mustang from two hundred of its kind. With no extra burden now to weigh it down, it ran like a bird on the wing, sweeping along with great, free strides. They had begun their sprint too early and rushed their horses along too fast, in closing the gap, those fellows from Benton Creek. Now they would pay for it. With every stride, the lithe bay gelding widened the margin between the fluttering tip of its tail and the leaders of that party of manhunters.

Jeffers began to laugh silently, a quick pulse and tremor of joy in his heart. He rounded a bend of the draw, and a bed of big pebbles began to rattle about the hoofs of the mustang. Quickly he drew rein, but too late. The bay stumbled, almost fell, and, quickly righting itself, tried to run on three staggering legs. It was hopelessly lame in the right forehoof!

Groaning, Bill Jeffers looked about him. A rifle might keep them at bay for a while, but he had no rifle. If there were an outcropping of big rocks, he might hide and keep them off until the coming of night gave him a chance to crawl away. But there was no shelter except the tall, spectral bodies of a few Spanish bayonets. All else was as bare as his hand. He slipped from the saddle, turned, and faced the onrush of the posse around the bend with his arms stretched above his head.

What a shout they gave. They were wolves giving savage tongue. They closed on him with a rush as though they would beat him into the earth.

The sheriff pitched from the saddle to the earth and clamped handcuffs over his wrists, yelling: "Now, Jeffers! I promised it to you, and you're going to get it! How I'd like to let you have the heel of my gun in the middle of the face. It'll be about twenty years for this little job, my boy. You'll get a free education out of this. Unless the boys hang you and save the law the money."

Jeffers looked about him with a strangely quiet eye. He saw that every member of that posse was a man he knew. He had played with some of them since boyhood. But now they were strangers. He had left the flock. He had become, to them, the wolf.

Tom Kinney, who had raced and fought and ridden with him those years ago, was making a cigarette, and grinning. "The greasers are going to mourn a whole lot about this," said Kinney.

"Let 'em mourn," said the sheriff. "Let 'em mourn and be damned. I tell you that it's the best day's work that was ever done around the town of Benton Creek. It's a weight off the mind of this county, is what it is. If you'd aired those trousers to let 'em dry, Jeffers, you fool, you wouldn't be out of luck now. But every crook is a fool, now and then."

Jeffers said nothing at all. He was silent all the way back to Benton Creek, but the news had gone before, and every man, woman, and child was out to see the "robber" pass. And there, in front of the general merchandise store, was Calhoun himself, standing up in the driver's place of his buckboard, with Anne Calhoun at his side.

Jeffers lifted his chained hands and raised

his hat to them. Neither of them responded with the slightest gesture. So he rode by them and felt the edge of the sword of pain enter his heart. Nothing mattered, after that.

They reached the jail. He passed through the door. They were cheering the posse. The whole population of Benton Creek was roaring applause for the capture of the desperado. The door, with its metal facing, clanked heavily, and shut out half the noise.

Before him were the glimmering bars of the cell room. All was steel. Steel would surround him, now, for all the best part of his life. Real life was ended. When he came out — well, the spirit dies, sometimes, before the body. And perhaps his spirit would be dead before he was a free man again. But he felt that something was dead in him already.

In the cell he lay face down on the cot.

"He's quitting. He'll be bawling like a baby, before long," said the harsh voice of the sheriff. "Just a lot of brag and no man about the great Bill Jeffers, all of these years. A yaller streak a mile wide."

But Jeffers hardly heard. His mind was still filled by the vision of the cold, stern face of Anne Calhoun.

XIII

His first visitor was Alvarez, and Dolores was beside him. She clung to the bars with her slender hands and shook them. The jailer told her to step back.

"Go back yourself," said Alvarez sternly to the jailer. "I'll make it worth your while. Get out of earshot. You'll be able to see that we don't pass him anything through the bars."

"It's a risky business," said the jailer, a big fellow with a sheen of uncropped red beard about his face. "But there ain't no money where there ain't no risks. Make it short, will you?" And he drew back a little.

"Why do you do it, Billy?" Dolores cried. "Why do you do it? Alvarez has the gold that was paid in by Trimble. I have the piece of gold that he gave me. I know that he was up and out that night. I can swear it. I know that he carried the sack of money into the house afterward. I heard the money clink, and I have a sample of it. That's enough to set you free, Billy. What's half of ten thousand dollars compared with a dozen years in prison?"

Alvarez nodded. "Everything she says is true. Why do you do it, *Señor* Billy? Let us say just one word."

Jeffers considered. He remembered the stern, set face of Anne Calhoun. After all, why should he ruin his life to let her marry a fellow who seemed to him a worthless rat? But something restrained that impulse toward freedom. How or why, he could not tell, but he found himself shaking his head slowly. Anne had chosen the fellow. He himself had worked for him, risked his life — and found a prison for repayment. And still he could not strike back for freedom.

"I can't do it," said Jeffers.

"But why? Oh, why?" moaned Dolores, still gripping at the bars.

"Hush," said Alvarez. "When you find a mystery in the ways of a man, Dolores, there is always a woman behind it. And where there is a woman, argument is a foolish thing."

"A woman?" said Dolores. "A woman? *Señor* Billy, it is not that other one . . . that blonde, pretty, cold one without a heart?"

Jeffers said nothing at all. It was true that Anne Calhoun was cold as stone. That had been what her face was like this day — like a stone.

He heard Alvarez arguing; still he shook his head.

"It is the woman," said the girl to Alvarez. "Leave him then. Why should I care about him? He cares nothing for me. Come away from him. Come!"

Alvarez went slowly out with her. At the very door of the jail they found Anne Calhoun and Trimble. He was saying: "No good of me going in. I can't help the poor devil. I'm sorry for him, but he has to take what's coming."

Dolores gasped.

"Come," Alvarez hissed, and his hand urged her forward.

She broke away with a sudden, passionate gesture. "Anne Calhoun," she said, "why do you go with a thief and leave an honest man in the jail?"

The American girl looked at her with that quiet, cold eye that seemed to Dolores so totally inhuman. She spoke to Trimble, not to Dolores. "Is this your friend, Dixie?"

"Ah, Anne," said Trimble, "you'll never forget that once I played the fool."

"*Señor* Trimble," broke out Alvarez, "this morning you paid my bill with new gold, and it was part of the gold that was stolen from the stage. Do you say anything to that?"

"Nothing," said Trimble, "except that it was money I borrowed from Jeffers."

"When I met you in the hall, and you were carrying the heavy sack," continued Dolores, "did you ask me to leave the country with you? Did you show me the money? Did you give me this piece of gold as a proof of what you have?" She held out the gleaming $10 gold piece.

Trimble shrugged his shoulders. "All the greasers love Jeffers," he said to Anne Calhoun. "At least they love him enough to lie for him."

He managed to laugh a little, but Anne Calhoun was not laughing. Her serious eyes went from the face of Dolores to that of Trimble. She seemed to be measuring and weighing a truth.

"And *Señor* Billy loved you enough," said Dolores to Trimble, "to risk his life for you when Muntaner and Oñate ran at you in the dark. He saved you then, and you betray him now."

"They'll carry on like this for hours, Anne," said Trimble.

"Wait a moment," said the girl. "She's not lying. She's trying to tell you the truth. Who are Muntaner and Oñate?"

"Two men who thought I was a fool to waste my time on this," said Dolores, with a gesture toward Trimble. "They had the lights turned out, last night, and they came at him through the dark. But *Señor* Billy came in time to save him."

246

"Do you mean that?" asked Trimble, suddenly turning crimson.

"Who else but *Señor* Billy would dare to do such a thing?" asked Dolores. "Who else would be willing to die for a friend? Who else would forbid *Señor* Alvarez and me to say what we know? But no matter what he forbids, we are going to tell everything. Why should he do such things for you and your man, *señorita?* Oh, if he could see your heart as I see it, as cold as a stone in winter."

Anne Calhoun, with a faint cry, ran suddenly up the steps of the jail. The jailer himself was shutting the door, but he pushed it open again so that she could enter.

"This way, ma'am," he said. "This ain't a jail, today. It's a kind of a reception hall for the friends of Bill Jeffers. I'll stand out of earshot, ma'am, but watch your hands that they don't pass nothing between the bars." He closed the door behind her and took her down the concrete floor of the aisle until she was in front of Jeffers's cell.

He stood up as he saw her. His formidable head sank a little, and he peered up at her from under his brows.

She twisted her hands together. She was like a child that wishes very much to come near, but is afraid. "Billy," she said, "is it all true, what they tell me? Did you steal the money?"

He looked at her steadily and said nothing.

"Is it true," she hurried on, after that clumsy, deadly pause, "that you saved Dixie Trimble last night from two Mexicans?"

"I don't remember," said Jeffers.

"You don't remember? You do remember." She came suddenly to the bars, pressing her face actually against them. "Billy, will you talk to me?" she pleaded.

"Sure," said Jeffers. "I'm wishing you luck, all the time. But it's no good talking. It's no use disgracing yourself, talking to a crook in a jail."

She extended one hand between the bars.

"Hey, ma'am, you can't do that," said the jailer.

She paid no heed to the warning, hurrying on: "I'd rather talk to you inside bars than to any man who's outside of them."

"Except Trimble, eh?" said Jeffers.

"I don't except anyone," she said. "I've been trying to be sensible. And I've only made myself a fool. But ever since I saw you at the dance, Billy, my heart's been lead. And when I saw you go by, this morning, with the irons on your hands, everything died out of me except the old love, Billy. I knew I had to see you. I didn't care what you'd done. When I was afraid of what you might do, the fear almost killed me. But when I knew what you had done, I saw that it didn't matter, except to you. I don't care what you are. If you've robbed ten thousand people, it won't change the way I feel."

The jailer had come to move her back from the bars, using force if need be. But he halted, as he heard this speech, and began to peer curiously from her face to that of Jeffers.

It was a flash of joy like a wave of fire that changed Jeffers's face, at first, and then came bewilderment. "Do you mean," he asked, "that I've done all this for nothing? That I've tried to make a man of him . . . and . . . and all the rest . . . is that for nothing? You never really cared about him?" He threw back his head and laughed. It was a mere gasping sound.

Before she could answer, a heavy, harsh voice came ringing from the farther side of the cell room: "Jailer! Jailer!"

"Yes?" said the jailer.

It was Trimble, who stood at the end of the aisle with his head lifted, his body rigid, his face still crimson, but with a white spot in either cheek. "Where's the sheriff?" he demanded.

"He's in his office. The second door," said

the jailer. "How did you get through . . . ?"

The hand of Trimble, knocking heavily against the door of the sheriff's office, checked the voice of the jailer. Then they could hear the sheriff speak, and once more this new, loud harsh voice that issued strangely from the throat of Trimble.

"Will you bring Bill Jeffers in here?" demanded Trimble. "And Miss Calhoun, who's talking to him now?"

"Sure," said the sheriff. "Why not? He made a show of me this morning, and the whole world knows about it. I'll make a show of him now, and the whole world can see him, too. Mike! Oh, Mike! Bring Jeffers in here and ask Miss Calhoun to come along."

That was how they happened to gather in the sheriff's office — Anne Calhoun, and the sheriff himself, with Trimble and Jeffers.

The fevered look remained in the face of Trimble. His eye was like the eye of a sleepwalker. "Bill," said Trimble, his strident, new voice filling the office with quick echoes that almost drowned some of the words. "Bill, will you tell me if it was you who stopped the Mexican that tried to knife me last night."

Jeffers shrugged his shoulders.

"Was there one of 'em, or were there

two?" demanded Trimble.

"I'd warned you to get out," said Jeffers, frowning. "There were two of 'em."

"You stopped them?"

Jeffers shrugged again.

"He did. He did," said the girl, suddenly radiant with pity and belief. "Oh, Billy, there must be some mercy for such a brave man."

The sheriff began to gnaw his lip. "Mercy be damned," he said. "If he. . . ."

"Why did you do it?" broke in the harsh voice of Trimble.

Jeffers said nothing.

"Was it because of her, in some way?" demanded Trimble.

Still Jeffers would not speak. Anne Calhoun began to tremble. She put her hand on the arm of Jeffers and looked up into his set face with fear in her own.

"Billy, what have I done to you?" she whispered.

"Was it because of her," said Trimble savagely, "that you came over to the Circle Eighteen and made me think that I was a man, and not a white-livered cur? Was it because of Anne that you did that?"

"Talking's no good," said Jeffers. "I'm through with talking to you, Trimble. I told you that before."

But Trimble, suddenly groaning aloud,

sank into a chair, bowed over the desk, and buried his face in his hands. "Now I can see it," he said, as though all his questions had been answered in full. "Sheriff, I'm in my right mind, and I'm going to confess a stranger story than you've ever heard. I want to tell you how Bill Jeffers came home to Anne, and found that she was looking with half an eye at another man . . . myself. And how Jeffers came to the ranch where I was working, and found me in a pinch, and saw that I was a rotten coward, and took pity on me. And how he managed it so that he smashed up the bully first, and then let me seem to beat down himself. But I thought that I'd found myself. I went wild. I spread my elbows at the board. Nothing between heaven and hell could hold me.

"And when my money was gone and I needed more, I went out to steal it. And I took the horse of the man who had saved my life that night. I took his horse so that I could cover up my traces. What happened to him, didn't matter to me. I would have thrown him to the dogs. I stole the money. He found I was gone. He rode out to trail me. He brought me back. He tried to cover up what I'd done. When you came, Sheriff, he took the blame. He didn't try to throw it on me. He wanted to save me because of

Anne. Do you see that? Can a man believe it? And when he'd escaped, and went off with me, he told me that I was a fool, and a thief on top of a fool. He took the stolen money away from me, to return it to the people who owned it. You caught him. I went free. I would have let him rot his life away in jail. And he was the man who had saved my life! He wanted to make a man out of me, but no manhood comes out of a cur, with the nature of a cur." His voice choked away.

The sheriff, having started to speak several times, stared helplessly at the pale, entranced faces of Anne and Jeffers, and then very slowly shook his head.

"It kind of don't seem natural," muttered the sheriff at last.

Jeffers was looking back, suddenly, to that night in the bunkhouse at the Circle 18 Ranch, and remembering the disgust and the pity with which he had looked at the noble face and the powerful body of Trimble, made weak with fear. That very sight of fear had inspired Jeffers to make the great attempt.

He remembered that moment. Then he laid his hand on Trimble's shoulder. "I hoped there was enough in you to make a man," said Jeffers. "But it looks as though

253

there's enough to make a hero. Nothing matters, Dixie, if a fellow comes clean before the end."

Trimble started. His face was still buried, but he reached up with one hand. "Do you mean that, Bill?" he asked.

Jeffers caught the hand with a great grip. "Aye," he said, "I mean it with my whole heart."

"With both hearts," said Anne Calhoun.

Afterward, the money was brought in. And when it arrived, the sheriff turned Jeffers loose. "Maybe there had oughta be some time in jail for you, Jeffers, too," he said. "It kind of burns me up, when I think of you resisting arrest and socking the sheriff, and all of that. And maybe some kind of a charge'll be put ag'in' you for aiding and abetting robbery. But since you was the means of saving the hard cash in the windup, and the means of a lot of other foolishness that I can't believe still, even with Trimble's yarn down in writing, I got an idea that folks are going to forget to press any case ag'in' you. Anyway, you go free till the judge says different. I aim to think you won't be running away from this part of the world for a spell."

When Jeffers and Anne Calhoun were out

of the jail, they looked back to it with silent trouble, for a moment. Poor Trimble would have to pay some penalty, they knew. Enough of his strange story would come out to make his sentence a light one, to be sure, but even the minimum was apt to be a lesson that he would never forget.

Then they went over the creek across the bridge to the inn of Alvarez. They had decided, carefully, that they should go together to give Dolores their thanks, for they knew that, if it had not been for her, the irons would still be on the wrists of Jeffers.

They found Alvarez in his little back room, beginning to build up his usual thick atmosphere of smoke. He got up hastily to greet them, amazed by the sight of Jeffers. "I had heard something I could not believe," said Alvarez.

"Dolores," said Jeffers. "Where is she, Alvarez?"

Alvarez blew out some smoke, caught at a puff of it, and then opened his hand as though he were letting a bird loose into the sky.

"She is gone, *Señor* Billy," he said.

"Gone where?" exclaimed Jeffers.

"I can't say," said Alvarez. "And if I knew, I wouldn't dare to speak. We shall never see her again, *señor*. A small wind may carry one a great distance, when the heart is empty."

■ ■ ■ ■

Outcast Breed

■ ■ ■ ■

In the mid 'Thirties Faust abandoned what had been his primary story market, Street & Smith's *Western Story Magazine,* due to decreases in the rate he was paid per word. During the transition, he published a total of eight stories in Star Western — seven in 1934, of which "Outcast Breed" was the sixth appearing in the October issue, and one in 1935. In this tale of revenge, John Cameron must find the killer of the only true friend he ever had as well as overcome the stigma attached to the Indian blood that runs in his veins.

I

Cameron saw the ears of the rabbit above the rock when he was a hundred yards away. He began to stalk with the care he might have used to get at a deer, meat in even small portions was so valuable to him and Mark Wayland. As long as the rifle ammunition held out they had fared well, but it is as hard to get within revolver shot of desert game as it is to surprise a hawk in the naked sky.

Through the dusty film of twilight Cameron took aim and fired, not exactly at the ears but at the imagined head beneath them, hoping to break off the edge of the rock with the weight of his bullet. But the rock shed the speeding lead as it might have slanted a drop of water. Not one rabbit appeared, but three of them exploded from the shelter, and each ran in a different direction.

Cameron stood up as tall as his toes would

lift him. The olive darkness of his face and the brown of his eyes lighted; he smiled a little; it was hard to tell whether it were cruelty or joy or a sort of pity that inspired this smile. And then the revolver spoke to north, west, south, rapidly, the nose of it jerking at each explosion. The first two rabbits skidded along the earth, dead. The one to the south leaped high into the air and that pitiful, half-human shriek that only a stricken hare utters sounded to the ears of Cameron. The pain of that jerked the head of Cameron to the side. Then his fifth shot accurately smashed the backbone of the jack rabbit from end to end.

Before Cameron moved again, halted as he was in mid-stride, he rapidly reloaded the Colt. It seemed a single uninterrupted gesture that jammed the five cartridges into the chambers. With the cylinder filled again, Cameron picked up the game, cleaned it, tied it in a bleeding bundle for the return trip, and then stood straight once more to scan the horizon. A fox or a wolf will do this after the flurry of the fight, when there is dead game to be eaten — a last look toward all possible danger before the feeding begins, and never a wolf had eyes brighter than those of Cameron.

It was during this rapid scanning of the

whole circle of the twilight that he saw the glimmer on the head of the mountain, up there between the ears of the height where stood his and Wayland's mine. That trembling gleam could be but one thing — the shimmer of flame!

The shack was on fire. In some way — it was inconceivable — Mark Wayland had permitted the cabin to become ignited. Once the fire caught on the wood — there was no water available for the fight — there was nothing to do but shovel earth at the flames. And perhaps the fire would spread into the shaft and burn the timbers; the shaft would collapse; the labor of the many months would be undone, just as they were sinking into the valuable heart of the vein, just as they were writing the preface to a wealthy life, an easy future divorced from the need of labor of sweat and worry.

Cameron, through the space needed for one long breath, thought of these things. Then he stripped the ragged shirt from his back, wrapped the precious meat in it, and slinging the shirt around his shoulders like a knapsack he began to run.

He ran with his eye on the flame-spotted head of the mountain. As for the roughness of the terrain, his feet could see their own way. The half-Indian blood of his mother gave him that talent. Like an Indian, he toed in slightly, his body erect in spite of the weight on his back, his breathing deep and easy, an effortless spring in his stride. There was something of the deer about him, something of the predatory wild beast, also. He would catch his game, if not at the first spring, then by wearing it down, and, when it was caught, he would know how to kill. If he had the body and the darkened skin of an Indian, he had the proud features of the white man, and the white man has always lived by blood.

When he came to the end of the valley, he started up the ascent of the trailless slope with a shortened step. The small weight of the rabbit meat was beginning to tell on him, now. The burning of his lungs, the trembling exhaustion of effort, the agony of labor was stamped in the heaving of his lungs and in his shuddering belly muscles, but it appeared only as a slight shadow on his face in the sweat that polished the bronze of his body.

So he came to the upper level, the head of the elevation where he and Mark Wayland had found the thin streak of color, long ago, and had begun their mine.

He had brighter light than that of the dusk, now. It came from the ruins of the cabin, weltering with flame. And out of the throat of the mine shaft issued a boiling mist of flame and smoke.

The cabin was gone. The labor on the shaft was ruined, also. Well, all of this could be reformed, redone. They had the plunder that three weeks of work in the heart of the vein had put into their hand — fifty pounds of gold dust — and perhaps it would be wiser anyway to take the money to town, turn part of it into hired labor, tools, powder, mules, and return to reopen the work with tenfold more advantage.

He thought of that as he stood on the edge of the little plateau and saw the flames. The fire made little difference. But where was the figure that he had imagined hard at work shoveling earth? Where was Mark Wayland? Where was that big, stocky body, that resolute face?

"Mark!" he shouted. "Mark! Oh, Mark!"

He had no answer. A dreadful surmise rushed into Cameron's mind, a sort of darkness, a storm across the soul. He ran forward past the mouth of the mine, past the crumbling, flame-eaten timbers of the hoist, toward the fiery shambles of the cabin. It had fallen in heaps. The fire was rotting the heaps away. Smoldering, charred logs lay here and there where they had rolled from the shack.

A more irregular shape was stretched on the ground, smoking. He had passed it when something more profound than the sight of the eyes stopped him. He turned back to that twisted shape and leaned over the body of Mark Wayland.

Strong wires had been twisted around the arms, fastening them helplessly to the sides. The legs had been wired together at the knees and also at the ankles. There was a gag crammed into the mouth, distending it wide. Fire had eaten the body. Someone had come, caught Mark Wayland by surprise, robbed the cabin, bound the victim, and trusted to the fire to rub out the record of the crime. And then Cameron saw that the eyes of the dead man were living.

A cry came from Cameron like the scream of a bird. He snatched the gag from the mouth of Wayland. He picked up the great, smoking hulk of the body in his arms to carry it to the life-giving waters of the creek.

The voice of Wayland stopped him. The voice was calm. "I'm dead," he said. "I'm already in hell. Don't waste . . . motions. Listen to me."

Cameron laid his burden back on the ground. He broke the wires that bound the captive. With his bare hands he stopped the red coals of fire that ate at the clothes of the victim.

"A gray mustang," gasped Wayland. "He was riding a gray mustang with a lopped ear . . . lopped left ear. A big . . . man. . . . Gimme that gun."

"No, Mark!" shouted Cameron. "I'll take care of you. I'll make you well."

"God," gritted Wayland. "Don't you see that I'm burned to the bone? My face'll rub away like rot." And again added, half sobbing: "Gimme that gun. . . . A big kind of man . . . a gray mustang with a Roman nose and a lopped left ear. . . ."

"Mark, you've been a father . . . for God's sake let me be a son to you now . . . let me try. . . ."

"Are you gonna show yourself a damned half-breed after all?" demanded Mark Wayland. "Gimme that gun."

Cameron was stiffened upright on his knees by the insult. But he drew out the revolver and dropped it on the ground. He whirled to his feet and began to run. He realized that he could not run beyond the sound of the gunshot and cast himself down on his face, with his hands clasped over his ears.

But he heard, nevertheless. It seemed as though the noise were conducted to him through the earth. His body drank it in not through the ears only but through every nerve. It was a deep, short, hollow, barking noise. And it meant that Mark Wayland was dead.

It meant that the years were struck away from Wayland. It meant that the years he had spent in rearing and caring for the outcast Cameron could never be repaid, nor that patience in teaching which had endowed Cameron with far more than his preceptor had ever known.

The whole future was snatched away from Cameron, the whole chance of making a return to his benefactor. And all the love that he had poured out toward Wayland would now have no object. It would blow away in the wind; it would be wasted on a ghost.

Cameron lay still on the ground.

But there was one thing to live for. There was the man — the big sort of man, who rode the gray mustang with a lopped left ear. Cameron got up from the earth as a cat rises from sleep at the scent of prey.

The trail could not be followed by night. Cameron spent the darkness in digging the grave. He carried to the grave the dead man with the flame-eaten body and the purple-rimmed hole in the right forehead. Into the pit he lowered the dead man. Over the body, with his hollowed hands, he first laid a layer of brush, because he could not endure even the thought of rocks and earth pressing on the dead face. Afterward, he filled the grave.

He wanted some sort of ceremony. Instead, he could only give his own voice. And his voice was too small for the moment. It could not fill the vast space of the mountains and the desert that the dawn was beginning to reveal, therefore, as he kneeled by the grave, Cameron merely lifted to the morning in the east his empty hands and made a silent vow.

Afterward, he took the revolver and went on the trail. There were only five bullets in that revolver, now. But he had enough rabbit's meat to last him for a time.

He followed the trail across the desert. It took him three days to get to the hills and to the town of Gallop. There the sign disappeared. But if he ever found the trail of that horse again, he would know it. He would know it by the length of the stride in walking, trotting, galloping. He would know it by the size of the hoof prints.

The only description he had of the rider was of a "big sort of man," and Gallop town was filled with "big sort of men." Therefore, he left the town and cut for sign in circles around it. Every day he made the circuit until at last, on the old desert trail, he found what he was looking for. He had not been able to spot the gray horse in Gallop, but he had found the trail of it leading from the place.

Two days he ran down that trail, for the rider traveled fast. For two days, the flesh melted from the body of Cameron as he struggled along the traces of the unknown. At the end of the second day, he saw a winking fire in a patch of mesquite beside an alkali water hole. He crawled to that fire on his belly, like a snake, and saw standing nearby, eating from a nosebag, a gray mustang with a Roman nose — a dirty-gray mustang with a yellow stain in the unspotted portion of its hide. And its left ear was lopped off an inch from the point.

By the fire sat a big man with a broad, red face, and red hair. When Cameron looked at him, he smiled, and took a deep breath. The weariness of the two days of running slipped from his body. The tremor of exhaustion passed away from his nerves. His hands became quiet and sure.

Then he stood up on the edge of the firelight. "Put up your hands," said Cameron.

The red-faced man looked up with a laugh. "You won't get anything off of me except a horse and a half a side of bacon, brother," he said. "What's the matter?"

"Stand up!" commanded Cameron.

The red-faced man grunted. "Aw . . . well . . . ," he said. And he rose to his feet.

"You've got a gun on your hip," said Cameron. "Use it!"

"What's the matter?" shouted the other. "My God, you ain't gonna murder me, are you?" Fear rounded his eyes. He looked like a pig, soggy with fat for the market.

A horror surged up in Cameron when he thought that this was the man who had killed Mark Wayland. As well conceive of a grizzly slain by a swine.

"Look," said Cameron, "I'll give you a fair chance. I'm putting my gun up and we'll take an even start. . . ."

This chivalry was not wasted. The man who looked like a pig snatched his own weapon out, suddenly, and started fanning it at Cameron with the flick of a very expert thumb. He should have crashed at least one bullet through the brain of Cameron except that instinct was as keen as a wolf in him always. It told his feet what to do, and, as he side-stepped, he whipped out his own gun.

If he could kill three scattering rabbits on the run, he could kill one red-faced swine that was standing still. Cameron drove a bullet for the middle of the breast. It clanged on metal, instead of thudding like a fist against flesh. The revolver, jerked out of the fat fingers, was hurled back into the red face. The big fellow made two or three running steps backward, gripped at the stars with both hands, and fell on his back.

Cameron picked up the fallen gun. It was whole. "Here!" he commanded. "Take up that gun and we'll start again."

The other pushed himself up on his hands. There was a bump rising on his forehead but otherwise he had not been hurt. "Who are you?"

"My name is Cameron. Stand up!"

"I ain't gonna stand up. God Almighty saved my life once tonight, but He won't save it twice. Cameron, I never done you any harm. Why are you after me?"

"You've done me more harm than any other man can ever do!" exclaimed Cameron. He came a little closer, drawn by his anger. Hatred pulled the skin of his face taut. "When you did your murder . . . when you wired him into a bundle and left him to burn in the cabin . . . you didn't know that he'd manage to wriggle out of the fire and live long enough to put me on your trail. But. . . ."

"Wired into a bundle . . . burn in the cabin . . . what are you talking about, Cameron? I never killed a man in my life."

"What's your name?"

"Jess Cary."

"Cary, tell me where you got the gray horse?"

"From Terry Wilson, back there in Gallop."

"What sort of looking man is Wilson?"

"Big sort of feller."

Surety that he was hearing the truth struck home in the brain of Cameron like the bell clapper against bronze. He began to tremble. It was as though God had indeed turned the bullet from the heart of Jess Cary, and only for that reason were the hands of Cameron clean.

Back there in the town of Gallop — a big fellow by the name of Terry Wilson — a man who had been anxious to sell the gray horse — that was the murderer of Mark Wayland.

Cameron backed off into the darkness.

II

He had a last picture of Jess Cary glowering hopelessly after him from the small, ragged circle of the firelight. Then he turned and struck back through the night.

There was big Terry Wilson to be reached, but Terry Wilson was a known name in Gallop, it appeared, and men whose names are known are easily found. Terry Wilson would have to die, and then some peace would come to the tormented ghost of Mark Wayland.

This thought soothed the soul of the hunter. During the last two days he had made great exertions following the trail of Jess Cary. So when he reached a run of water in the hills at the edge of the desert, he stopped the swinging dog-trot with which he covered ground and lay down to rest. Infinite fatigue made the earth a soft bed. As for the hunger that consumed him, a notch taken up in his belt quieted that appetite. In a moment he was sound asleep.

He had five hours of rest by dawn. Fatigue still clouded his brain, so he stripped, swam in a pool of the stream, whipped the water from his brown body, and then ran in a circle until his skin was dry. After that, he dressed and ran on toward Gallop with the same effortless pace that always drifted him over the trail. A jack rabbit rose from nothingness and dissolved itself with speed. He tipped it over with a snap shot and ate half-roasted meat, sitting on his heels at a hot, smokeless fire of dry twigs. Afterward, he lay flat for twenty minutes, sleeping, and then rose to run as lightly as ever toward Gallop.

That night he slept three hours, ran on again, and entered Gallop in the early morning when life was beginning to stir. He had two bullets left in his gun, but two bullets would be enough.

The blacksmith had the doors of his shop open and was starting a fire in his forge.

"Terry Wilson . . . can you tell me where I can find him?" asked Cameron.

The blacksmith looked up from the gloom of the shop. "Terry Wilson. Sure. He's got the corral at the end of the town. He's the horse dealer."

The horse dealer! The lightness went out of the step of Cameron as he turned away. He had thought that vengeance was about to fill his hand. Instead, it was probable that Wilson was only another milestone pointing down the trail of the manhunt.

He reached the corrals of the horse dealer in time to see a new herd driven through the gates of the largest enclosure. They washed around the lofty fences like water around the lip of a bowl. Dust rose in columns, a signal smoke against the sky.

Dust spilled outward in billows, and in that mist Cameron found a big fellow who was pointed out to him.

"Mister Wilson," he said, "you sold a lop-eared gray to Jess Cary, didn't you?"

The man turned his eye from the contemplation of the horses. "Jess stick you with that no-account mustang?" he asked.

"Where did you buy the gray?" asked Cameron.

"Tierney," answered Terry Wilson. "Will Tierney." His eyes changed as he stared at Cameron. "Ain't you Mark Wayland's 'breed?" he demanded.

The question stiffened the spine of Cameron to ice. Something broke in his brain and a mist of red clouded his eyes. He had to force himself to turn on his heel, slowly, and walk away.

It was not the first time he had heard the word. 'Breed, usually, or half-breed in full, slurring from men with no friendliness for any part of Cameron's heritage. Was it always to strike at him like poison in his shadow? And why? He could wish that he had not led such a secluded life with Mark Wayland, riding, shooting, working as hard as any man, and then, in the evening, stretching out beside the campfire with one of Wayland's books.

He knew something of grammar and books; he knew the wilderness, but he knew nothing of men. Of the human world he had had only a few score glimpses as he passed through with Mark Wayland. And now it seemed that the strange insult of the word half-breed was to be cast in his face from every side. But why?

His mother's mother had been a beauty of the Blackfoot tribe, a queen of her kind. Was there not honor in such blood? And a chieftain of the frontier had married her. Was not their daughter able to hold up her head even before thrones?

Three parts of his blood were white, and, as for the other part, he could see in it nothing but glory. Yet the world called him half-breed as it might have called him cur.

Will Tierney was asleep at the hotel. "I'll go up and wake him," said Cameron.

"The hell you will," answered the hotel clerk. "He'll take your skin off if you wake him up before noon. Tierney ain't a gent to fool with. I guess you know that."

Cameron left the lobby. He could wait till noon, easily enough. Behind him his acute ear caught the phrase: "That's a 'breed, ain't it?"

"Yeah. Walks like one."

Why? What was the matter with his walk? Had Mark Wayland kept him purposely in the wilderness during those long prospecting trips so that his skin would be tough before he was exposed to the tongue of the world?

He found a tree in the little plaza opposite the hotel and sat on his heels to smoke a cigarette and think. Sun was filling the world. Over the roof of the hotel he could look up the gorge of Champion Creek and see the white dazzle of the cliffs on its western side. There was beauty and peace to be found, but where white men moved in numbers there was insult, cruelty. . . .

The morning wore away. The sun climbed. The heat increased. A magnificent fellow came down the steps of the hotel and strode along the street. There was a flash and a glory about him. He had that distinction of face that is recognized even at a distance. He bore himself with the pride of a champion. And if his blue silk shirt and silver conchos down his trousers and glint of Mexican wheel-work around his sombrero made a rather gaudy effect, it would be forgiven as the sheen of a real splendor of Nature.

So that was Will Tierney? Cameron could have wished the name on a fellow of a different aspect, but nevertheless he would have to accost the handsome swaggering giant. He was up and after him instantly, and followed him through the swinging doors of Grady's Saloon on the corner. A dozen men were inside breathing the cool of the place, and the aroma of beer and the sour of whiskey.

"Step up, boys," Tierney was saying. "Line up . . . it's on me."

A trampling of feet brought everyone toward the bar as Cameron stepped to the shoulder of Tierney and said: "Mister Tierney, you sold a lop-eared gray mustang to Terry Wilson. Do you mind telling me where you got the horse?"

Tierney turned with a sudden jerk. His upper lip pulled back in a sneer that showed the white of his teeth. His eyes were the black of a night that is polished by the stars. He gave to Cameron one glance, and then nodded to the bartender. "Grady," he said, "since when have you been letting 'breeds drink in your place?"

The bartender grunted as though he had been kicked in the stomach. "Is that a 'breed? By God, it is. Throw him out. Get out, you damned greaser!"

A bow-legged cowpuncher with a bulldog face and neck shook a fist under the chin of

Cameron. "That means you. Get!" he growled.

Tierney stood back against the bar with one hand on his hip, the other dangling close to the butt of a revolver that was strapped to his thigh. He was laughing.

"You . . . Tierney . . . it's you that I want to talk to!" exclaimed Cameron. "Where did you get that gray horse? Will you answer me that? It's a fair question."

"Grady," said Tierney, "do I have to talk to the greasers you keep in your place?"

The cowpuncher with the face of a bulldog drove a big fist straight at the head of Cameron. His punch smote thin air as Cameron dodged — right into the sway of another powerful blow. There were a dozen enemies, all bearing down. He tried to shift through them. Hands caught at him. Fingers ground into his writhing flesh like blunt teeth. His gun was snatched away. A swinging Colt clipped the side of his head and half stunned him.

Then he was through the swinging doors. The sunlight along the street was like a river of white fire that flowed into his bewildered brain. Hands thrust him forward. He was kicked brutally from behind and pitched on face and hands into the burning dust of the street.

"Where's a whip?" called the clear, ringing voice of Tierney. "We'll put a quirt on the 'breed dog!"

A whiplash cut across the back of Cameron and brought him swiftly to his feet in time to take another lash across his shoulder and breast. Then a rider plunged between him and the Grady crowd.

The horse was skidded to a halt. A girl's voice shouted: "What a crew of cowards you are! A dozen of you on one man! A dozen of you! Will Tierney, isn't there any shame in you? Jack . . . Tom Culbert . . . Harry . . . I'll remember that you were all in this."

They scattered before her words as before bullets. Two or three hurried down the street. The rest streamed back through the swinging doors of Grady's saloon. Their shouted laughter beat on the brain of Cameron.

He had dragged off his ragged hat and looked into the gray eyes and the brown, serious face of the girl. She wore a blouse of faded khaki, a well-battered, divided riding skirt of the same stuff. But every inch of the horse she rode spoke of money. That was not what mattered. The thing she had done talked big in the mind of Cameron. And it seemed to him that he could look into the beauty of her face as far and as deep as into the loveliness of a summer evening in the mountains.

"It was rotten of them," the girl flared. "I don't care what you were doing . . . it's rotten for a dozen to pick on one man."

He put his hand over his shoulder and tentatively felt the welt that the whiplash had left. It was still burning and growing. He could feel it easily through his shirt.

"I was asking a question of one of them . . . and they didn't want me in there. So. . . ." He made a quick gesture. "So they threw me out," he said, and, in trying to cover his expression of rage, he smiled.

"Ah?" said the girl. "The drunken hoodlums. I'm Jacqueline Payton. Who are you?"

"John Cameron," he replied.

"Cameron's a good name. I like it," she said. "I like you, too. I like the look of you, John Cameron. Are you down and out?"

"I've been down just now," he answered. He turned his head and looked steadfastly at the door of the saloon. "I'll be up again, though, perhaps."

"You want to go back in there and fight them? Don't be crazy," she commanded. "You come along with me. Dad needs a new man or two, and he'll give you a job. You come along with me." She dismounted. She touched his arm and his eyes drew down from the picture of the vengeance that had been growing across his mind.

"Yes . . . I'll go a ways with you," he said. "You get on the horse again."

"I don't ride when a friend is walking," she answered. "Come along, John Cameron."

He walked beside her down the middle of the street.

She was not very tall. Her forehead would touch his chin, just about. That, it appeared, was the right height. She was not heavy and she was not light, except in the quick grace of her movements. She had a voice that he must have heard before. He said that aloud: "Have I heard you speak before today?"

"I don't know. I'm pretty noisy. I do a lot of talking." She smiled. "Have you been around this town?"

"No," he answered. "But it seems as though I've heard your voice before. The sound of it strikes in a certain place and makes echoes. It makes me happy."

She slowed her step and looked up at him with a frown. "Are you saying that just for my benefit, because you think it sounds nicely?" she demanded.

"Are you angry?" asked Cameron. "I'm sorry."

"No, I guess you mean it, all right," she

281

decided aloud. "But just for a minute I wondered . . . well . . . let it go. What are you doing in town, John Cameron?"

"I'm looking for a man . . . and I think I've found him," he said.

"Is that good news or bad news for him?" said the girl.

"I have to kill him," said Cameron slowly.

She looked suddenly up at him again.

"Shouldn't I have said that?" he asked her.

"Great Scott, John," she answered, "do you mean that you're out on a blood trail . . . you . . . at your age . . . ?"

"I'm twenty-two," he said.

"And going to kill a man? Why, John?"

"Because he murdered my friend," said Cameron.

"Murdered? But there's the law. You can't. . . ."

He lifted his hands and looked down at them curiously. "If the law hanged him, there would be nothing that filled my hands . . . there would be no feeling . . . there would be no taste," said Cameron gently.

"Good heavens," said the girl. "You do mean it."

"You're angry," said Cameron. "And that makes me unhappy."

"Not angry. But horrified. Really on a

blood trail. Are you sure that your friend was murdered?"

"He was tied with wire and left in a burning cabin," said Cameron. "And I came back before he was dead."

They were beyond the edge of the town. The girl halted, looking straight up into the eyes of Cameron, but he was staring past her at the vision from the past.

"He lived long enough to tell me what sort of horse the murderer rode. He told me that, and then he asked me for my gun. Then he killed himself."

"No!" cried the girl. "No, no, no! It isn't possible that you gave him the gun and let him kill himself."

"He was burned," said Cameron, "until his face was loose with cooking. It was ready to rub away. He was burned like a roast on a spit. That was why I gave him the gun. Before he had to begin screaming with pain. Ah . . . I'm sorry."

For the girl, making an odd bubbling noise in the back of her throat, had slumped suddenly against the shoulder of the horse.

III

He could not tell what to do, but the sight of her helplessness made him feel strangely helpless, also. He touched her with his hands and his eyes, reverently, and this reverence seemed to restore her strength. She was able to stand straight again. The mare turned her head inquisitively toward the mistress and was pushed away by a touch that was also a caress. The path for the girl's mind had to be cleared of everything else so that she could stare at the problem of Cameron.

"*That* is what I saw in your face?" she demanded.

"What else could I do?" asked Cameron.

"I don't know. I only know it was terrible. I never heard of anything so terrible. It makes me want to help you. How can I help you, John?"

"By letting me come to you whenever you're in trouble . . . whenever you need any sort of help. By letting me walk up the road with you."

"Walk up the road?" she repeated, bewildered.

"This is the happiest thing I've ever done," he answered. "Walking up this road with you, I mean."

At this, her eyes avoided him and her color grew warmer.

"That was a wrong thing to say. I've hurt you by saying that," he declared.

"No," she said. "It's not the wrong thing to say. John, I don't think you could say the wrong thing."

He felt his face grow hot. He swallowed, and said after a moment of silence: "I haven't seen very much of people, and I don't know how to talk." He walked on beside her. "But is this a happiness for you, too?"

"Yes."

"As though, when the road climbed that hill, we'd find something wonderful on the other side of it?"

She laughed. "A sort of road through the sky?" she said.

"Exactly that! How did you happen to think of that? How did you know what I was thinking."

"I don't know. It's strange," she said.

He began to laugh and he laughed with her and their voices made together a music of two parts, high and deep, but with only one theme. He was aware of that. It delighted him and it delighted her, also. Their laughter stopped, and they looked at one another with shining eyes.

But still they were walking on, and at this moment they passed the top of the hill beyond which, he had said, they might find that the road was laid through the sky.

What they saw was a string of a dozen or more Indians riding across the main trail, blanketed Indians who only lacked feathers in their hair to give them the exact look of the old days. They crossed into the trees and were gone.

"I knew we'd see *something* strange," said the girl. "They're heading up toward the new reservation."

Something had stirred in the heart of Cameron, and he looked earnestly after the vanished file of riders. But now a turn of the trail brought them to the Payton Ranch — the confusion of the big corrals, a grove of cottonwoods, and the low, broad forehead of the house itself showing over the rim of the rise.

Her father would be inside, she said. She gave her mare to a boy who loitered near the hitching rack and took Cameron straight into the house. He hung back.

"What's the matter?" she asked.

"My clothes are ragged. They're dusty and dirty."

"Your skin is clean, and so are your eyes. That's what counts. You come along in and don't be afraid of anything. Father needs a man like you on the place."

The living room was a big, barn-like place where a dance or a meeting could have been held. Over in a corner, in a leather chair, sprawled a man with gray hair and a grayish care-worn face. He looked up from some paper spread out before him and rumbled: "Well, Jack, what have you brought home?"

"John Cameron," said the girl. "And he's a lot to bring. He wants a job and you'll give him a place. You need him."

Payton smiled a little. "You know how these dog-gone' girls are, don't you?" he asked. "The newest dress and the newest man are the only things that count."

Cameron did not smile. He was too seriously and deeply examining the fatherly kindness of that face.

"I want men who can ride and shoot," said Payton. "We have some rough horses and some pretty handy gents with long loops have been helping themselves to the herds. They got one of our own men last week. Can you ride and shoot?"

Cameron laughed. With Mark Wayland, he never had had horseflesh to ride unless it were wild-caught, fiercely savage, vengeful, cruel. "Yes, I can ride," he said. "I can shoot pretty well, too."

"Good with a rope?"

"I never had one in my hands," said Cameron. "But I can learn."

"Yeah," growled Payton. "Boys can learn

how to handle a rope. But only God can teach 'em to shoot fast and straight. Let me see how good you can shoot. Here . . . come over to this window . . . got a gun on you?"

"No."

"Take this. Look yonder . . . you see that crow on top of that fence? Knock him off of it."

"It's not fair, Dad!" exclaimed the girl.

"Sure it ain't fair," said Payton. "But there's nothing any closer for him to blaze away at."

He passed his gun to Cameron, and they saw him stand a little straighter, with his head raised in a peculiar pride and eagerness. Many unfortunate men were to learn the meaning of that lifting of the head before the end of his trail.

He gave to the target a single glance. His hand swept up, bearing the flash of the gun. The nose of it jerked as the weapon exploded. The crow leaped from the fence post and swung into the air.

"Missed!" said Payton.

"Try again!" cried the girl. "It was a close one."

"It will fall," said Cameron calmly. "It is dying on the wing."

Payton shrugged. "What makes you think you hit it? No feathers flew."

"I always know when the bullet strikes," said Cameron.

"What tells you?" scowled Payton.

"I can't say. But I know."

Payton glared at the girl and she shrugged her shoulders as she answered the glance. This sort of calm egotism was not to her taste any more than it was to the taste of her father. But now Payton exclaimed: "By thunder! Look!"

The crow, flapping hard, circling for height, seemed to fall suddenly from the edge of his invisible tower in the sky. Down he came, blown into a ragged bundle of feathers by the wind, and struck the ground with a thump that was audible to the three watchers. Cameron gave the gun back to Payton.

"How did you know you'd slugged that bird?" demanded Payton almost angrily.

"Well . . . I feel which way the bullet goes," said Cameron. "I've hunted a good deal when every bullet had to be turned into a dead rabbit, or a deer. You learn to feel just where the bullet is going."

He made this speech with such simplicity that all at once Payton began to smile. "All right, Cameron," he said. "I want you on this place. You're hired."

Hoof beats swept up to the front of the

house, paused. And almost at once there trampled into the room three big men. One of them was Will Tierney.

"There's a dance at Ripton!" called out Tierney. "Going with me, Jack?" Then his voice changed as he barked out: "What's the idea, bringing 'breeds home, Jack?"

"What do you mean?" asked the girl. She cried it out and made a quick step away from Cameron.

" 'Breed?" growled her father. "Have you got greaser in you, Cameron? By God, you have!"

Big Tierney and the other two men were striding closer. "Throw him out," said Tierney. "Think of the gall of him, coming out here. By God, think of it. Jack, what's the matter with you? Can't you see the smoke in the eye?"

Cameron looked not at all at this approaching danger. He considered the girl only, and saw her eyes widen with horror and disgust. She caught up a hand to her breast as though she were struck to the heart by some memory. He knew what that memory was. It was their walk together up the road. It would stay in her mind, now, like dirt ingrained in the skin. It would be a foulness in her recollection.

Hands fell on him. But they could do

nothing to him compared with the look in the great, stricken eyes of the girl as she turned away from him.

Then Cameron turned toward the others. The two tall, fair-haired men had something of the look of Jacqueline about them. They were her brothers, perhaps.

"Kick him out!" shouted one of them. "We don't want no damned 'breeds in here!"

"I'll leave the place and never come back," said Cameron. "But if you handle me, I'll return and kill you, one by one, I swear to God."

"D'you hear him, the dirty half-breed!" cried Tierney, and he struck Cameron across the mouth with the flat of his hand. They swept Cameron to the window and hurled him through it. He landed on his head and shoulders, rolled over, and came staggering to his feet.

"And if I have a look at you again," called Tierney, "I'll take a whip to you myself!"

IV

In a wind-swept ravine among the hills the campfire blew aside, sharply slanting, fluttering the flames to blueness, making them shrink close to the sticks that were burning.

The circle of blanketed figures around that fire was very dimly illumined; young John Cameron, standing in the center of the circle, near the fire, could be seen more clearly. Instinct had made him select the leader of the party. He had to face the wind in order to look at the old man. He had to stiffen his lips and raise his voice against the blast. Sometimes he was almost shouting. And his breath was short as he came to the end.

"I have told you everything. The white men kick me out of their way like dirt. The white women loathe me. Therefore, I am not one of their people. If I am not a white man, then I am an Indian. Let me come with you."

There was a slight turning of heads as all looked toward the old man. He rose, tapped the ashes out of his pipe, and stepped close to Cameron. He was very old. The million wrinkles on his face were like knife cuts, but the eyes, folded back behind drooping lids, were as bright as youth itself. He laid on the breast of Cameron the tip of a forefinger as hard as naked bone.

"My son," he said, and the words blew with the wind and entered the mind of Cameron. "My son, when the heart is sick, men turn to new places. But they find no happiness except among their own kind. What is your kind? The white people will not have you. But you have an eye too open and wide. You are not an Indian. We cannot take you. You would bring new ways to us. You are neither white nor Indian. You must live your own life in your own world. Or else you must fight the white men or the Indians until they take you in. All people are glad to have a man of whom they are afraid. Find the best man among many and ask him. He will tell you what to do."

The wind was at the back of Cameron, helping him, and it was still early night when he came again into the long, winding main street of the town of Gallop. Fire still burned in the forge of the blacksmith. He was still hammering at his anvil when the voice at his door made him look up and see the same agile, light form that he had noticed that same morning.

"Will you name the best man in Gallop?" Cameron was asking.

"The best man?" The blacksmith laughed. "Les Harmody is the best man, all right."

"Where shall I find him?"

"He's in the old Tucker house, down the street. He moved in there the other day and unrolled his pack. Fourth house from the corner, in the middle of the big lot."

Cameron found the place easily. His mind was weighted by the sense of a double duty. He had to find Will Tierney and make sure that Tierney was indeed the murderer of Wayland. But when he killed Tierney, it must be not as a sneaking man-slayer but as a man of accepted name and race.

Les Harmody might be the man to tell him what to do. He had heard the name before, but he could not tell how or where. Wayland himself must have spoken of Harmody. But the name had always been attached to something great. He was an old man, no doubt, and loaded with the wisdom of the years.

So Cameron tapped with a reverent hand at the door of the shack. A faint light seeped through the cracks in the flimsy wall.

"Come in!" thundered a great voice.

He pulled the door open and stepped inside. The wind slammed the door shut behind him because what he saw loosened the strength of his fingers. He never had seen such a man; he never had hoped to see one.

Somewhere between youth and grayness, young enough to retain speed of hand and old enough to have his strength hardened upon him, Les Harmody filled the mind and the eye. He was not a giant in measured inches or in counted pounds, but he struck the imagination with a gigantic force. He was magnificent rather than handsome. The shaggy forelock and the weight of the jaw gave a certain brutality to his face, but the enormous power that clothed his shoulders and his arms was the main thing. His wrist was as round and as hard as an apple, filled with compacted sinews of power and the iron bone of strength underneath.

He was eating a thick steak with a mug of coffee placed beside it. Gristle or bone in the last mouthful crackled between his teeth now.

"Are you Les Harmody?" asked Cameron. The other nodded.

"I've come to ask you a question," said Cameron. He stepped closer to the table.

"You're Wayland's 'breed, ain't you?" asked the great voice.

Cameron stopped, stiffening suddenly.

"I don't talk to 'breeds. I don't have them in the same place with me. Get out!" commanded Harmody.

"I go without talking?" said Cameron. "Like a dog?"

"All 'breeds is dogs," said Harmody.

"Dogs have teeth," answered Cameron, and, stepping still closer, he leaned and flicked his hand across the face of the giant.

Harmody rose without haste. His eye measured several things — Cameron, and the distance to the door that assured him that the victim could not escape. He leaned one great hand on the table and in the other raised the mug of coffee, which he emptied at a draft. He wiped his dripping lips on the back of his hand as he put down the cup.

"I've come to ask a question and I'll have your answer," said Cameron. "I'll have it . . . if I have to tear it out of your throat."

Harmody did not walk around the table. He brushed it aside with a light gesture, and all the dishes on it made a clattering. "You'll tear it out of me?" he said softly, and then he lunged for Cameron.

Up there in the mountain camps, patiently, with fists bare, Mark Wayland had taught his foster son something of the white man's art of self-defense. Cameron used the lessons now. He had no hope of winning; he only hoped that he might prove himself a man. Speed of foot shifted him aside from the first rush. He hit Harmody three times on the side of the jaw as the big target rushed past. It was like hitting a great timber with sacking wrapped over it.

Harmody stopped his rush, turned. He pulled a gun and tossed it aside. "I'm gonna kill you," he said through his teeth, "but I don't want tools to do the job. A greasy 'breed . . . a damned, greasy breed . . . to make a fool out of me, eh?"

He came again, not blindly, but head up, balanced, inside himself as a man who understands boxing advances. Even if he had been totally ignorant, to stand to him would have been like standing to a grizzly. But he had skill to back up his power. He was fast, bewilderingly fast for a man of his poundage.

He feinted with a left. He repeated with the same hand, and the blow grazed the head of Cameron. It was as though the hoof of a brass-shod stallion had glanced from his skull. The weight of the blow flung him back against the wall and Harmody rushed in to grasp a helpless victim.

His arms reached for nothingness. Cameron had slid away with a ducking side-step. He had to look on his own fists as tack hammers. They would only avail if they hit the right place a thousand times, breaking down some nerve center with repeated shocks. The swift blows thudded on the jaw of Harmody, as he swayed around. He tried the left feint and repeat again. The blow was side-stepped.

Wings were under the feet of Cameron,

and he felt them and used them. If only there were more room than this shack afforded — if only he had space to maneuver in, then he could swoop and retreat and swoop again until he had beaten this monster into submission. But he had to keep a constant thought of the walls, the overturned chairs, the table that had crashed over on its side and extended its legs to trip him. And one slip, one fall, would be the end of him.

Those dreadful hands of Harmody would break him in an instant, but every moment he was growing more sure, more steady. He changed from the jaw and shot both hands for the wind. His right thumped on the ribs as on the huge round of a barrel, but the left dug deep into the rubbery stomach muscles, and Harmody grunted.

A second target that made. And then he reached Harmody's glaring eyes with hooking punches that jarred back the massive head. He reached the wide mouth and puffed and cut the lips. They fought silently, except for the noise of their gasping breath.

And always there was the terrible danger that one of Harmody's blows would get fairly home. Then the devil that was lodged behind his eyes would have its chance at full expression.

A glancing blow laid open the cheek of Cameron. He felt the hot running of the blood down his face. But that was nothing. Nothing compared with the stake for which he fought. Not merely to endure for a time, but actually to win, to conquer, to beat this great hulk into submission.

He fought for that. He never struck in vain. For the eyes, for the mouth, for the vulnerable side of the chin, or for the soft of the belly — those were his targets.

A hammer stroke brushed across his own mouth — merely brushed across it — but slashed the lips open and brought a fresh downpouring of the blood. In return, he stepped aside and tattooed the body and then the jaw of Harmody.

The big fellow was no longer an exhaustless well of energy, but now he paused between rushes. His mouth opened wide to take greater breath. Sweat dripped down his face and mingled with the blood. But the flaming devil in his eyes was still bright.

Exhaustion began to work in Cameron, also. He had to run, to dance, to keep himself poised as on wings. And the preliminary tremors of weakness began to run through his body constantly. He saw that the thing would have to come to a crisis. He would have to bring it to an end — meet one of those headlong charges and literally knock the monster away from him. It was impossible — but it was the only way.

He saw the rush start, and he moved as though to leap to either side. Instead, he sprang in, ducked the driving fist that tried to catch him, and hammered a long overhand right straight against the jaw of Harmody. The solid shock, his running weight, and lashing blow against the rush of Harmody, turned his arm numb to the shoulder.

But Harmody was stopped. He was halted, he was put back on his heels, he was making little short steps to the rear, to regain his balance.

Cameron followed like a greedy wildcat. The right hand had no wits in it, now. He used the left, then, and, with three full drives, he found the chin of Harmody. He saw the great knees buckle. The head and shoulders swayed. The guarding, massive arms dropped first, and then Les Harmody sank to the floor.

Cameron stepped back. He wanted to run in and crash his fist home behind the ear — a stroke that would end the fight even if Harmody were a giant. But there were rules in this game, and a fallen man must not be hit. So Cameron stood back, groaning with eagerness, and saw the loosened hulk on its knees and on one supporting hand.

"Have you got enough?" gasped Cameron.

"Me?" groaned Les Harmody. "Me? Enough? Damn your rotten heart. . . ." He lurched to his feet. Indignation seemed to burn the darkness out of his brain, and again he was coming in.

Once more Cameron stepped in to check the rush. This time his fist flew high — his right shoulder was still aching from the first knockdown — and he felt the soggy impact against the enormous, blackened cushion that covered the spot where the eyes of Harmody should have been shining.

It was a hard blow, but it was not enough to stop Harmody. Before the eyes of Cameron loomed a great fist. He tried to jerk his head away from its path, but it jerked upward too swiftly. The shock seemed not under the jaw but at the back of his head. He fell forward on his face. . . .

Consciousness came back to him, after that, in lurid flashes. He had a vague knowledge that told him he would be killed, certainly. He was dead already. It was his ghost that was wakening in another world. Then he was aware of lights around him, and the wide flash of a mirror's face. There were exclaiming voices. There was a greater voice than all others, the thunder of Les Harmody. A mighty hand upheld him, wavering. A powerful shoulder braced against him.

He looked, now, and saw his own face, dripping crimson, swollen, purple here and running blood there. He saw the face of Les Harmody beside his own — and the big man's features had been battered out of shape. On the left side there were no features. There was only a ghastly swollen mass of bruised, hammered flesh.

This monster was shouting, out of a lopsided mouth: "Here's the fellow that stood up to me . . . me . . . Les Harmody! By God, I thought that the time would never come when I'd have the pleasure of standin' hand-to-hand with any one man. Look at him, you coyotes, you sneakin' house dogs that run and yammer like hell when a wolf comes to town. Look at him . . . here's plenty of wolf for you. Look at the skinny size of him that fought Les Harmody man to man, and knocked me down. And then, by God, he stood back and give me my chance to stand once more. I tell you, look at him, will you?"

The big bandanna of Harmody dipped into a schooner of beer. He drew it out, sopping, crushed the excess liquid out, and

302

then carefully sponged the bleeding face of Cameron.

The cold and the sting of the beer helped to rouse him completely.

"Speak up, one of you . . . d'you see him?" thundered Harmody.

There was a murmur.

"Grady, you fat-faced buzzard, d'you see him now? Is he a white man?"

"He's anything that you want to call him, Les."

"I ask you, is he white, damn you?"

"Sure. He's white, Les."

"The rat that ever calls him a 'breed again is gonna have me to reckon with afterward. No, he don't need no help. He can go by himself. But, by God, he'll have fair play, man to man. Listen, kid . . . are you feelin' better? I wanted them to see you, and what you done to me. I wanted the whole damn' world to see. Kid, will you drink with me? Can you stand, and can you drink? Whiskey, Grady. Damn you, move fast. Whiskey for the kid. Here, feller, I've been searching the world for a gent with the nerve and the hands to stand up to me. Here's to the man that done it. Every one of you *hombres* liquor up on this. Take a look at him. He's a man. He's a M-A-N! Drink to him. Bottoms up!"

V

There was music in the Payton house. Joe Payton thrummed a banjo; Harry and Will Tierney sang; Jacqueline was at the piano, and her father, Oliver Payton, composed himself in a deep chair with his hands folded behind his head, a contented audience. They had not heard the pounding hoofs of a big horse approach the house, but they were aware of the creaking of the floor in the hall as someone walked toward them, and now the great figure that loomed in the doorway silenced the song in the middle. Oliver Payton jumped to his feet.

"Hey, Les Harmody!" he called. "I'm glad to see you, old son. Come in and sit down. You know everybody. What you drinking?"

Harmody accepted the extended hand rather gingerly. "Thanks, Ollie," he said. "I'm not drinking. And for what I've got to say I reckon that standing will be the best. Sorry to break in on you folks like this. Hello, Jacqueline. Hello, Will. Hello everybody. Glad to see you . . . and sorry to see you, too."

"What's the matter, Les?" urged Oliver Payton, frowning anxiously. "You talk as though you had a grudge, old-timer?"

"By a way of speaking I ain't got a

304

grudge," said Harmody. "But in another way, I got a pretty deep one. I've come from a friend, and a better friend no man ever had. You know John Cameron?"

"The 'breed?" asked Tierney.

Harmody started. "That's the wrong word for him, Will. I've stood up and told people that 'breed ain't the word for him. But maybe you weren't around when I did my talking. His grandmother was a Blackfoot girl that could've married a chief and done him proud. His father and all his line are as white as white. Understand?"

"Blood is blood," said Tierney calmly. "He's always a 'breed, to me."

Harmody took in a big breath. "We'll find a better place to argue it out, one day," he said.

"Any place and any time would be good for me," said Tierney, and his bright eyes measured Harmody steadily.

"Quit it, Will!" commanded Oliver Payton. "It only riles up Les. Can't you see that? Les, I wish you'd sit down."

"I'll say it standing," answered Harmody. "I've been away in the hills for pretty near a month with Cameron. It takes time to learn to know a friend, but I've learned to know him. On a horse or on his feet, with his hands or with a gun, I never found a better man. But he's got ideas."

He paused, when he said this, and ran his eyes over the group, his glance dwelling for a moment on the face of the girl. She had grown pale. "Jacqueline," said Harmody, "maybe you know what news I've got?"

"I can guess it," she answered.

Her father stared at her.

"I've done a lot of talking and reasoning with him," went on Harmody, "but the main thing is that he feels he's given his word, and he's given it to God Almighty. So he'll keep it. Right here in this room he gave his promise."

"He did," said the girl through colorless lips.

"What promise?" asked Oliver Payton.

"When Will and Joe and Harry had their hands on him, he told them that if they threw him out, he'd kill them. He swore to God that he would."

"What kind of damned rot is this?" demanded Oliver Payton. "I heard that, too . . . but it's rot."

"Why, he's a crazy fool!" declared young Joe Payton.

"Harmody," said Oliver Payton, "you mean to say that that fellow . . . that man Cameron . . . that . . . he's going to come on the trail of my boys?"

"He gave 'em a fair warning," said Harmody. "There was three of them, and he gave them a fair warning not to handle him. And then they done it. I tell you, Ollie, a promise is a mighty sacred thing to that Cameron."

"There's a law," said the rancher, "and I'll have the sheriff and his men out."

"Hell, Oliver," said Harmody, "you might as well ask the sheriff and his boys to try and catch a wild hawk. I'm telling you the truth. They'll never see hide nor hair of him."

"You mean that the young snake is down here now?" shouted Payton.

"He ain't near," replied Harmody. "The fact is that he's the kind that never hits below the belt. I've talked and argued with him. I've begged him to think it over because a killing is most usually murder in the eyes of the law. But he can't get it out of his head that he's made a promise to God Almighty to kill the three of 'em. Arguin' won't budge him." Then he added: "But he wants you all to be warned fair and square that he's coming after you. You'll kill him or he'll kill you."

This struck a silence across the room. Harmody went on: "You're the special one, Tierney, and he mostly wants to have the killing of you because he says that you sure killed his partner over at their mine."

"He's a madman," said Tierney. "Accusing me of murder, eh? All that a mad dog can see is red."

"He says that there was around fifty pounds in gold dust. And he points out that inside the last ten days you've made a payment on the land where you're going to live with Jacqueline, yonder. You've made that payment. . . ."

"I don't follow all this!" exclaimed Tierney loudly.

But Harmody said: "You can't drown me out till I've made my point. You made that payment with thirty pounds of the same sort of gold dust."

"Will!" cried the girl.

"You damned sneaking blackguard!" shouted Tierney. He strode at Harmody, but Oliver Payton stepped between and stopped the younger man.

"I know that you're a mighty brave and bright young man Will," said Payton, "but don't you start anything with Les Harmody. He's just too old and tough to be chawed up by youngsters."

Harmody backed up to the door. "I come in here being sorry that I had to bring bad news," he said. "But the longer I've stayed here, the more I've felt that the kid is right. There's something damned rotten in the air. Tierney, I think the kid is right about you . . . and, if you done that job, God help your soul."

He was gone through the doorway at once.

Behind him, Tierney was saying: "Something has to be done about this. A skunk like that 'breed going about the county poisoning the air with his lies. . . ."

"Will," said the girl, "is it a lie?"

He spun about on his heel and confronted her and her white face. "Jack, are you *believing* him?" he shouted.

She stared at him for a moment. "I don't know," she said. "I don't know what to believe, except that John Cameron is an honest man."

She saw everything clearly. It would be a battle of three against one, and poor John Cameron must die unless Harmody threw in with him. Even so, that meant a battle. There was one way to stop the fighting. That was to induce Cameron to leave the country. And if she could find the way to him. . . .

This thought got her out of the room at once. In the corral she caught up her favorite mare and was quickly on the road. Far away — north on the trail or south on the trail, east or west on it, or more likely wandering straight across country, big Les Harmody was traveling now. She turned in the saddle with a desperate eagerness, scanning the horizon, and so made out, very dimly, the movement of a shape over a hill and against the horizon.

She struck out in that direction at once. It was the eastern trail and she flew the mare along it for half a mile. After that she slowed to a walk and heard distinctly, out of the distance, the clacking of hoofs over a stretch of stony ground. She would have to go very carefully; she would have to hunt like an Indian if she wished to trail this man and remain unheard.

As she came up the next rise, it seemed to her that she heard other hoof beats behind her, but that was, no doubt, a sheer mental illusion, or a trick of echoes. Before her in the night there was no longer sound or sight of the big horseman. She pressed on at a gallop, giving up all hope of secrecy in her pursuit. "Les," she began to cry aloud, "Les Harmody!"

A deep-throated shout answered her at once; she saw the huge man and the huge horse looming against the stars on the next hummock.

"That you, Jacqueline?" asked Harmody, as she came up. "What's wrong?"

"Cameron will probably kill my two brothers," she answered, "or they'll kill him, and that won't make me any richer."

"What do you want to do?" he asked.

"I want to beg John to leave the country."

"It's no use," said Harmody. "He won't go."

"I want to try, though. I have to try to persuade him."

"D'you like Cameron?"

"I like him a lot."

"Come along, then. A woman can always do what a man can't manage. I've begged him hard to give up this job. He's been like a stone, though."

They rode on together, leaving the trail presently and plunging into a thicket of brush higher than their heads. Finally, through the dark mist of brush, she could see the pale gleam of a light that showed them into a small clearing where the ruins of a squatter's shack leaned feebly to the side, ready to fall. By the fire Cameron answered the call of Harmody.

"Who's coming with you?" he snapped. "What made you . . . ?" He broke off when he saw the girl. He had been thinner when he last talked to her, but he looked older now. Across one cheek bone was the jagged red of a new scar that time, perhaps, would gradually dim. He wore better clothes. Perhaps they helped him to a new dignity.

She went straight up to him when she had dismounted, and offered her hand. "The last time, I insulted you by keeping silent when I should have spoken up," she said. "Can you forgive that, John?"

He took her hand with a touch softer than that of a woman. His grave eyes studied her face. "They told you the truth," he said. "I *am* a half-breed."

"It isn't the blood . . . it's the man that counts," she answered. "And I'm beginning to realize what a man you are. I guessed it when we walked up that road together. I knew it when I heard what you'd done to Les Harmody. It's because I know what a man you are that I've come here tonight."

"Les should never have brought you," he said.

"She follered me, John," protested Harmody. "Don't be hard on me about that. What was I to do? And, besides, I thought that she might show you the best way out of this whole mess."

"That's it, of course," said Cameron gloomily. "I have to be persuaded. But there's no good in that, Jacqueline. There's no good at all. I've given a promise that I'll have to keep."

She was silent.

"You see how it is?" said the grumbling voice of Harmody. "Nothing can budge him."

"There's only one thing I wish," said Cameron, "that none of them meant anything to you."

"Why do you wish that?" she asked him.

"You remember when we walked up the road together?"

"I'll never forget that."

"If I could keep you from sorrow, I'd like to. You know, Jacqueline, now that I see you here and remember that some of your look is in your brothers, I don't think that I could harm them. But Tierney . . . I know you're going to marry him . . . Tierney has to be rubbed off my books."

"He's nothing to me," said the girl.

"He has to be. You're marrying him!" exclaimed Cameron.

"I give you my word and my honor, he's nothing to me, tonight. Because I think . . . I really think . . . that he did the frightful thing you say he did."

"You're through with him?"

"Yes."

"I don't believe that," said Cameron sternly. "If you love a man, you'll never give him up, even if he has a thousand murders

313

on his back."

"It was never love. It was simply growing up together, and going riding and dancing together, and being encouraged by everyone."

"Ah?" said Cameron. "Would a woman marry a man for no better reasons than that?"

She felt the scorn and the horror in his voice. She flushed. "I'm afraid we do," she answered. "John, have you become so hard, so stern? Is there no use, my trying to talk to you?"

"I can listen to you better than I can listen to running water in the desert. Sit down here, Jacqueline. Here by the fire. That's better. I can see your eyes now, you know. Whenever they stir, my heart stirs. When you look up at me like this, my heart leaps like a fish."

"Hey," said Les Harmody, "you can't talk to a girl like that."

"Can't I?" asked Cameron, startled. "Have I said something wrong?"

"Not a word," said the girl.

"Help me to teach him something," said Harmody. "All he knows is hunting and reading. He don't know nothing about people. You can't let a gent talk to you like that."

"Why not? I like it," she said.

"But, dog-gone it, Jacqueline, unless he loves you, or something like that. . . ."

"I do," said Cameron. "Does that make it all right?"

"Hey, wait! Wait!" shouted big Les Harmody. "What's the matter with you? You've only met her once before."

"It's true," said Cameron. "But that was more happiness in a few minutes than all the rest of my life put together."

"Well, then you gotta learn not to say everything you think right out loud to a girl. They ain't used to it. You gotta spend a lot of time approaching a woman. You gotta be more dog-gone' particular than when you come up on the blind side of a horse. Ain't I right, Jacqueline?"

"Not about John," she answered.

"Hold on! What's his special edge on the rest of us?"

"I don't know," said the girl. "But I like everything he says."

"Hold on, Jacqueline!" shouted Harmody. "Hold on, there! If you get ideas into his head, you'll never get them out again."

"I don't want to get them out again," she answered.

"Don't say that. I mean," explained Harmody, "that if you give him half a chance, he'll start ragin' like a dog-gone' forest fire."

The girl smiled up at Harmody. "You know a lot about girls, Les," she said, "but John Cameron happens to know a lot about me." She put out a hand and touched the arm of Cameron. "That's why I've had the courage to come up here tonight," she said. "It *couldn't* go on. John, you couldn't take the blood trail behind my brothers."

"No," said Cameron breathlessly, leaning toward her. "I couldn't lay a finger on them."

"And Tierney . . . leave him to the law. There is a law for that sort of a man."

"I can't leave him. I told you that before. If you were I . . . if you'd been raised by Wayland, and then found him dying as I found him . . . wouldn't you despise yourself if you waited for the law to do your work on the murderer?"

She held her breath, fighting back the answer that rose into her throat, but it burst out in spite of her. "Yes, I would!" she exclaimed. "I don't blame you a bit."

"Quit talking that way," commanded Harmody. "D'you know that you'll have him out raisin' hell right away, if you talk to him like that?"

"I'm only begging one thing," said the girl. "You've held your hand for a month.

316

Will you wait another month before you take that trail? Will you let the law see what it can do, first of all?"

He dropped his face between his hands and stared at the fire. Les Harmody, making vast, vague signs of encouragement from the background, tiptoed to a little distance. The girl looked up at the giant with a flashing smile of confidence.

And John Cameron had raised his head to answer, the trouble gradually clearing away from his eyes, when the voice of Tierney barked from the edge of the brush: "Stick up those hands! Fast!"

"What in hell . . . ?" began Harmody.

"You're out of this, Les!" shouted the voice of Joe Payton.

Cameron had risen to his feet.

The girl threw herself in front of him. "Joe, don't shoot!" she screamed. "Will, don't shoot at him! The poor fellow didn't mean anything . . . he only has half a brain, Will!"

VI

Will Tierney came out from the brush at a strange, gliding pace, his feet touching the earth softly for fear that he might upset his aim, and his revolver held well out before his body.

"Get away from him, Jack!" he shouted. "Step away or I'll get him through you, by God!"

Cameron had waited a single second, stunned. His gun belt and gun had been laid aside. His hands were empty, and death was stalking him, but what really mattered was that the girl had called him a half-wit.

Had she come merely for the purpose of holding him and Les Harmody helpless while her fighting men came up to wipe out the 'breed? He thought of that. Then he turned and dived for the brush. He ran as a snipe flies, dodging rapidly from side to side and yelling: "Harmody, it's my fight! Stay out of it!"

He heard the scream of the girl, then the guns began to boom. Bullets whistled past his head, right and left, and then the sudden thunder of Les Harmody's voice broke in. The gunfire continued. But the bullets no longer whirred past him.

The brush crashed before his face. He was instantly in the thick gloom of the foliage, safe for that moment, and he heard the shrill cry of the girl: "Will! You've killed Les Harmody!"

That voice struck him to a halt. He stood gripping at the trunk of a young sapling until the palm of his hand ached, and behind him he heard Harmody's deep, broken voice exclaiming: "I'm all right, Jacqueline! Don't worry about me. I'm all right. But I tell the rest of you for your own good . . . don't go into that brush after Cameron. If you go in there, he'll kill you as sure as God made wildcats. Keep out of the darkness . . . he ain't got a gun. But he's got hands that are almost as good as a gun."

They did not press into the brush, but Will Tierney exclaimed: "Here's hell to pay! It's the 'breed that ought to be lying here, not Harmody. Les, it's your own fault. If you hadn't got in between me and my aim, I'd have Cameron dead as a bone. He dodged . . . damn him . . . he dodged like a bird in the air. I never saw such a rabbit."

"You never saw such a man-eater, either," declared Harmody. "And he'll chaw your bones one day, Mister Murderer Tierney."

"Murderer?" shouted Tierney. "You mean to say that you believe his yarn about me?"

"Stop talking, Les!" commanded the girl. "Save your breath. Help me carry him into the shack. Joe . . . Harry, take his shoulders. Does that hurt you, Les? Gently, boys."

Back to the edge of the clearing ventured Cameron, and from the thick of the brush he watched the men carrying huge Les Harmody through the open door of the shack. Will Tierney, coming back into the clearing, kicked some more fuel onto the fire and made the flames jump. This brighter light seemed to be a comfort to him. He walked in an uneasy circle around the fire, staring toward the brush constantly.

In the meantime, the conference inside the cabin could be heard clearly as it progressed. They were examining the wound of Harmody. Once he groaned aloud as though under a searching probe. Then the girl was saying: "He ought to have a doctor. I'll stay here with him. But he ought to have a doctor by the morning. The three of you go straight for town."

"I'll stay here with you, Jack," said Harry Payton.

"You'll do nothing of the kind," she answered. "What if John Cameron knew that there was only one man here?"

"He hasn't a gun," said Harry Payton.

"He has his wits and his hands, and that's enough," said big Les Harmody. "Jacqueline is dead right. The three of you stay close together all the time."

Tierney stepped to the door of the shack. *"Bah!"* he snarled. "I'd like nothing better than to tackle him . . . alone! I'd love it."

"I think you like murder better'n you

would ever like fighting," said Les Harmody.

"When you're on your feet," answered Tierney, "I'll give you your chance at me, any time."

"Thanks," said Harmody. "I'll take you up on that, one day."

"Be still!" commanded the girl. "The three of you start riding . . . and start now. Keep bunched. Head for Gallop and get Doc Travis. We don't have to worry about Les for a while. Those big ribs of his turned the bullet a bit. And it's better to have broken ribs than a bullet through the heart. Will . . . you fired to kill."

"The fool came in my path," said Tierney. "What else was I to do? He came between me and Cameron."

"Who gave you the right to murder John Cameron?" she demanded.

"You talk as though I were a butcher, Jack."

"I think you are," she answered.

A strange joy rushed through the brain of Cameron as he listened.

"Jack," cried Tierney, "does it mean that you're through with me?"

"I never want to see your face again," she replied.

Tierney strode into the shack, shouting something that was lost to the straining ears of Cameron, because all the men were speaking at once.

Then, through a pause, Cameron could hear Tierney crying out: "You prefer a 'breed, maybe?"

"I prefer John Cameron . . . I don't care what you call him," she answered.

Not care? Not care even when he was called a half-breed? Did she, in truth, prefer John Cameron? He, lingering on the trembling verge of the firelight, the shadows wavering across his eyes, felt a weakness in the knees, a vague and uncertain awe.

The brothers were protesting. Harry Payton was thundering: "Jack, you don't mean it! You can't mean it. A dirty half-breed? I'd rather see you. . . ."

"Shut your mouth, Harry," said the profound voice of Les Harmody. "Don't you speak to her like that."

The three men came striding out of the shack a moment later. "It's no good," Tierney was saying. "You can see that she's hypnotized by that rat of a Cameron. Joe, I'm going to have the killing of him."

"Not if I can get to him with a gun first," answered Joe.

They went away across the clearing, hastily, and, as the brush closed after them, cracking behind their backs, there was a great impulse in Cameron to run forward to the shack and show himself for one instant to the girl he loved, and to Les Harmody who with his own body had stopped the bullets that were intended for his friend. Some rich day would come when he would have a chance to show Harmody that he was ready to die for him.

He could understand, too, why the girl had called him a half-wit. It had been her first gesture toward stopping the attack of big Will Tierney, to assure him that his rival was a creature of no importance.

But there was something more for Cameron to do than to speak to the woman he loved or to touch the hand of his friend. He had to strike Tierney. If God would let him, he had to strike at Tierney now, and he was on foot, he was weaponless, and there were three men against him, two of whom were sacred from any serious injury at his hands.

As the idea dawned in the mind of Cameron, it seemed at first totally absurd. But he knew that Tierney would probably get out of the country as fast as possible. Tierney had lost his chance at the rich marriage; there now hung over his head the accusation of murder, and there was nothing to hold him in this part of the world except, perhaps, a desire to wipe out Cameron. But the great chances were that Tierney would ride with the Paytons, go as far as Gallop, deliver the message to the doctor, and then slip away toward an unknown destination.

There was no time to catch him, therefore, except on this night. And already the horses of the three were galloping steadily away.

They would turn down through the hills and take the long, straight road offered by Lucky Chance Ravine, which pointed straight on at the town of Gallop. It was his consciousness of the probable course they would follow that taught Cameron what he could do. The riders would have to wind down through the hills to come to the head of the steep-walled ravine. For his own part, he could strike straight across and climb the walls wherever he chose.

As he ran, he made his hands work. He snatched off his shirt, tore it into strips, and began to knot the tough strings together. He could have laughed to think that this was his weapon against three mounted, armed men.

Meantime, he had been running as few people can. He had left the woods, slipped through a pass between two hills, and so found himself on the rim of Lucky Chance Ravine. It ran straight east toward Gallop, bordered with cliffs to the north and south, sheer faces of rock.

It was not hard to get down the cliff face. On the level floor of the ravine, Cameron dodged among the rocks until he came to a narrows where the only clear passage was a ten foot gap between two very large rocks.

This was the strategic point for him. It was the thought of this gap through which the riders must pass in single file that had started him for Lucky Chance Ravine. And now he heard the distant clattering of hoofs that moved toward him with the steady lope that Western horses understand, that effortless, pausing swing of the body, slower than any other gallop.

He had very little time for his preparations, but his plan was simple enough. He knotted one end of his clumsy rope around a ragged projection on the side of one boulder, then he crouched beside the other great rock with the loose end in his grip. The slack of the twisted rope lay flat on the ground.

He had hardly taken his place before he saw them coming. He was crouched so low that he could see the heads and shoulders of the two in the lead against the stars, so that they seemed to be sweeping through the sky. Well behind them came the third. He prayed that the last rider might be big

Will Tierney.

He gauged his moment with the most precise care, then jerked up the rope and laid his weight against it. Well below the knees of the horse the rope struck. There was a jerk that hurled Cameron head over heels, but as he rolled he saw horse and rider topple.

As he scrambled to his feet the mustang was beginning to rise, snorting, and the rider lay prone and still at a little distance. Cameron caught the reins of the mustang and led it to the fallen rider. He had to lean close to make out the features of the man in the dull starlight, and with a groan he recognized Joe Payton.

He thrust his hand inside Payton's shirt and pressed it above the heart until he felt the reassuring pulsation. Not dead, but badly knocked out. He got Joe Payton's gun and flung himself on the back of the horse. It was at full gallop in a moment, speeding after the distant beat of hoofs.

At full speed he rushed the horse, pressing its flanks with his spurs, and so the leading pair of riders came back to him through the night, growing visible, then larger and larger.

"All right, Joe?" shouted Harry Payton.

He uttered a wordless whoop for answer,

and the leaders sped on, unsuspicious. He could distinguish them one from the other, now. Will Tierney was in the lead. Harry Payton was two or three lengths behind Tierney. Therefore it was beside him that Cameron rushed his mustang, bringing the horse up so fast that Payton had only time to twist in the saddle and cry out once in astonishment — for he could see, now, the gleam of the bare skin of Cameron.

His cry was cut short; a clip across the head struck with the long barrel of Cameron's revolver dropped Payton out of his saddle. Cameron, catching the loosened reins of the other horse, jerked the mustang to a halt. And at the same time the yell of Will Tierney flashed across his brain.

Men said that Will Tierney feared nothing human. He must have thought, then, that half-naked Cameron was a devil and not a man, for he dropped himself low over his saddle bow, gave his horse the spur, and raced it toward the distant lights of Gallop.

Cameron had a strange feeling that luck was with him, that, having helped him past the first two stages of his night's work, it would not fail him in the last important moment.

But he found that Tierney was drawing away from him. Big Will Tierney, twisting in the saddle, tried three shots in rapid succession, and missed his mark. But to Cameron there would be no proper revenge in merely shooting a fugitive through the back. That would not repay him for the death of his friend. So he held his fire, and rode harder than before.

In another moment he had his reward. The far finer horse of Tierney had opened up a gap in the beginning, but the much greater weight of Tierney made up the difference after the first burst of speed. His mount began to flag, while the tough mustang that labored between the knees of Cameron gained steadily.

Tierney dodged his horse through a nest of boulders. The mustang followed like a true cutting horse on the tail of a calf. Cameron was not a length behind when Tierney turned and fired again.

And the mustang went down like a house of cards. The earth rose. Cameron's head struck fire through his brain. He fell into a thick darkness and lay still.

When he roused, at last, he was dripping with water. Another quantity of it had been sloshed over him by the figure that stood tall and black against the stars. A groan had passed involuntarily through the lips of Cameron.

"Coming to, kid?" asked Tierney's voice cheerfully. "I thought you'd never come around. Feeling better?"

Cameron tried to move, but found that his legs and hands had been bound together with something harder and colder than twine. Then he realized that he had been bound with wire — hard bound, so that the iron ground the flesh against the bones of his wrist and his ankle.

He stared up at the stars and found them whirling into fire. Nearby, there was the sound of swiftly whispering water. And gradually he realized what had happened, and the sort of a death that he was likely to die.

VII

"I'm to go the way that Mark Wayland went, eh?" asked Cameron.

Tierney had been carrying the revivifying water from the creek in Cameron's hat. Now he swished the hat idly back and forth, the final drops whipping into Cameron's face.

"Sure you're going the way of Mark Wayland. But to hell with him. Think about yourself."

"Wayland," said Cameron, as the confession came from Tierney, "never did harm to any man. Why did you murder him?"

"Want to know what he did to me?"

"Nothing wrong," declared Cameron.

"If you say that again, I'll kick your face in," said Tierney. "Listen . . . five years ago, when I was feeling pretty good, I got into a fight with a greaser fool . . . I never had any use for 'breeds and greasers."

"I know," agreed Cameron. He was trying to think. Mark Wayland had always said that a good brain could cut a man's way through any difficulty. What device could he find to free himself from the danger of death now? At least, he might keep Tierney talking for a little time. Every moment saved was a chance gained, in that sense.

"This greaser," said Tierney, "got me down on the floor of the barroom, and I pulled out a gun and let him have some daylight through his belly. He kicked himself around in circles and took a long time to die. You never heard anything like his screaming. I hung around and listened to the last of it, and that was where I was a fool. There were half a dozen people around but they felt the way I did . . . that killing a greaser was always self-defense. Then another man came . . . Mark Wayland. He heard what had happened and started for me. I pulled the gun on him, but he was a little faster."

Tierney rubbed his right arm. "Clipped me through the arm so that my gun dropped, and then he turned me over to the sheriff. The sheriff didn't want to pinch me, but, after Wayland had done the pinching, the law started working. Nothing but murder. And me headed straight for the rope. But I managed to work my way out of the jail, one night. That's one of the good things about this country . . . their cheesecloth jails."

He recommenced on the theme of Wayland. "You were saying that Wayland never did anybody harm. If I'd hanged, that would have been harm, wouldn't it? And living these years, never knowing when somebody might turn up and recognize me . . . that wasn't harm, eh?"

"Did Wayland recognize you?" asked Cameron.

"I had a mask over my mug. I lay up there behind the rocks and watched you start out hunting. Then I slipped down to the shack and whanged him over the head. It was easy. I wired him up, and touched a match to his clothes to wake him up. He wakened with a holler, too, like the sort of a noise that the greaser made on the barroom floor."

It was strange and at the same time a horrible thing to look straight into the mind of a man without the slightest sense of right and wrong.

"He wasn't yelling at the end," remarked Cameron.

"No, he'd shut up as soon as he realized. Too much brute in him. Like an Indian. Pride, and all that."

Big Will Tierney sat down on a convenient rock and lit a cigarette. "I thought that he'd break down," he said, "when I pointed out what I was going to do . . . light the cabin and let him roast like pork. But he locked up his jaws and didn't say anything. A queer thing, Cameron. I was almost scared from just sittin' there and lookin' into the cold of his eyes. It almost made me think of hell . . . you know."

"And you went ahead," muttered Cameron.

"Wouldn't I have been a fool not to? I'd found the gold in the sacks. I needed that money, and I needed it damn' bad. Old Payton was too dead set against me marrying his girl unless I showed that I was able to take care of her. He said that he'd never put up the money for me to live easy. He's always seen through me a little. He's the only one of the Payton family that has . . .

332

until you came along, damn you."

There was no particular venom in that last speech. He shrugged his shoulders and went on: "Not that I give a damn about having Jacqueline wise to me. I never cared a rap about her. But I wanted her slice of the Payton money when it came due. That old swine has a couple of millions. Know that?"

"I knew that he had money. Where did you kill the greaser?"

"You'd like to use that on me, wouldn't you? Why, it was a little side trip I made down to Phoenix when I was a kid. If you live till tomorrow, you're welcome to use the news wherever you please."

Tierney laughed. He had a fine, mellow-sounding laughter, and the strength of it forced back his head.

"But damn the Payton money," he went on. "I'll get along without it. I would have had to play a part with Jacqueline all my life, anyway, and I don't like to do that. Unless I decided to raise so much hell with her that the old man would buy me off with a good lump sum. But I've never had to work my way, and I never will have to. Always too many suckers like you and Wayland. They dig out the coin and the wise birds like me get it." He laughed again.

The brain of Cameron was spinning. "Tell

me something, will you?" he asked.

"Sure. I'll tell you anything you want to know. It's the sort of pleasure that I've never had till now . . . talking what I please to a fellow who's going to be dead inside of a few minutes. It's like whispering secrets into a grave, kid." He began to laugh again, highly pleased by this thought.

"Well . . . tell me if you ever had a friend."

"Friends? I've had a dozen of 'em. Look at the two Payton fellows. I've got the wool pulled over their eyes a yard deep. Sure I've had friends. I get a friend, use him, chuck him away. That's my idea. Now, let's talk business."

"What kind of business?"

"The way you're to die."

"There's the creek."

"You'd like that," agreed Tierney. "Sure you'd like it. But I want to have it longer and sweeter. Maybe you're not like Wayland. Maybe you'll pipe up some music for me, the same as the greaser did?"

"Maybe," said Cameron, through his teeth.

Tierney stood up and stretched. "Tell me something. D'you think you broke the skulls of both Harry and Joe?"

"No. They're only a little knocked out," answered Cameron.

"Too bad," murmured Tierney. "They're a pair of wooden dummies, and I'm tired of 'em. But what am I going to do about you, old son? I've got matches. How about lighting you up here and there and watching you roast? As long as you liked Wayland so much, you might as well go to hell the same way he went." He leaned over Cameron. "I think I'll have to take that pair of spurs, though," he decided. "Where'd you get golden spurs?"

"My friend gave them to me. Les Harmody."

"The hell he did! Why would Les be chucking away money on a 'breed like you?"

"He said it was to show that he thought I was as good as any white man."

"Did he? Well, you're not. Understand? When I've taken these spurs off, I'll show you what I think about you."

He leaned still farther. With an instinctive reaction, Cameron pulled his feet away, doubling his knees high.

"Good," said Tierney. "Going to be some struggling, eh? That's what I want. That's what I like. Put up a good fight, kid. I hate to hook a fish that won't do some wriggling. I'll have you screeching like the greaser on the barroom floor, before I'm through with you."

He stepped forward to catch Cameron by one foot. His head was low. The target was not unattainable. And Cameron let drive with his heels at the head of Tierney — with the golden spurs of Les Harmody he struck out, making his supple body into a great snapping whiplash.

Tierney, seeing the shadow of the danger at the last instant, yelled out and tried to dodge. But the spurs tore across the flesh of his chin and the heels themselves thudded against the bone of his jaw. He fell on his face.

Cameron came to life, moving as a snake moves. He got the revolver from the holster at the side of Tierney, first. The big fellow already was beginning to move a little as Cameron held the weapon in both hands and with two bullets severed the wires that bound him at the knees and at the ankles.

It was a harder, an almost impossible task to get a bullet through the wires that confined his two wrists. To manage that, he had to hold the Colt between his feet, pressing his wrists over the up-tilted muzzle of the gun until one strand of the wire was against the muzzle of it. But he could not keep the flesh of the wrists from pressing over the muzzle together with the wires.

He managed to get the middle finger of

his left hand over the trigger of the gun; another extra pressure and the explosion followed. Hot iron seemed to tear the soft flesh inside his wrists — but his hands were free.

And there was Tierney on his feet at last, staggering a little, then snatching at a second gun as he realized what had happened. Cameron shot low, aiming between the hip and the knee, and saw the big fellow pitched to the side. He struck on both hands, the gun spinning to a distance. Then he reclined there as though he had been struck down by a spear and pinned to the ground.

"By God, it's not possible!" shouted Tierney. "Cameron, don't shoot . . . for God's sake, don't shoot!"

Cameron went to the fallen gun and kicked it back to Tierney.

"I ought to cut you down and kill you the way you were going to murder me, Tierney," he said. "But I'm not going to do that. Wayland taught me a different way of living. There's the gun inside your reach. Grab it up. Fill your hand and take your chance."

"What chance?" groaned Tierney. "I'm bleeding to death. Cameron, do something . . . help me! If you try to shoot it out now, I won't lift a hand. It'll be murder. It'll damn your soul to hell. For the sake of God, don't kill me!"

"Look," said Cameron. "I'm sitting on the ground exactly like you, now. I'm putting the gun down just the way yours is laying. Now fill your hand and fight . . . you yellow dog."

But Tierney, spilling suddenly forward along the ground, buried his face in his arms and began to groan for mercy.

VIII

That was why Cameron, his soul sick with disgust, brought Tierney into the town of Gallop with the feet of his prisoner tied under the belly of the horse. A crowd formed instantly. Men ran from the saloons, and some of these were sent off to rouse the doctor and prepare him for a trip.

Tierney, when he saw familiar faces, began to make a frantic appeal: "Bob . . . Sam . . . Bill . . . hey, Bill! . . . help me out of this. The damned 'breed shot me from behind. I'm bleeding to death. Bill, are you going to let me go like this?"

He held out his hands in appeal. Cameron rode beside him with no gun displayed. He made a picture that filled the eyes of men, however, and kept them at a distance.

For blood had run and dried from a thousand scratches, and, naked as he was to the waist, he looked like a savage come back from war with a captive.

Harry Payton and the gray-headed sheriff appeared at the same time, Harry shouting: "There he is, Sheriff! There he is now. I'll help you get him!"

Harry Payton had a thick bandage around his head, but otherwise he appeared perfectly well. He was pulling out a gun as he ran.

The sheriff stopped that. "If there's any gun work wanted, I'll call for it," he said.

The crowd had become still thicker. Men held back from actually stopping the progress of Cameron, but they drew nearer and nearer.

"Are you the sheriff?" Cameron called out.

"I am," said the other, wading through the crowd.

"Then I'm turning Tierney over to you," said Cameron. "I'm charging him with the murder of Mark Wayland."

The sheriff came up, panting. Harry Payton was at his shoulder, glowering, ready for battle.

"You let me down, Harry, damn your heart!" snarled Tierney.

"What's this charge of murder?" demanded the sheriff. "Are you wounded, Tierney? This looks like a damned black night's work for you, Cameron. Hold that horse. Harry, help me get Tierney off his horse. Cut that rope."

Now that the horses were stopped, the men pressed suddenly close from every side. There was a shout from the rear of the crowd: "Hang the damned 'breed! Lynch him!"

Cameron leaned from the saddle and gripped the shoulder of the sheriff. "Are you going to listen to me?" he demanded. And the green glare of his eyes struck a sudden awe through the man of the law.

"I'm listening to you," said the sheriff, scowling. "What's this talk about murder?"

"He killed Mark Wayland. He confessed it to me tonight."

"Confessed? What made him confess?"

"When he had me lying on the ground and tied with wire . . . the way he tied Wayland before he burned down the shack at the mine."

"What kind of a liar will you listen to, Sheriff?" demanded big Will Tierney. "He shot me from behind. . . ."

"Here's one proof," said Cameron, and he held out his wrists, with the blood still trickling from them, and the powder burns

340

were horrible to see. The sheriff frowned and a curse of wonder escaped his lips.

"It's true!" he said suddenly.

"You'll find the wound in his leg, whether he was shot from behind or not," said Cameron. "And if you want to know more than that, send down to Phoenix. They've wanted him for murder there for five years. They'll want him still." He said it loudly, and the muttering of the crowd was blanketed in a sudden silence.

The sheriff said: "Look at me, Tierney. Is this true? Have you been a damn' wolf in sheepskin, all this time?"

"Wait a minute!" yelled Tierney. "You wouldn't believe a 'breed against a white man's word, would you? You wouldn't. . . ."

"Shut up," said the sheriff. "You're under arrest. Cameron, I can see that I've got to thank you for doing a job that I should have handled myself. Tierney, you look as guilty as hell, and hell is where you'll wind up, with a hangman's rope to start you on the way."

It may have been that the loss of blood and the successive shocks to his nerves had weakened Tierney, but now at the very moment when he should have rallied himself to make a last desperate appeal to the crowd that might have favored him, his nerve gave way. With one hand he gripped at his throat as though already he felt the rope about it, and slowly turning his head he stared at Cameron — a look that Cameron would never forget.

Then they carried him toward the jail.

The sheriff lingered to say, loudly: "The next man I hear calling Cameron a 'breed had better come and call me the same thing. There's no dirt on his skin that soap won't take off."

It was the same fellow who had yelled for a lynching who now started a new demonstration. Cameron marked him clearly. Perhaps, seeing how the wind was blowing, from this unexpected quarter, the man wanted to bury his other remark under new fervor. But he it was who proposed cheers for — "Cameron, who's all white." — and the crowd, falling into the spirit of the thing, cheered itself hoarse, and then trooped back into the saloons to start a celebration.

Cameron himself by that time was riding at the shoulder of the doctor, with Harry Payton on the other side of him, and Joe Payton in the rear. The brothers said nothing. They were not the kind to waste words, but neither, Cameron was sure, were they the sort to nourish grudges. And that was how they came back to the shack where big Les Harmody was lying.

When he heard them coming, Harmody shouted a question. The voice of Cameron answered. And a cry of happiness broke from the throat of the wounded man.

There was not much need of talk. When Harry and Joe, who had started with Tierney, returned with Cameron and the doctor, it was a fairly clear proof that everything was altered in the affairs of Cameron.

There was one anxious pause while the doctor made his examination of Harmody, then the medico looked up with a smile. "Luck and an extra heavy set of ribs have saved you, Harmody," he said.

An involuntary gasp of relief broke from the lips of Cameron, and, hearing that, Harmody held out a sudden great hand toward him. "Old son," he said.

Cameron caught the hand and gripped it as hard as he could. "The two of us, Les!" he exclaimed.

"Fine," said Harmody. "But suppose we make it three?"

He looked across at the girl, and she, from her place beside the bed, forced her head up until she was looking with great eyes straight at Cameron. She began to smile in a way half fond and half foolish, and Cameron knew that he had reached the end of pain.

ABOUT THE AUTHOR

Max Brand is the best-known pen name of Frederick Faust, creator of Dr. Kildare, Destry, and many other fictional characters popular with readers and viewers worldwide. Faust wrote for a variety of audiences in many genres. His enormous output, totaling approximately 30,000,000 words or the equivalent of 530 ordinary books, covered nearly every field: crime, fantasy, historical romance, espionage, Westerns, science fiction, adventure, animal stories, love, war, and fashionable society, big business and big medicine. Eighty-one motion pictures have been based on his work along with many radio and television programs. For good measure he also published four volumes of poetry. Perhaps no other author has reached more people in more different ways.

Born in Seattle in 1892, orphaned early, Faust grew up in the rural San Joaquin Valley of California. At Berkeley he became a student rebel and one-man literary movement, contributing prodigiously to all campus publications. Denied a degree because of unconventional conduct, he embarked on a series of adventures culminating in New York City where, after a period of near starvation, he received simultaneous recognition as a serious poet and successful author of fiction. Later, he traveled widely, making his home in New York, then in Florence, and finally in Los Angeles.

Once the United States entered the Second World War, Faust abandoned his lucrative writing career and his work as a screenwriter to serve as a war correspondent with the infantry in Italy, despite his fifty-one years and a bad heart. He was killed during a night attack on a hilltop village held by the German army. New books based on magazine serials or unpublished manuscripts or restored versions continue to appear so that, alive or dead, he has averaged a new book every four months for seventy-five years. Beyond this, some work by him is newly reprinted every week of every year in one or another format somewhere in the world. A great deal more about this author and his work can be found in *The Max Brand Companion* (Greenwood Press, 1997) edited by Jon Tuska and Vicki Piekarski. His next Five Star Western will be *Train's Trust.* His Website is www.MaxBrandOnline.com.